I0654422

SHIPS OF VALOR

Persona Non Grata

Persona Non Grata

Persona Non Grata

SHIPS OF VALOR

Aaron Kennedy

Published in the United States by Templar Press. Templar Press and the mounted Templar Knight colophon are registered trademarks and may not be reproduced.

TEMPLAR
PRESS

Persona Non Grata
A Ships of Valor Novel
Copyright © 2016 by Aaron M. Kennedy

Library of Congress Control Number: 2016915077
ISBN-13: 978-0-9980656-0-1
ISBN-10: 0-9980656-0-9

Cover artwork, copyright © 2016 Jeffrey J. Burger
Legionnaires logo, copyright © 2016 Jeffrey J. Burger
www.shipsofvalorbooks.com

For Emmy, with whom I share the grandest Adventures.

Persona Non Grata

Acknowledgements

Thank you to all my beta-readers who helped refine this from a passion piece into something approaching what I hope is a good product. Thank you to my fellow authors Travis I. Sivart, Kevin Gardner, and Jeffrey Burger for all the advice along the way. Thank you to my friends for putting up with me for the last year as I plugged away at this.

AK, Midsummer 2016

Persona Non Grata

Chapter 1

There was almost no line for Terra, which I found was odd in itself. I would have expected it to be as packed as the Mars or outbound queues, but maybe I caught a lull. I made my way to the counter and the desk-jockey looked surprised to see someone wearing a scarlet Legion jacket.

I've had this jacket going on twenty years. It was my first major investment after becoming a shareholder. Made from synth-leather and damn near indestructible. It's not exactly a flagrant display of being in the Legion, but the large gold chevrons on the right sleeve tend to draw attention even if the embossed club patch is missed. The jacket will survive temps ranging from stupid cold to insanely hot, and I'm not sure a knife can cut it. I know the seamstress had a hell of a time putting the stripes on it. She eventually gave up trying to sew them on and ended up moly-bonding them instead. Worth every credit I paid.

The clerk looked at me as if I had grown a second head when I asked for a ride down to Terra two days hence. Kind of slack-jawed like I wasn't speaking Standard. At first, I assumed it was a clerk level issue. I'm not saying all clerks are on the low end of the intelligence spectrum, however, a great many people placed in public facing positions did not get there through feats of amazing competence. I showed my Terran passcard, and the rest of my idents, creating a reaction I hadn't expected. The security doors on his booth slammed shut. I stood there, somewhat shocked for a minute until I realized he still had my idents.

I knocked gently on the partition a couple times, hoping maybe he hit the wrong button by mistake and waited. I slowly breathed in and out, counting to one hundred, willing myself not to rip the down the barrier. I wasn't sure I could, but I also wasn't sure I couldn't. Legionnaires go through some extensive genemod when we join. We're strong, and we're not affected by gravity the same way most folks are. I had recently come off a tour in one point two standard gravs and combined with this metal arm meant I had a lot of power.

I felt it twinge as I actively thought about it. The Doc used to tell me it was phantom pain, all in my head. I told him a lot of things in response, little of which should be repeated in polite company. None of that changed the fact that I could feel the pain all the way from the top of my bicep through my deltoid and into my shoulder blade itself. My arm felt as if I had slept on it wrong. As though it were possible to sleep wrong. Then again, I had spent much of the last hour propped precariously in what passed for a chair with my head leaned back against the wall.

Nothing brings pain about faster than thinking about the area where the pain might be. The doctors replaced most of the bone structure in my left arm a little over a decade ago. It was stronger and lighter than normal bone but made going through any kind of security checkpoint a nightmare. The alloy was military grade, instantly flagging me for additional screening even though my idents clearly exempted me for this specific reason. Maybe that was it.

I stood there standing like a fool trying not to get too irate and agitate the Horin behind me. The last thing I wanted was some report saying I had gotten into an interspecies altercation. That would be just my luck. Horin are ugly sons of bitches. They're huge and scary being both taller than humans and double our mass. Although Horin walk on their rear legs like humans do, the majority of their muscle is in their shoulders and front arms, so when they aren't moving, they lean forward on gigantic four-fingered hands. Add to that their resting state is sort of a shivering movement, in a fur covered aggressive red color three shades brighter than the scarlet jacket I was currently wearing. They draw attention to themselves, not because Horin want to, but because their natural camouflage makes them blend into their home world. That camouflage doesn't make them blend in anywhere else. Like right behind a comparatively small human trying to get through security in one of the drabbest buildings in this part of the sector.

As I mulled this over and talked myself out of doing something idiotic this close to being home, two people dressed in dark navy business suits approached.

"Lieutenant Gadsden?" the shorter asked cautiously. I corrected with sergeant, then corrected with mister saying I was retired. "Could you come with us, Sir?" He handed me my idents. I asked if there was a problem, and he shook his head but pointed towards a corridor that practically screamed official use only. I followed them to an ash gray runabout in the back where they sat me in the rear seat. Not a police model, at least. They did not speak, only escorted. Off we went making our way through side streets, and into access tunnels below the dome.

I have a decent sense of direction, but combining vertical with lateral on a sphere things get rough. I attribute it to some clerk's idea of a joke. I think I made some receptionist mad when I joined, so the Legion loaded me up with data processing ware while in deep-sleep. Everyone in the Legion does a rotation, usually for five years. I was lucky, if that's the right word, and ended up doing eight. We're paid the same whether asleep or awake, so it doesn't make much of a difference. Aging isn't an issue, not that we do anyways, what with all the nanites, and they've got us plugged into the grid for auxiliary training. So my brain runs numbers fast. It's got some advantages, though. Anything dealing with math, I generally don't have to think about until it gets to levels requiring people with post-nominals. Unfortunately, the human brain has only so much storage space, so although I'm able to compute it fast I don't truly understand it. It's all instinct. I know the answer but not how I got to it.

In this case, I estimated we were heading towards LC, and I knew we were heading deep, but I couldn't say how deep or how far in. Too many twists, too many turns. At a guess, I would say Central Administration, because we passed passenger vehicles often enough not to be deep mining.

Chapter 2

I was getting really sick of simply moving from point A to point B when I should already be at my destination. I had spent the last month on the *Compass Rose*, a five megatonne spaceliner. And before that, two of the longest weeks of my life on a dirtball of a planet called Nalath 4 watching the locals being exploited by the resident corporations.

The Kabrins were dumb as a box of rocks. They were about eighteen to twenty-five kilos on average, topped out intelligence around a human toddler, and looked like a cat and a monkey had a love affair. They were beta level predators, communal, and not someone to piss off. They had a social memory that humans, like myself, have a hard time grasping. The little catmonkeys can be annoying at times, like a younger cousin, but will bend over backward if treated at least halfway right.

When I left Nalath, they were playing at baggage jockeys and ironically doing a better job than most humans I had encountered. I wouldn't trust the Kabrins with anything breakable, or that could get lost, but I knew they wouldn't steal anything. They were honest to a fault. Their social memory bit bordered on telepathy making it impossible to lie to each other and hard for them to even understand the concept of deceit. However, they were predators and very good ones at that. If it wasn't for their size, they would be really dangerous. Kabrins intuitively understood when someone was untruthful and it did not turn out well for those who took too much advantage of them.

I wished I had a similar ability when we finally arrived at our destination. I doubted my escorts had come down there very often as they handed me off to a gray-suited lady who introduced herself as a functionary second class something-something. I stored the name for later and forgot it for the moment. She escorted me from the drop off to an elevator and made small talk. Nothing makes my battle senses tingle like small talk. I had already been on edge since the door slammed in my face and wherever I was going was significantly farther up the food chain than someone like me rated. Days like this I'm glad I wasn't a real officer. Something was off, really off, and I was lucky enough to be part of it.

I probably should explain that last bit. I was a brevet Lieutenant. I wore bars but got paid stripes. In essence, not a real officer, but I played one in vids. The command decided to promote me to a staff position during my last tour. I think the idea was to keep me from getting killed so close to retirement more than anything else. Not that I really subscribed to gods or fate, but lady luck seemed to have watched over me a long time and made sure I've received equal doses of both her hands. Eventually, she would get tired of me, much like a cat tires of a mouse and just eat it. My leadership team seemed to be aware of my penchant for interesting situations and decided close supervision was needed. Either that or the brass wanted to give me a taste of power to keep me in. I'm not really sure actually.

I'm getting ahead of myself, though, everyone in the Legion starts out the same. Based on skills, folks are promoted up the chain. We keep it fairly simple, and there's a lot of up and down based on needs of the service and the Peter principle. Nothing wrong with going back down if things didn't work at the next rank up.

Everyone is a Legionnaire first and foremost. That's the no stripe rank. We have corporals, then sergeants, then lieutenants, captains, colonels, and finally brigadiers. It's a much more streamlined system than some of the traditional rank structures out there, lacking several intermediate ranks. A unit is small enough that everyone knows everyone else, and rank is never truly an issue. It's more about pay and dealing with outsiders. A sergeant is a senior combat specialist and handles internal issues while being a lieutenant was more about dealing with planetary governments than anything. Had it not been a brevet promotion, I actually would have ended up with a pay cut. For whatever reason, saying Lieutenant Gadsden was more impressive than Sergeant Gadsden. I never actually understood that aspect.

When we finally made our way down to the appropriate floor, she knocked once on the door and opened it, and ushered me in. Rising behind the desk was a woman in a severe cut indigo suit. Tall, probably had two centimeters on me, and I'm no slouch being over 185, but low-g grows people tall. Not pretty but striking. Couldn't guess age, but mature. At least as old as me. Brows were brunette but the hair was auburn so guessed dyed. She exuded confidence and power through crisp blue eyes the same color as the Terra sky. She was in charge, and in charge of a lot. All of this was secondary thoughts that flashed through my head and I shoved back down almost as quickly. I only wanted to find out why I was here.

The functionary disappeared by the time I was in the room. "Ari Gadsden, right. Pleasure to meet you. Sorry under these circumstances. Please have a seat. Would you like a drink?" I shook my head, but thanked her, and took a seat in what was an amazingly comfortable chair. A man could retire in a chair like this.

"My name is Lysha Kellinger. I'm Managing Director of Luna Corporation." All right then. My original assessment of being in charge was correct. I guessed low, by a lot. When estimating her being in charge, I figured a large company, in the realm of several thousand. Luna Corporation was several million. In actuality, the moon was a sovereign nation, but legally couldn't be called one.

Nobody owns the moon. The big thing to remember is the moon is free territory. People control it, but no single country owns it. Luna Corp. controls it, at least, the side facing Terra. There are smaller subsidiaries controlling other sections, but in reality, it was Luna Corp.

"I understand you just got back to Sol. I hope the trip wasn't too unpleasant." Statements, not questions. It was easy to understand why she was in charge. Her presence was comparable to anything I saw in the Legion. She would have put a couple brigadiers to shame honestly. "How familiar are you with the current political realities on Terra?"

I replied that I had never tracked politics at home, and she gave me a rundown of the last three decades. The situation was frankly disconcerting. A lot of this won't make sense without a history lesson, but here's the down and dirty.

The Sol System consists mainly of Terra, Luna, Mars, and the outlying moons. Terra and Mars have independent governments. Luna is a Corporate Trust, and each of the outlying planetary moons like Ganymede and Titan are properties of those three. Fairly simple. Outside Sol, everything works pretty much the same. Each system has its own government or corporate set up that works best for them.

Luna is effectively the Galactic Seat. The Luna Corporation makes sure the moon stays free territory. They're greedy bastards but they're fair greedy bastards. Seems strange, I know. They'd been around in one way or another since we started colonizing. Originally, a construction company they expanded into frankly everything, but on the moon they were management. Luna Corp kept the population breathing, working, and running.

The Legion, my organization, is a peacekeeping force. We don't get involved in politics. We actually don't care about politics at all. What we do care about is galactic stability. The last thing anyone needs is some knucklehead with atomics killing off settlers, or some pirate causing people to have a bad day. So we stop those kinds of shenanigans. When each new government or corp joins up, they apply for Galactic Citizenship. All that means is ships can travel to and from those planets' space-ways unmolested and the Legion can patrol that region of space. If someone wants to join the Legion more the better, but we don't conscript. It's actually against our charter.

It's a voluntary arrangement. Planets can leave anytime, and some do but normally not for very long, because trade routes are what keep planets alive. Most new places aren't self-sufficient, at least not for a hundred years or so. They don't have the tech or the people.

But what happens if an old planet pulls the plug? That's what Terra did. It left the Galactic Union. I didn't understand all the complexities of what Lysha was telling me, but I was getting the gist of why this was bad. The major problem with this was that Luna was Terra's Moon. This created a major pissing contest, having since been resolved with some very large military and financial threats, but one of the sticking points was that Legion wasn't allowed on Terra. I was Legion. I wasn't allowed home. I was persona non grata.

I asked if the offer for a drink was still open, and received some very good rye. We sat there talking over several other details including things like my existing holdings, the status of my Terran Citizenship, all of which blurred past me until I finally excused myself and Lysha escorted me up and out. "Ari, I know this is a shock. If there's anything I can do to help or just talk, please call. You have my direct number."

The return from central admin dragged as I tried to work out exactly what had happened. Ms. Kellinger's explanation was simple and straightforward, but it didn't explain why. I think my escorts saw my frustration peak and let me out sooner than was absolutely necessary as I found myself in the center of Luna City in a bit of a fog and decided to make my way to the closest thing I had left to a home, White Caps.

Chapter 3

To call White Caps a bar would be doing her a grave injustice. White Caps was the bar for Legionnaires. She had originally started out as a small shack next door to the recruiting desk back when Luna City was a couple imperial centuries old. The recruiters would put the new guys up for the night there before shipping them off to basic at Peary Basecamp near the northern pole of Luna. A few years deeper into its history, one of the bartenders got smart though and started offering extra services. Little things at first, like long-term storage lockers, and basic kit issues. He used that idea to expand the footprint, building up to the dome, and down further than anyone knew.

Then a guy named Clemmons came up with an inventive idea. He made us shareholders. We all own a piece. We all benefit. When a Legionnaire gets out of basic, they're shipped back to Luna city for a little R&R before heading off to their unit. Of course, we all end up at White Caps, with half a years' back pay in our pockets, and itching to go crazy. Clemmons started selling stock in the bar. A single share would cover room and board anytime a Legionnaire was in Luna City and that happened a lot back in those days. The share didn't pay for booze, but it made sure Legionnaires had a place to stay for the night, and people to guard their backs. It also paid the locker fee for the Vault. Somewhere to store the stuff from before joining or collecting along the way. White Caps had been around over a hundred years at this point. She wasn't going anywhere, and after the first batch of guys signed up, the rest followed in droves.

They used the share money to cover operating expenses, expand as needed, and turn the place into a home. The old pensioners are taken care of, and the new guys see they never truly leave the Legion. Make it out of the Legion alive, and there was a place to live forever.

But I digress. I had been walking from the Luna City Administration Center towards White Caps for almost an hour when she finally came into view. Most of LC is under the large central dome, and there are a few smaller underground caves linked via tunnels and access ports. The thing about domes is they have defined limits. The sky is essentially a large white painted ceiling, and there is no real horizon because so many buildings butt into the inner wall. White Caps was one of those buildings. Originally, she started several hundred meters away from the closest wall, but over time expanded to the point where she touched the dome itself. She took up about five percent of the wall in total. In essence, she was a monster. I could see her, and I was still several clicks away. A landmark of the city.

When I finally got to the entrance and palmed my way through the secondary door, I took the lift to the Legion section. The main door is for tourists and recruits. It's their last chance to bow out before joining, but most can't. Not after seeing the shrine this place is. Old banners, trophies, and photos of our fallen brethren. White Caps has more memorabilia than Legion HQ by several orders of magnitude, and that's not including the personal items in the Vault. Every so often, we get word of a Fallen, and a bequeathment and find some new item for the collection. We have an active custodian who tries to keep things in rotation, both above and below decks, but the last word I heard she and her team only has a small fraction even categorized.

The Legion section is built more like a hotel than anything. Once on the main level, head towards a reception area, towards housing, recreation, or dining. Since it had been several years since I had last been in LC, I headed to the reception. Checking in is never a problem, flash idents, and a clerk issues a room key. For pensioners, we can let them know they'll be staying permanently, and arrangements for a permanent room are made as soon as one opens up. Although I'm technically a pensioner, I wasn't planning on being on Luna very long so I checked in with an indef key, which is basically a weekly key that can be renewed. If the key isn't extended, at the end of the week the staff move any personals they find into the private vault for pick up later. After stowing my duffel, I headed down to the vault to dump a few items and get a couple others out.

The vault comes with the share. Each share gets a one-meter cube as part of the default, but the Legionnaire can upgrade as needed. Every chance I've gotten, I've bumped mine up, because I'm a bit of pack-rat. My vault was sitting at twenty-seven cube, or a three by three by three meter, which is about the same size as a personal stateroom on ship. Funny considering, I shared my last one with three other guys. It's not the biggest vault size available, but the next one up is hangar size and I wasn't sure I could quite justify that yet. I tend to keep mine about eighty percent full, but it's mostly mementos. One nice thing is vaults have their own addresses, meaning they can receive mail. Whenever I get back, the items are waiting inside almost like having an extra birthday finding the stuff I mailed previously. The last time I had cracked the door, I had the pleasant surprise of finding a case of cryo-sealed plums from my grandad.

I could spend all day going through decades' worth of memories, but my goal was to pull out a couple specific things. I kept a bag prepped at the door, as well as a table so I got to work. LC is a nice place, but most of the rest of Sol proper can be less hospitable. If I ended up on Ganymede, I likely wouldn't need what I was pulling out, but on Titan or Mars, I'd be a fool not to have it.

An ancient slug-thrower covered in protective oil, waiting for me to pull it out of storage. It was a simple steel model I found years before as part of an auction and worked diligently to get operational Not as nice or as fancy as the energy weapons we used in the Legion, but it was just as effective. The slugs were a centimeter in diameter, and the thing kicked something fierce, but it was effective. The goal being to poke enough holes in a smart suit to just end a fight through pure catastrophic damage.

The worst battle footage I ever saw, if it could even be called a battle, was a Legion platoon who went up against what we thought was an abandoned outpost using weapons similar to these things. Lost six guys in as many seconds because they were overconfident and didn't anticipate energy displacers not working on kinetic energy transfer. Our suits are great, but massive blood loss inside a suit that's sealed is as dangerous as getting a hole burned through. What works for modern doesn't work for ancient. Hard lesson.

Another nice part about these old school weapons is most scanners won't pick them up. That's not to say all, but much of the new stuff ignores them as mechanical devices. I placed the gun and holster beneath my left armpit, thinking my arm should mask it enough to where I wouldn't have any too many issues. I grabbed a couple other minor pieces of equipment, secreted them about my person, and then headed down to the bar proper.

Schmiddy was staffing the bar. Schmiddy was ancient when I joined, and he was still ancient when I came in. When I said we don't age normally, I meant it. Between the nanites repairing any incidental damage, the genemod therapy the Legion subjects us to when we join, and spending so much time in zero-g our clocks slow down. We have Legionnaires pushing triple centuries, and to the best of my knowledge no one knows how old Schmiddy is, but old timers have heard him mention others who were old timers to them.

As I said, I'm good at math. Part of the training while in deep-sleep. From what I've been able to gather, Schmiddy was a payroll clerk, a long long time ago, and he got the same kind of treatment.

He just knows Legionnaires. Remembers us all. Not just our names, but little things as well.

He greeted me with a "Hey Rattlesnake," and poured me an Arnold Palmer. Lemons! I hadn't had lemons in years. Trees take up so much physical space we don't generally grow them in the hydro labs on ships. It's easier to grow vine plants, so we juggle nutrition around the use of space. Luna had a lot more space and with it, the luxuries of things like citrus fruit, and even apples. I'd have to be careful, I could eat myself broke if I didn't watch myself.

I drained the drink, and Schmiddy got me a second before I realized what I was doing. He gave me a look and then slowly said "Hell of a thing." Word travels fast. If had I come to White Caps first instead of straight to the ticketing center, someone like Schmiddy would have warned me and I probably wouldn't have spent the last few hours traipsing around LC.

I nodded and left it at that. I was still trying to wrap my head around the idea myself. The old saying regarding never really leaving the Legion is true, but I couldn't hang my hat up in Luna City either. I'm young by pensioner standards. Most of the old timers have me beat by triple digits. That's not to say I wouldn't be welcome, but I wasn't the right age group yet. Most guys don't settle in until they're near bicentennials. Sort of an unwritten rule, to keep the space available for those who need it. The guys who couldn't work any longer. I was barely a quarter of that, and with deep-sleep excluded, closer to a fifth.

I needed to find other employment, and other pastures. LC would remind me I couldn't head back to Terra, at least for the foreseeable future. I wasn't even sure what I was qualified to do on Luna. At least on Terra I could turn my Legion skills into something marketable.

The thing stuck in my mind was the one on one the Kellinger woman. I couldn't quite shake it, so I asked Schmiddy. "Ah, she's a hands-on type. Delegate the good, but handle the bad herself. Remember Bris?" I nodded. "Like him. She's come down here a couple times when the corp messed up a shipment to figure out where their process failed. A bit of a looker."

Brigadier Brisendine was one of the slickest combat commanders I had ever seen. A tactical genius who made sure his guys, guys like me, knew and believed in the plan. Not only did he empower his troops in case things changed on the fly but when things spun out, he liked to take the wheel. Not a bad thing, just gave him a chance to make instant decisions and coordinate top down. Matched his leadership style and worked for him.

If Schmiddy was comparing this Kellinger to Bris, then she deserved respect by proxy. A nod from him was enough to convince me she was worth following into battle.

Schmiddy and I talked trash and war stories for a bit while I drank and ate. He got me caught up on where some old buddies were hanging their suits at the time, which was his way of pointing out employment leads. He's super old school. Big on making sure no one loses face. Lots of Legionnaires are prideful sons of bitches, myself included.

Eventually, my internal clock caught up with me and I excused myself. That's the thing about living in space, is I set my clock based on local time, or the ship itself. When patrolling a specific sector, adjusting to the local government became a matter of course making communication easier. The *Compass's* clock was set to LC so adjusting wasn't a big deal, but that didn't mean anything since Luna runs all day and night. Having a big dome above and no actual sunlight, there isn't any real night or day, so it's a matter of what I was used to and the other people on the same schedule. My personal schedule was about a quarter day of sleep right after midnight. I could survive on as little as half that, but retirement had its perks. I ducked up to my room and crashed for the evening.

Morning came with all its normal routine. Quick hygiene in the included pod followed and breakfast down in the canteen. It had been a few years since I'd been back, so rather than dedicating real thought to my problem, I played tourist and grabbed some basics from out in town. Luna is a major hub, making it easy to get the most recent tech, and replace old gear on the cheap. It's not that I couldn't get items elsewhere, only I didn't want to pay an arm and leg for it, and the old stuff worked well enough while I was still in. I picked up some replacement jumpsuits, a new set of dampers, and more books. I can never have too many books.

I have an extensive library already but always on the lookout for more. Some folks like paper claiming to love the feel of a real book in their hands. I've always looked at the space issues, though. My vault is only so large and it gets hard to justify shipping at a certain point. Don't get me wrong I'll take whatever I can get but generally prefer data, whether aud, vid, data-stream, simply because I can take those wherever I go. The vault is for memories, touchstones, and things I did. Reminders of friends who have somehow slipped away for a little bit. Irreplaceable things.

My trip through Luna city that day was about replacing items, though. It's amazing what gets lost each time a person moves. Little things that don't seem important until you need them. When I had gone through my duffel in the morning, I found I was missing one left shoe. I hadn't needed it up until then but it's always fun to find out what gets forgotten in the shuffle. This led to me spending a couple hours wandering around wasting creds before getting back to White Caps to find I had a message waiting for me.

Chapter 4

Messages themselves are not very strange. A lot of time what happens is we check in and admin sort of catches up over the next few days. People expect our arrival and they send messages in advance but mail can't be delivered until we get there. I figured mine was one of those. More than likely someone back home, like family or a buddy, reiterating what I had discovered the previous day, rubbing salt in the wound.

It wasn't one of those types of messages. This message was from Luna Corp. I waved the comm chip at the screen expecting a recording to begin playing the message. Instead, I got a connecting call prompt followed by "Kellinger, here. Oh hi, Ari! You got my message. Thanks for ringing me back." She was in workout clothes in what looked like a higrav gym. I had obviously caught her mid training. I upgraded my assessment from striking to very attractive, at least as displayed on the screen in my room.

"The reason I called. I had a dinner companion bail on me last second for a State event. I could use a friendly face who doesn't work for me. Those are hard to come by around these parts, and I was hoping you'd be willing to help me out?" I could hear the disdain in her voice when she said State event, but something else when she said friendly face.

I'm not terribly fond of groups but there wasn't really a polite way to address my social anxiety issues with someone I just met, let alone a person who had tried to do me a favor and was asking me for an exceptionally minor one not costing cost me anything. I told her I didn't have anything for formal wear, and she said that wouldn't be a problem, as long as I didn't mind someone delivering a suit. As that was the only reasonable objection I could come up with, I agreed and she said she would have her driver stop by this evening to pick me up.

A few minutes later, a new incoming call rang up. The assistant I met the previous day, Terry, I recalled. She wanted to know if I wanted suits delivered for fitting or the driver, Robert, to pick me up a couple hours early and run me by the tailor. I'd like to believe I'm hard to catch off guard, but a tailored suit was completely unexpected so I responded with whatever is easier and found myself being picked up earlier than originally anticipated.

Robert was waiting for me when I stepped outside. He was everything I'm not. Or everything I was when I was much younger. Clean cut, dark hair, bright eyes. I found it hard not to hate him just for spite. I'm sure my mood was feeding into the first impression. Then I saw him move. He moved like a cat. I would have guessed Legion, but not the right kind of movement. Some other kind of training and lots of it. But he didn't size me up. He didn't need to.

I'd like to believe I'm fairly alpha and can roll with the best of them mainly because I've managed to survive a lot of scraps, but Robert would have torn me apart. I'm relatively tough because of lots of seasoning and years of mistakes and learning from them. Robert, on the other hand, was good because he trained not to make mistakes in advance. Approaching the same end goal from different directions. The major contrast was he wouldn't end up losing an arm through his own fault. Probably wouldn't be stuck staring at home from the moon either. There's a reason he drove for Lysha.

Shortly after he had me in the back of the runabout, we were moving fast through the dome. Based on his driving I could tell he'd done this hundreds of times. The level of mastery had passed outside conscious thought into the intuitive level. That's not the flavor of patience I was blessed with.

It had been years since I'd driven myself, but giving up control is a hard habit to develop. For whatever reason there's an urge to second guess the person next to you and assume a higher level of proficiency. None of those issues were present with Robert though. He was able to be social without me worrying about his driving. Unlike the assistant, he didn't go for small talk. When he spoke, it seemed like genuine interest.

It wasn't long before we were on the other side of the Old Dome, in what could best be described as the merchants' district. Robert parked us on a side street and escorted us to what was possibly the most nondescript building I had seen since leaving Terra. The only thing separating the spot from any of the surrounding buildings was the cornerstone, reading Mason & Redback Est. 2076. No windows, no signage, only a simple stone front from actual lunar rock, with what appeared to be a real wooden door.

Robert knocked briskly, and we were ushered into the building by one of the most distinguished-looking people I have ever seen. Something about his bearing. He exuded it, like a fog. Not only dressed better than I had ever been, but absolutely comfortable in his skin, something I have never been able to accomplish in public. If pressed for details though the only thing I could actually describe after the encounter would be the mauve necktie he wore and his intense brown eyes. Robert gave a quick introduction, "Master

Redback, this is Ari Gadsden. The gentlemen we spoke of earlier." After a few seconds of shock, he had me at ease, and we were discussing what I needed for the evening. Luckily, Robert was there and knew the particulars.

Including what I had on, I owned perhaps five sets of clothes. The Legion gives, and by gives I mean sells, everything needed for daily wear. I hadn't worn civilian attire in over half my life. Excluding my jacket, boots, and a few jumpsuits, arguably military themed, the only clothing I owned was underwear. All the kit I had stayed with my old unit. Who needs two dozen drab ship-suits?

After I changed, Robert helped collect my gear and told me he would have it delivered back to White Caps. I thanked him and headed over to the triple mirror to look at myself. The last time I had been in a suit was before I left Terra. I had forgotten the feeling. I had opted to keep my boots, as Master Redback assured me they wouldn't clash. We went with a midnight blue dinner jacket, peak collar, and a vest the same color as my Legion jacket instead of a cummerbund. Simple studs and a gorgeous pair of cufflinks showing the opposite sides of Terra's hemispheres. The final addition was a Legion lapel pin showing a simple shield with the moon and the galactic arms. I'm not sure where he got it, as we're not big on swag.

Sure, we have things like the club patch on my jacket, but it's never been necessary to advertise when showing up with ten thousand very well armed folks. The residents tend to get the idea.

I looked good, I don't mind saying, especially as I had trimmed my hair to a respectable level, and even managed to shave without cutting an artery. I looked more like a real soldier than my usual shaggy Legionnaire self.

I should probably explain the last bit. The Legion isn't really a military in the traditional sense. We're more akin to a para-military organization with a charter allowing military operations. Goes back to our founding and who could be trusted to employ us.

Militaries are armed services belonging to governments. Governments are political entities, and politics change over time. When the human race made it to space, a few very smart people realized time and distance could create disastrous effects when added to politics. So these smart people found rich people. Stupidly rich people and got them on board with a concept of an apolitical watchdog organization. Somebody beholden to no government, no corporation, and no man. Idealistic, I know.

That was the seed of the idea becoming the Legion. The question that followed was where to place an organization like the

Legion? We were formed early in space travel, before the hyperspace era, back when we still called it the Sun and the Solar System, instead of Sol. This was when we still called Terra, Earth. We were still only in the early stages of colonizing Mars and Ganymede. Titan and Venus weren't viable yet. So, the moon became the natural choice. Since the moon can't be owned by anyone, no one can use the location to exercise control over the Legion. We became partners in a sense. Legion HQ is located off the south pole of the moon, training command is off the northern pole, and we recruit from Luna City proper.

Since we don't have the underlying bureaucratic structure accompanying a government, we never developed the mindset of a real military requiring all of the regulations that come with them. Instead, we promoted a philosophy. That doesn't explain the lack of uniforms, shaving, or grooming standards. A lot of those boiled down to saving creds and keeping only the things that worked.

So, yes, we have things like ranks, because they make sense, and allow us to communicate better with governments who understand hierarchies, but we don't have dress uniforms because they're not necessary for what we do. Instead, we focused on kit that's used during actual operations,

Our charter was very simple, and a few things set us apart were we weren't as regimented as normal military and had no real intention of becoming so. The only uniforms we had were combat gear as opposed to dress uniforms. We don't do medals. We don't believe in unnecessarily stringent levels of hygiene, like shaving every day or haircuts once a week, unless the mentality served some real purpose like keeping us from killing each other aboard ship. We weren't trying to become something we weren't. We were trying to be our own thing and we succeeded. We took the best aspects of organizations available and left the worst ones.

So there I was, cleaned up nice, looking somewhat respectable, and on my way to a state dinner as the guest to the head of Luna Corp. A situation I was wholly unprepared for. After getting back in the runabout it finally dawned on me to ask Robert what the dinner was about.

"They happen about twice a month. Most of them are social events. It's been my experience real business takes place at the dinners as opposed to during the scheduled business meetings." This jived with my experiences as well. The meetings are for show. They're great for azimuth checks and getting people together, but things don't get done during them.

As an example, we had weekly commander's call. The Old Man passed word, and so would everyone else with half an ounce of silver. But nothing really happened. Where things really happened was over beers at night or at chow when the teams got together. This was no different. We were heading to what was comparable to a bunch of Legionnaires sitting around beers trying to figure out how to get a bunch of jump jets ready by system-fall.

The dinner was taking place outside the main dome at the old observatory. Replaced long ago, a convention center with a restaurant occupied the old observatory grounds. One of the few places to see Terra with the naked eye. As the old saying goes, go big or go home.

The observatory was one of the first things built on Luna, actually predating the Old Dome in many ways, as it was finished first. Since most things on the moon are under the protective canopy of the domes, light pollution isn't an issue. It's actually a heck of a lot easier to see into space than back on Terra. Or at least it was back when the first observatories were built.

We started getting smart. Since the moon doesn't really have an atmosphere to speak of, it made sense to put solar panels on the outside of every available constructed surface whenever a dome went up. May as well take advantage of free power. Not like Sol is burning out anytime soon. The vast majority of our power is nuclear, in the form of thorium generators, but solar helps offset things quite a bit, at least during Lunar day, which is half the month, and makes a great industrial level job for those with the knack.

When we left the domes through a secondary tunnel, I was greeted with a view of Mankind's largest solar farm. Built atop the main dome hundreds of thousands of panels shared my anxiety. They waited for the sun while I anticipated a dinner with a woman I hardly knew. The tunnel's transparent walls acting as a poor surrogate jacket, as we crested the horizon and approached the old observatory.

It's not exactly a big building compared to some of the structures under the dome, but it's the tallest single structure outside the dome. Coming in at over 120 meters above average surface level. And that's not including the telescope proper. Surrounding the main telescope were three old school receiver arrays. The old parabolic types, designed to listen for any signs of intelligent life out there in the cosmos. Of course, we made them before we stumbled into the other races but that's a story for another day.

Robert pulled the runabout into the parking bay occupying the entire bottom floor. It had originally been more a hangar than anything, back before the building had its tunnel leading to it. Needed for rovers and even to park shuttles to protect them from meteors on the surface. A large open area, little more than a flat piece of concrete, with open blast doors on one end, and airlocks leading to elevators on the side. After parking the vehicle, Robert waved us through the security at the lock, and we headed up to main levels.

When this place was originally constructed, the observatory needed a lot of computing power. And back then the computers were a lot bigger, so entire floors were dedicated not only to computing but to communication as well. Hence the monster antenna outside. Well, technology gets better over the centuries, so what used to take floors, eventually takes broom closets. And the fact this place wasn't active allowed them to strip out the old gear.

When the engineers retrofitted the main floor, they decided to have a little fun. They added high res screens to the floors and ceilings. The floor was currently displaying the Sol system, with the Sun as the centerpiece. The ceiling was displaying our section of the Milky Way.

There were perhaps a hundred people in the room. Tables arranged around the outside in what was arguably a school circle so everyone could see everybody else. On the one side without tables, was a bar. Robert drew my attention, with a slight nudge to the ribs, to a particular fetching woman at the bar, and it took me a moment to realize she was my date for the evening. I thanked him and headed to the bar.

Lysha was wearing something I could only describe as downright amazing, slinky, and shade a red matching my vest. I wasn't sure if she planned it or not but based on the way the dress draped over her that was inconsequential to me. I am no expert on women's fashion, but I know what I like, and this plumage fell distinctly into that category. Going into more detail would not do the gown or her justice; I would seem like a pervert for trying. "Hey sailor, buy a girl a drink?" she said as I approached. Again, I notched up my assessment and wondered how in the hell I got it wrong the first few times.

She gave me a quick peck on the cheek and waved over the bar-back. I'm cautious to bring this up because I hardly knew her at this point and it wasn't intentional but she smelled like fruit. I love fruit. Absolutely love it. Can't get enough of it. I've wasted more money on fruit than I have on books, and that's saying something.

I'm jumping off topic, though. I've spent about half my waking life on ships. Recycled air really doesn't have a smell. People living on boats are careful about their personal hygiene. Those who don't quickly find themselves the subject of involuntary baths, or worse. Even too much soap can set someone off after spending a year together due to the cabin fever effect.

I'm hyper aware of smells, particularly body odor, but her quick peck and the smell of oranges and vanilla had me reeling. I did my best to hide my reaction during the couple of seconds as the bartender approached. I requested a scotch on ice while she nursed what looked like a white wine of some type. I have decent skill at identifying drinks, but it's been my experience most are named after regions, and after getting into intergalactic travel, the possibilities quickly become infinite. I learned as a young trooper; never drink the local stuff unless knowing exactly what it was, and what its effects would be.

Back when I was much younger and way dumber a few of my squad-mates and I got lit on what we later found out was distilled arachnid venom. By later I mean about four drinks in when the local guides invited us to hunt our own drinks and we thought the idea was great. Until we realized our prey weighed almost three kilos. Five drunken Legionnaires hunting giant spiders in the jungles of a low-g world. I'm not sure how much of my memory is a drunken haze, and how much the story has grown from the retelling, but spiders jump. And battle hardened Legionnaires have no problem running from them, screaming like little girls when those spiders do.

Those visions always gave me shivers when I thought about drinking new or local stuff and after being gone so long; the local stuff may as well have been brand new to me. Who knew what new and crazy concoctions had seeped in, so I stuck to the old standbys, at least until I re-acclimated.

"So glad you came. I really dread these things, but they come with the job." I caught a genuine smile in the eyes when she said that and told her I was happy to help. We chatted for a bit, getting a feel for each other, mostly about nothing until we were slowly ushered to our seats. As the resident authority, she sat center-stage, and as her date, I was on her right. On my other side were the representatives from Mars. The seats to her left were empty.

The event, a misnomer, began without much fanfare. A server provided water and presented a few meal options. Having been aboard ship for a long time, I've been effectively vegetarian for as long as I've been in the Legion. I'm not meat adverse, but it's a luxury more than a necessity at this point. When I do eat it, I lean towards animals who aren't self-aware.

I've run into enough other intelligent species in the galaxy, I don't want to be on the wrong side of that arrangement, and I'm hoping I build up enough karma in the present to pay off in the future. The last thing I want is to be dinner on some higher predator's table.

I selected the least objectionable, but still a palatable option, and introduced myself to the Marsans to my right. Folks from Mars are a hard people. They have to be. Mars has never been a kind place. Worse than the moon in many ways.

Not that I'm stereotyping, it's the first colonists went over on big sub-light transports, and rather than using deep-sleep, they chose a combination of genemod and psychological conditioning instead.

When people talk about Marsans not having a sense of humor, it's not a far stretch. Near impossible to get them riled up. It's not that they can't be made to laugh, it takes an understanding of what Marsans think is funny. For Terrans, we tend to lean towards the pain of others. It's a sad fact. We take a perverse little joy in seeing others hurt. Not necessarily injured, emotional pain is near as funny. Laughter is our release. Looneys love satire. They love fiction hitting way too close to the truth. Marsans love epic misunderstandings. The bigger the better. If someone could die because of it, the joke can have them rolling on the floor. They don't want to see people hurt, but the potential due to a misunderstanding is hilarious to them.

Back on the *Rope,* I met a Marsan whose call sign was Guano. Most of us get them either in basic or in our first unit, or we go by our last name. Mine's Rattlesnake, in part from the flag bearing my surname. Being significantly easier to pronounce than Gadsden. People seem to have a hard time with the double-ds. As for the Rattlesnake, at least that's what I tell people. Back when I was younger, I had a bit of temper and the name stuck.

Well, this guy apparently was given a snipe-hunt during some downtime in basic. Someone told him to clean out an old thorium reactor on the camp. Normally, involving getting into full scrub-gear, deconning up, and spending the better part of an afternoon. Well, as I said, Marsans are hard people and don't really have a sense of humor. He grabbed a mop and started scrubbing the place down. About three hours in, the senior instructor went looking for him to end the fun, figuring he should be about thirty minutes from actually going into the reactor, only to find him inside, wearing nothing but shorts and a smile.

Thought the prank he had killed him. Thorium can be nasty stuff. Luckily, Marsans are damn near immune to that level of radiation. Earned himself the nickname, and a vacation sitting in a decon chamber for the next week while he regenerated off the tan he gave himself. When Guano told his family back home, they thought the event was hilarious and sent the squad cookies with the frosting decorated with little reactor symbols.

The pair I was sitting next two were comparable to ambassadors, not that Mars really has them. Once a Mars cycle, lots are drawn and a batch is sent to each of the major worlds. They treat the trip like a vacation. The pair I was talking to had been on the moon for a quarter year and were enjoying the lower gravity, the abundance of people, and all the delights Luna had to offer.

Mars isn't really a bad place these days. But it's all relative. I'm from Terra, and comparing her to the Luna is hard. Comparing Mars to Terra would be impossible. The nice part of Mars is no domes. The not so nice part of Mars is no domes. The first Marsans

Terraformed it using big ships like the *Compass Rose*. Landed there and changed the place into something sort of like Earth of old. Terraforming works best on places with an atmosphere and no population. Mars was perfect for it, unlike Luna. It's not that we couldn't convert Luna, only it didn't make sense because of the number of people already living there. Mars, on the other hand, was desolate in comparison. The Marsans relocated the few settlers into the ships while the beginning processes happened. Once kick-started and with a breathable atmosphere, the rest was relatively easy. In another 500 years or so, Mars will actually be like Earth was, before she became known as Terra. A lush green planet. That's assuming they can get enough water on it, and keep the atmosphere there. But as I said, Marsans are hard folks and conditioned not to give up.

It's what can kindly be called an arid plain. Water is liberally rationed but still rationed. Lots of food is grown. More than the planet can use, and they trade it for water, and elements. All to make the place better. Mars has a plan, a schedule, and does not run behind. They're the perfect trade partner for the Luna Corp.

At first, I thought this was the reason for the honored position but turned out to be much more mundane reasoning. The host sits at the head table I understood. To avoid any perception of added influence, everyone was arranged by proximity to each other. So the head table was Venetians, Terrans who were not present, Luna Corporation, Marsans, and then Ganymede's representatives. The next batch of tables was organized in a similar fashion, trying to keep things as close as possible.

These are all asides. I had this running in the background of my head, as I engaged in the conversation at the table, to the best of my very limited ability. Since I had been out of the system for so long, I wasn't able to speak intelligently on matters relating to Sol, so I swapped to an old standby I kept my mouth shut, and asked questions, trying to learn as much as I could, as quickly as I could without looking like too much of an imbecile.

Humans, no matter where they are from tend to be talkative creatures. What's more is that a solid portion tends to be extroverts, unlike me, and are willing to share their knowledge with only a little prompting. The group I was with gave me an advanced course on local history, rivaling anything I could pick up from the net, but with far better context, and actually made sure I understood it, and how each piece affected every other bit.

As the meal ended Lysha grabbed my hand and dragged me to the dance floor. I apologized for bringing work into her work dinner, and she laughed. A full-throated one that was infectious. "It's fine. You actually made it somewhat enjoyable. That's the first time I've seen the Marsans actually talk to the Venetians about something other than ammonia or vapor trading. You have a way with people." She leaned into my chest as we danced. The floor zooming in and out on the system and galaxy as we did. We were there for a half dozen songs before I begged us away for another drink.

I lost track of time, but we spent the rest of the evening with the two of us chatting, laughing, and enjoying far too many libations. Eventually, I looked around and realized we were the last of the night's guests. I could see Robert standing off in the corner. I wasn't quite sure if he was trying to usher his boss off, or merely waiting patiently. Lysha caught my glance and followed it. I think she ran the math and realized the time.

The thing about living in space is the acute internal clock that comes with it. It's a product of necessity. Not only the daylight piece but good old fashioned Oxygen. Planet-side, O2 isn't usually an issue, but on station or ship, there's a need to track it. It's a number that's always running in the back of the head.

Robert approached and gave me a nod, "Ms. Kellinger, upstairs is ready for you." She stood, and took my hand and we slid up to what appeared to be one of the observation decks. Our timing couldn't have been more perfect. Across the moon's horizon suspended a near perfect duplicate of my left cufflink.

I don't know how long I was staring, but I know my eyes were dry and my cheeks were wet when I finally pulled my eyes away. Homesickness is a hell of a thing. I apologized and thanked Lysha for what I assumed was supposed to be a beautiful gift, and was.

I stole glances between her and home. Memories flooded back. But they were the memories of youth. Nostalgia. How things were before I joined. Not the Terra of now. She was still the blue marble. Smudged a bit more, but she was mine.

Chapter 5

I found myself dividing my time between a few key locations, but the majority was either seeking employment or spending whatever leisure time I had with Lysha.

We had a unique relationship mainly because we didn't have any conflicts of interest. We were looking at each other's problems with fresh eyes. That isn't to say we didn't have the occasional spat. She was absolutely correct to light me up when I would get into a funk and I'd have to remind her humans need food beyond the occasional takeout. But we were actually able to talk like adult human beings. I hadn't dated much before the Legion, and what I did while in was mostly at the fling level. I never really knew how long my ship was going to be anywhere, so I never tried to put down roots. Lysha had dated, but her issue was one of peer group. At a certain point, there were only so many people at the same relative level that it became self-limiting. Combined with her and their work schedules, she had almost decided to become a confirmed bachelorette.

My surprise stay on Luna gave me a chance to try something new. This was a positive out of this storm of negativity. Without her, I would have likely retreated to my White Caps' room and read myself into oblivion trying to avoid thinking the situation. I was still trying to work through my frustration regarding not getting back home. She helped a lot.

It wasn't even that I needed to go back to Terra immediately. Going back could wait, but I had set myself up with a plan, and I felt like the rug had been ripped out from under me. Pissed me off more than anything. I couldn't really understand what was going on down there, and I couldn't seem to get a straight answer regarding it. No, that's not right. Everywhere I went; from the news to Lysha I got answers. I wasn't happy with them was the problem, because I couldn't change things. That slammed me back to when I was a corporal and learned sometimes policy would tie my hands so badly I wanted to scream. I had to focus on something, anything else at least for a little while.

Lysha was that something. Although her schedule was eclectic, it mirrored up nicely with my ability to eat at any time and limited need for sleep. I became her regular dinner companion and we would attempt to do something simple before she was called in for the newest emergency. We were normally able to spend a few minutes in the evenings together usually lightening my mood tremendously.

I asked her one time what she saw in me, and got a quick shake of the head and "First, you're nice to look at. And tall. I've always liked tall men. But it's not like I have a whole lot of opportunities to meet people on a social level, and having you drop in my lap was a bit of godsend. You are a bit oblivious sometimes." I caught the gentle teasing, and a quick kiss. "But I like that too. It's endearing. You don't try too hard. You're yourself. I've never gotten the impression you are trying to impress me. It's rather pleasant. A great many people try too hard." I let her know it was all a very good act and I was doing nothing but, and was called a liar for my efforts.

But back to my job hunt. I was happy to temp work and had picked up day labor to keep myself busy. Manual labor was a great way to keep my mind off Terra, unfortunately, it made me a bit self-conscious around Lysha as well. I knew she didn't care, and I was only doing it as a hobby, but she's the kind of person that makes you want to be better just by being near her. Therefore, I had resolved to stay local, and I wasn't exactly sure where my relationship with Lysha was going, but I really liked the direction and speed. If we lasted two weeks or a decade I think I would have been happy. She was interesting, kind, and listened to me, and I really needed her. It's not that my past life wasn't exciting, but it was also monotonous at times. Spurts of adventure with huge amounts of downtime and the same few dozen people to talk to.

The benefit of working temp was every day was a little different. Different made it interesting, even if it was tedious work. Most of the longer-term employment I had encountered was outside system or significantly outside my skills set. The few inside tended to be mercenary in nature. I wasn't quite ready to cross that line yet. From what I understood, I would never really know whether what I signing on for was exactly as advertised, and my ethics sway a lot closer to black and white than gray. Unless I was starving, that option was going to be the last ditch.

The best work I came across was dock work. Sure it was grunt work, but it was appreciated and also essential. My genemods made me as strong as an ox on Luna compared to almost everyone else, making me a cheap buy. I could move more, and faster than most others. I was worried about showing up my cohorts at first, but Looneys have a heavy streak of pragmatism that runs deep. Working faster means more work for everyone. My crew ended up getting better slots, better shifts, and better bonuses. They were happy to have me, which really was a relief.

My circle of friends was light and adding a couple of work friends was nice. I had also taken to working out with Robert a couple of times a week. I hate to say it, but I picked up a few new moves. I did manage to actually hit him a couple of times, taking it as a sign I wasn't too rusty.

I found out he was Imperial Army from way back. He'd been deep frozen for longer than I've been alive on a transport boat and made a complete *h*space jump without them ever needing him. He was quite a bit older than me chronologically; it's hard to judge because of awake time. Experience adds a lot. I had a lot more combat time under my belt, but his hand-to-hand and close quarter training trumped me by a significant level.

I'd love to present myself as a hardened war veteran, who engaged in countless operations, and constant training, but in reality, there was a hell of a lot of downtime while I was aboard ship. Using those skills only a few times a decade breeds complacency. I filled the gaps as best I could can, but sometimes fighting routine was far more important than practicing basic skills.

Space is a big place. Massively huge. Unfortunately, because of the way *h*space travel works and the lack of a real way to communicate effectively over anything larger than several light-minutes, we needed to patrol through inhabited space. The Legion does this by using big command ships like the *Europe*, who have dozens of smaller ships with them. Each ship is either *h*space capable or will fit into one that is.

These Legion divisions have about ten thousand people, not including Mariners and they head from one planet to another on a rotation. Some trips take days, some take months. Theoretically, most conflicts didn't happen instantly, so there is always a division inbound once or twice a year as well as supplies.

There really isn't much of a quick reaction except in areas where we have outposts. Normally, those are manned by a command staff and a Mariner ship full of deep-sleepers. We can't really justify having a full complement sitting in the middle of nowhere eating and getting fat. My first tour had been deep-sleep, and my second was essentially the latter. Looking back, deep-sleep was actually more productive in a lot of ways, as the loss of skills wasn't as pronounced.

A nice part about White Caps, in addition to the bar and the bunks, was the sub-basements had a full-scale range, which let me loosen up a bit in the mornings before my shifts. For my last couple of years in the Legion, I'd really only carried my sidearm. I'd been outside the main fray of things to the point where the only time I went to the range was during qualifiers. But shooting some of the relics reminded me of being a young stud, and the endless cleaning following the practices. Slowly replaced with less time at the range, and actually looking forward to it as the years passed and finally my weapon had become little more than an accessory, and nostalgia made me wish for those long ago days.

The range officer started me off slow, thankfully, but after a couple of quick refreshers, I was up to date on everything from the industrial age to modern. I'd need a few more weeks of gun time, but anything I picked up felt comfortable.

It was after one such workout when I got back to my room, and found two messages. One from the docks canceling my scheduled shift since the transporter had sublight engine problems. The second was from Lysha asking if I was available for dinner the following day. I called her back and confirmed, not thinking much of it.

Chapter 6

This dinner was a little more casual than our first date, if only by a hair. Lysha and Robert met me outside and we headed to a swank place over in Dome 6. I asked what the occasion was, and she looked at me as if I had grown a third eye then started laughing. I truly loved that sound. Robert, on the other hand, remained stoic in the driver's seat with barely a hint of a smile at the corners of his eyes. I'm not sure if he was more amused at my ignorance or discomfort not knowing.

"You really don't know do you?" after a few seconds staring at me. I confessed I had no clue and begged forgiveness for my ignorance. "It's your half-centennial, fuel for brains." Then she laughed some more. "How is it that you don't know this?"

I started working the math out in my head. It had been a gigasecond since I joined the Legion, right after my eighteenth birthday on Terra. After dealing with metric for so many years, I had to actually think about the conversions, even when calendars say the actual date on them.

I hated using metric time. Since I hadn't grown up with it, the concept wasn't intuitive to me like some of the younger folks. A kilosecond being a thousand seconds, or sixteen minutes and forty seconds, but I always just ended up thinking of it as a quarter hour for simplicity's sake. Hects were easy, count to one-hundred, but megaseconds and gigaseconds were where things got wonky. Who in the hell used eleven-day increments? As for gigaseconds, I knew that one intimately, being on the tail end of one, having officially retired after completing over thirty-one and a half years of service. Those thirty years were hard on the chassis.

Add in a month being back, etc., and yep, I'd be fifty, or I could look at the date and know that. But I'm male and don't think about things like birthdays because they don't really matter. Not since I reached majority and was able to place my thumbprint to join the Legion. My birthday was only a date on a calendar taking up space in my head.

Apparently, this was a birthday dinner. After recovering my wits, seeming to be a growing habit around Lysha, I thanked her. "Don't thank me yet, you haven't seen your present." That scared me and I've literally lost an arm. I had a feeling this night was going to get extremely interesting very quickly. My fears were confirmed with I saw the catlike grin from the driver's seat.

When we were inside the restaurant, the maitre d' hastened towards Lysha, without actually appearing to hurry. A slick move if I do say so, having all the elements of speed and precision but without any indication of rushing. She greeted him by name, and he was somewhat informal, but in a reserved way. About two seconds in, I realized she either owned the place or knew the person who did so well it didn't matter.

He ushered us to a semi-secluded area where an older gentleman was already seated. A man I had not seen in a decade. His was a face I would never forget. The first face I saw after waking up with the new hardware I call a left arm. General Adam Campbell.

I could spend days talking about this man. Legend really. Last I had heard he had settled on Luna because it was the one place no one could draft him. He'd been a strategic adviser for almost every colony for the last two centuries, not because of his war-fighting prowess but because of his peacekeeping skills. He was the man called when other diplomats failed.

During my incident, while patching me up, he had been a passenger on the *Europe*. He was there when I came to, personally debriefed me, and gave me a piece of advice that has always stuck with me. "Don't revisit decisions you can't change. Whatever you did at that point was based on the information you had at that time. You already know whether you did right or wrong. No point in trying to justify it. All you can do is learn from any mistakes with the new data you have."

These were the words running through my head as he rose and shook my hand. "Son, you're looking fit. Pop a squat and let's have us a chat." I helped Lysha sit then did as directed. Within moments, the wait staff was serving the meal. Apparently, everything was prearranged. No need for menus on this evening.

He regaled us with stories as we dined. Some I had heard, or read, but never from a first person account. I found it epically hard not to fawn like an awestruck teenager. I failed miserably, but, the General hid any disappointment he had in our meeting.

Eventually, as we switched from food to coffee, there was a subtle shift in the tone of the conversation, and the General asked a single pointed question. "Do you know why we don't have the problems out here like we do on Terra?"

I replied I didn't, and he expanded. "Terra is unique. It's the one planet in the Union with multiple nations. It holds to the old ways." He sipped at his coffee and looked at me for a moment. "I'm old, but I'm a Looney by birth. I'll always be a Looney. So is Lysha. You're Terran though, but that doesn't really mean much to you, not the same as us. I've read your file, and know you're from North

America up near the polar caps, but that doesn't mean anything to me. It has no context. I imagine being cold, which is hard. I've spent the vast majority of my life either here or on ships. The few times I've stepped planet-side it's been in very controlled environments."

"But Terra still has countries sitting next to each other. They bicker. Like children living in the same house. We don't have that out here. Except for the corporations, everyone spread out and established their place in the universe. No need to fight for space."

"I have my suspicions your problems at home are rooted in that." Another pause as he waited for me to acknowledge my understanding. I nodded for him to continue.

"There's an old adage in the diplomatic corps. 'There are no enemies or allies. Just countries whose interests currently align.' I have a feeling our interests may align at the moment." A very deep pause and a telling glance at Lysha. "You want to get back to Terra, and I'm in need of someone to go there. Lysha is under the impression you may be willing to skirt some of the restrictions currently placed upon you, and I think we can make all of this work to our mutual benefit."

Hell of a birthday present. I like to be surprised, but this was like dropping atomics. I had figured the dinner was the gift. Hell, even meeting my hero outside of work was a bonus. Going home, even for a mission was so outside the realm of my possibilities.

"This situation with Terra hit us out of the dark. Completely blindsided us. I've been trying to figure out how for months, and I'm still stumped. There's normally some sort of ramp up to something like this. I can't find it. I can't find the triggering events. And it's bugging me.

"We need eyes on the ground. It's really as simple as that. It's become increasingly difficult to get a clear picture of what's going on there. If we don't have that, we're going to get blindsided again, and the next time it's going to be catastrophic.

"What I'm proposing is we send you down. You'll scout the lay of the land, and we'll figure out a plan of action from there."

This is the point where my questions started getting in depth. Not that I was trying to be ungrateful, but Terra has a population pushing eighty billion, and Luna had about half a billion at any given point. So the real question I had to ask was why me.

"It all really boils down to exclusions. If we take the people we currently have available and start looking at them, most aren't a good fit. A Looney isn't going to pass for a Terran." He was right. Low-g would give them away in a second. Lunar gravity is 1.62 m/s^2, but Terra is rocking 9.81 m/s², meaning a Looney, is running around at six times their normal weight. That's a huge difference. Most Looneys haven't been conditioned for gravity like that. A Marsan would be closer, but they would still be dealing with over double.

"So we need a Terran, not only because of the physiological issues but because of the cultural concepts. We're all humans, but Terra is going to be a foreign land to anyone who hasn't spent extensive time there. It's not I don't think you are the right man for the job, but we also don't have many qualified people. Lysha vouching for you and your personal desire makes you the prime candidate."

He had a point. It's easy to take for granted little things, like slang or body language. I had talked about how humor was different between Looneys, Terrans, and Marsans. Something as small as that could give someone away in minutes. Toss in the training I already had, and the personal connections, and the logic did make a lot of sense. Especially since this did not seem like a sanctioned operation.

As I said, Looneys have a healthy dose of pragmatism. They're not about to let bureaucracy get in the way of getting something done. Not when the alternative is as bad as implied.

I'd love to say it took a lot of convincing to get me on board with the concept of running essentially a black op into a sovereign planet. I'd also love to say I wasn't chomping at the bit. I can't say either of those things. A man whom I had the utmost respect for was offering me a devil's deal, and I wasn't strong enough to turn it down.

Chapter 7

Legionnaires all have the same basic level of training. Our original design was based on classic shipboard combat with an expeditionary mindset so we could head down to planets and conduct ground combat as needed. Sea based infantry became our historical examples for modern operations. Depending on aptitude, we go on to more specialized areas. My official designation was demolitions, but all that really meant is I knew how to tear things apart, usually with lots of explosives. It also meant I had spent quite a lot of time looking at structures ranging from mud huts to dams figuring out their various strengths and weaknesses. I'm not the best, but I'm very good.

I don't want to give the impression I'm arrogant about my skills. I'm not. However, I am confident. I've got a lot of proverbial gun time under my belt and I know what I'm doing when it comes to my specialty. I also know what the limits of those skills are. I've popped smoke before when I wasn't good enough or when I knew there were better folks more suited for the task. Nothing wrong with calling in help or asking for a second opinion. Too much pride will get you killed, and I like my skin.

The General and I started with my baseline micro level knowledge and bumped it up to the macro. Rather than looking at bridges and buildings, we went global with towns and cities. He pushed me harder mentally than I had ever been before. A completely different experience from being part of a larger class. Unfortunately, without others, any lulls or breathers were removed from the training process. I felt like I was going from simple math to rocket science in less than a month. In big classes, it's only possible to learn as fast as the slowest person. By reducing the number of people, it speeds up the rate at which information can be mastered. The focused one-on-one training accelerated my learning to migraine inducing levels. Pain is an excellent motivator though because it makes you remember. The General wasn't trying to cause harm but he had priorities.

On top of that, my workouts with Robert went from twice a week to twice a day. He had been holding back on me, and I was starting to feel the increased regiment by workout number three. If not for the nanites I would have been constantly bruised and bloodied. Even with them, it took a couple of weeks to get past the soreness of the new enhanced workout routine. I think he was pushing them to the upper limits while the General did the same to my mind.

Once the General was satisfied I had my head wrapped around global logistics to a passable level, he shipped me off to the DLF training facility near Tycho Crater. The DLF or Defense of Luna Force was the police on Luna. Not as though one was needed, not like on most planets. Looneys do not call for help preferring to take care of things themselves. The DLF dealt with the possibility of someone thinking invasion was a good idea. Anybody thinking so was in for a bad time. Looneys had no problem hunkering down, venting a dome, and then picking off anyone stupid enough to try one by one until they ran out of air, water, or food.

But the DLF was a sort of a first and last line of defense. They maintained the defensive arrays and were able to go head to head in land-based combat if they ever had to. Their mission was different, but the training was directly comparable to the Legion. No one really attacked the moon, though, so most of the DLF's time was spent as something more akin to beat cops. They were part of the community and maintained a sort of brand awareness. The best kind of policing is being visible. The vast majority of criminals fall under the stupid or lazy category. By having the DLF cops seen, Luna avoided a megatonne of problems. Additionally, when everyone and their cousin was invested in the well-being of the domes, most issues don't happen. Not to say Luna didn't have its own share of turmoil, but Looneys took a direct view of handling it.

Most of their members were militia, reserve types. Luna has a two-year mandatory service requirement. It didn't have to be military as service could be done in almost any sector, and many folks knocked it out doing janitorial before they reached their majority at eighteen. Looneys viewed Citizenship as coming with obligations, including a payback for education, training, and just breathing. People like the General had completed theirs through the Diplomatic Corps. It turned out Lysha was a qualified ship mechanic and others opted for the DLF, mainly because they offer genemod.

Genemod or genetic modification is where the scientists tweak the DNA sequences a bit. It gives us humans a few advantages. The big one people are familiar with is gravity acclimation. The human body adapted to grow in Terra's gravity, what most people refer to as normal grav. That's 9.81 m/s^2, but someone spending their entire life in 1.62 m/s^2, like the moon, and they aren't really fit to travel anywhere else.

With the right kind of genemod and intensive training, a person ends up insanely strong, fast, and able to travel anywhere without having to worry about it. This is something Terrans take for granted, but Looneys have to think about. Folks like the General didn't need same types of acclimation, so visiting anywhere with more gravity than Luna became a huge issue. Lysha had gone through some of it during her payback because mechanics need to have a good amount of physical strength even in low-g. But Luna treated the process as an investment as a strong Citizenry is a strong Nation. For others gravity isn't really a big deal most of the time. Tech helps and all, but something as simple as wanting to go on vacation becomes infinitely more complex for folks from low-g worlds.

On top of acclimation are immunities. Some humans have a predisposition towards specific disease and sickness. We mapped the genome almost two centuries back, and although we don't know what causes every sickness, or how to cure it, every generation we get a little closer. When someone knows there's a potential ticking time bomb somewhere in their future, why not trade a couple of years when they're young to get rid of the possibility in the future?

The DLF was a great resource because of not only location but also access to several tools, beneficial to our mission. General Campbell needed me on Terra and the simplest way to do that actually was have me fly down solo. But I had absolutely zero training. Legion farms combat pilot school out to the Mariners based off Titan, but the DLF also had a moderate sized flight school, which was why I was at Tycho Station.

When I got there, I met by the crustiest Sergeant Major I had ever seen. I'm not sure what crypt the DLF pulled him out of, but he had to be pushing two-fifty. He could have given Schmiddy a decent run for who was going to expire first. He spotted the abundance of stripes on my arm and grabbed my arm like we had been buddies since basic. Hell of a thing, as Schmiddy would say. There's some sort of kinship that develops when you start pinning them on. Like wearing your resume on your chest. The Legion doesn't have Sergeants Major, which from our view is more of a billet than a rank. They're the guys commanders go to for advice about the men and morale. I don't have the right kind of personality to fill that role being good with individuals, not groups. I'm more of a technical expert, which is why I wear the gold mastery insignia of my branch on my collar. It made us peers in grade if not equals in position. As he walked me around the base, I found out he was a pensioner from a century back. Served on the original *Ozzie,* the sister-ship to my own *Europe.*

After he retired, and eventually settled back on Luna he decided to turn his skills to training. The kind of training that kept young bucks like me alive in the far reaches of space. Book knowledge is amazing but comes from scientists and writers. The kind of training this old soldier gave was hard-won and contained a full century of actual experience. As time goes by human kind becomes more and more reliant on tech, the old timers like him and me, to a much lesser degree, keep the new guys grounded in non-tech solutions. DLF was a good fit for him keeping him engaged, active, and all that expertise wasn't lost.

Since the main mission of DLF is to keep things from getting bad, he loaded me up on what he called "a little light reading." I'm not sure if he was joking or not, but it looked like every book DLF had on reconnaissance and undercover work. He then turned me loose and said flight school would start the following day. He seemed less worried about that since the ship's onboard computer should be able to handle most of the heavy lifting. I needed to be able to look the part, and talk my way through approach and landing.

I had been hooked up with a stateroom so I hunkered down and started plugging away at the books until I felt like I couldn't fit any more in my head and crashed. When I was much younger I was a horrible student, but I have always loved to read. I've had to learn how to study in the Legion to stay proficient. Dealing with explosives gave me exactly the push I needed to refine my education standards. My survival on Terra was no less important to this mission so I had the incentive I needed to keep pushing.

The next day, we went through probably the most boring morning of my adult life. I don't even get bored, but if I had a spoon on me, I would have scooped one of my own eyes out, to get a slight reprieve from it. I can't blame my instructor, because just I didn't have the background, and he was trying to figure out how to make a comparable model for someone well past his learning prime. Despite looking half my chronological age, at least by Terran standards, I was essentially an old man trapped in a young body. That made picking up new concepts a hell of a lot harder than back when I was a kid.

A product of a living in space is we forget the outer wrapping doesn't necessarily match our insides. It gets even weirder when you add in deep-sleep. For a guy like me, I looked about twenty-five but had about forty-two years of awake time, and fifty linear. The General was triple that, but only looked fiftyish in Terran terms, and someone like Schmiddy or my new Sergeant Major buddy looked like the walking dead. For Thomas Knox, all he saw was a young buck needing training and approached the issue like he would every other wannabe pilot.

My instructor, was a Mariner who was originally from Ganymede, but wanderlust and the stars made him join the Space Mariners' Guild as soon as he could legally thumb on. Unlike the Legion, the Mariners' Guild didn't really have a retirement program. They just worked folks until their pilots quit. I'd personally never heard of anyone doing that, though. The guys who ended up as Mariners had a different kind of outlook on life centered on exploration and travel. Thom was no different. He was back on Luna as part of a training tour as a mid-career breather waiting to get back out to the stars.

He'd been back on Luna for about a year and a half and had been itching to leave for about twelve months. He had a cool steady confidence of someone who was very good at his job, unfortunately, because he knew it so well and had spent years around others in the same career he spoke in a hodgepodge of trade-speak and jargon, mostly flying right over my head, forcing me to stop him every couple of minutes. Each question I asked would spiral into several additional questions to the point where I felt safer not asking questions at all. It was hard to avoid that urge because I knew the mentality was not only lazy but also dangerous.

He was pounding regulation, theory, and standard control layouts into me. Once we got to the last part, things started to click a little, since almost everything from hoppers to angrav sloops used almost the same setup. I'd used hoppers back in Alaska when I was a kid, and I loved watching them race, so I went from death by vid to wide awake almost instantly. Thom saw my level of engagement jump and asked if I wanted to try my hand in the simulator. Hell yes, I would!

"We're going to start you off on something small. We'll use a light shuttle. A little ten-seater. Lots of maneuverability and wide open space. It will give you a feel for the controls. Since we're in a sim, I'll let you crash, but co-chair if you have any questions." He plopped down beside me and I watched how he moved. If I was going to pretend how to be a pilot, I needed to mirror the little things too.

He fired up the system, and for practice walked through a launch sequence, as though we were leaving a satellite, then turned the controls over to me. I have to admit there was a bit of an adrenaline rush. The grav system tied directly into the sim, so as soon as we pretend launched, I felt the loss of gravity, and lifted out of my seat. Then a shift as we accelerated. Like I said, it's the little things. I quickly buckled my restraints, as Thom laughed, and pointed to the grav controls "keep her at point one five standard grav, which is comfortable for most folks, and bump the decel damps to ninety-three cabin, 100 all others. You'll want to feel the boat moving in here, but we don't want fluids flying back there." I did as instructed, adding the advice to my mental checklist.

"Sorry about that, but the best way to learn is to feel the drop firsthand. You tend not to forget after that. The guy who taught me, Grimes, dropped us off a cliff at four gees to drive the lesson home. I figured you didn't need as much a push" He smiled. I told him I appreciated it, and he pointed me towards a nearby moon on the display telling me to make my way there.

After a few minutes "Not bad, you have a bit of a knack. You sure you don't have any training?" I told him nothing larger than a hopper back home, back when I was a kid. "Hmm... let me try something here, you keep us going towards that moon. All right?" That was when the real fun began.

For the next hour, his hands were a blur on his panel, as I did everything in my power to keep us pointed in the same direction. I was sweating bullets by the time he said: "I give up." Huh? I gave him a look inviting him to tell me what he meant. "Someone's been screwing with your head. Probably a long time ago. Your sense of spatial geography is too good." He paused the sim a second and pulled up a display showing how I did. A lot of green on the board, and only a few orange. "These should have killed us both. And nothing on this screen should be above yellow past here."

I knew I had extensive dataware, but I had always assumed it was only math based. Bad assumption apparently. I told Thom about my first liner trip, and he laughed. "Yah, I've heard of them doing them doing that before." He hesitated for a moment then said. "That pineapple on your collar is for ordnance right?" I nodded, not correcting him about the bursting bomb insignia. "The Legion probably did it to give you an edge with that. This is a side effect.

Doesn't take with everyone, and the Guild doesn't like mixing too much ware because of our own conditioning. The human mind is fragile, and you can only bend it so much. Causes issues if not done right or you're under too long. But, now we know what we're working with, let's have some fun with some bigger boats." Why did I not like it when people in authority used the word fun?

We kept going until we got to ships so big the sim didn't have the computing power to deal with us. About that time Pembroke, the Sergeant Major who greeted me originally came to end our fun for the day. Rather than getting more solo lessons, he had me auditing classes with his guys. It was a welcome break from the entire one-on-one time, which had started to stress my abilities. It's a sad state of affairs when a completely new skill set is the least stressful only because of the shared experience. His included everything from video surveillance to computer usage. As we weren't exactly sure what I was going to need, but we figured more knowledge was going to be better and tried to get me as solid a core as possible.

Over the next month, this routine repeated at a near constant pace, until I eventually graduated from sims to real shuttles, and eventually larger ships, and Pembroke had me doing light training runs back in Luna City. Nothing significant, but feet wet level type things. Get as much practice in as possible. One of the most interesting things was having me try and spot some of his undercover agents and trainees if I could. With that exercise, I was most surprised by the false positives or people I thought were potentials than those who I completely missed.

I started dividing my time between the two locations, and we started fleshing out the actual plan since we had a real grasp of what I was capable of and what I was comfortable with. It also gave me a chance to spend some more quality time with Lysha, sorely lacking since I had started my training over at Tycho.

On one such occasion, she dragged me into the bowels of Luna, far deeper than I knew even existed. Eventually, we ended up in the largest hangar I have ever seen. I think the *Rope*, the *Ozzie*, and the *Compass* could have docked inside and there would have been room to spare. A multi-level affair, filled with hundreds of ships of all sizes, but three stood out in particular. They were on the main launch pad and looked ready for takeoff. The smallest was an executive yacht, which I assumed was Lysha's. The next larger parked beside it was an old *Liberty* class, heavily modified, and updated. I'd guess in the fifty-tonne range. Light and agile. The last boat was hard to make out but looked to be over two-hundred meters long, and in the hundred kilotonne range. I was very familiar with the body design having served on the *Gerdes*, but this looked older and had the wrong coloring being a deep royal. If I didn't know better she was a *Valor*-class hospital ship. I pointed her out to Lysha.

"You've got a good eye, that's *Heart*. We're going to see him." I gave her a questioning look when she said him since we usually refer to ships as women. Having one called him struck me as odd. She caught my expression and smiled. "You'll see." As we got closer, I realized the ship was indeed a *Valor*-class, but not one of the second or third generations, like the *Gerdes*, but one of the first generations. When she said *Heart*, I had assumed the name was short for something else like *Heart of the Sea* or *The Dragon's Heart*, but this was the *Heart*. One of the original four ships of the class.

The hangar was huge, even with slide-walks, but we eventually made our way to the *Heart*. Lysha palmed us through the portal and out of habit; I requested permission to come aboard. "Granted, Lieutenant Gadsden. You are always welcome aboard." A distinctly male voice. I looked to Lysha.

"Hey, *Heart*! We're coming up to the bridge, can you light the way for us?" She announced to the air. "And please pull out that package I sent down if you would?"

"Of course. It is already waiting." The speakers adjusted volume towards me. "Lieutenant Gadsden, it is a pleasure to finally meet you. Miss Kellinger speaks very highly of you." I told the disembodied voice to call me Ari, almost saying sergeant by mistake.

Since Lysha didn't seem to be disconcerted talking to a discorporate voice, I tried not to be either. I asked if this was the original hull, and caught a little bit of pride "Yes, everything is original, except the expanded computer systems and a few minor internal modifications. That is why you are able to talk to me! When we, the *Star* and I became hyperspace capable, we woke up."

That explained it. The *Valor*-class was a decent sized ship class, but not hyperspace ready originally. They had great sub-lights as hospital ships. Massive engines and decent comps for their time. As they started aging, they were sold off, and a few folks started retrofitting them.

Making a ship *h*space capable isn't as complex as the process sounds. The only thing needed is more computing power if the ship has enough mass. We can push any amount of matter through *h*space, but the more mass it has the longer it can stay inside. This doesn't affect real distance, but it does affect the paths a particular ship can take. More time in *h*space meant more potential paths or greater coverage of the galaxy. Basically, the bigger a ship is the more places it can end up going.

The universe is like a giant spinning clock in many ways, and the *h*space pathways appear constant, as opposed to relative. So as everything inside the universe is moving and space is expanding it becomes essential to have the best computers available to calculate not only where to enter, but what the conditions will be on the other side of a jump.

The major issue is computers get both better and smaller as time goes on. This allows more computing power to fit into the same physical space making them even smarter. Eventually, by continually upgrading the ships' computers, they start getting smart enough for some ships wake up becoming first gen AI.

With military and colony craft, it didn't happen because most of them were already large enough and were *h*space ready. Upgrading them resulted in more storage space, while the ones that weren't, didn't need as large of computer upgrades so the connections needed for consciousness didn't occur. With the smaller sized craft, enhancements had the physical space limitation of the ship itself, netting the same result. Their computers weren't quite there yet. At least not during that the first era. But for ships about the size of the *Heart*, doors for computer-based intelligence opened.

As Lysha led me through *Heart* towards his main control bridge, I saw he was in pristine condition for a ship approaching a hundred and fifty years. I ran my hands along the bulkheads as we walked and admired the craftsmanship. Lysha caught me staring and slowed our walk pointing out areas as we went. Although we were taking a direct route, she made sure to point out anything I stared at for more than a few seconds. In the few minute walk, it became obvious she was not only an expert on *Heart's* inner workings but on ships in general.

"My great-grandfather bought him and *Star* from the salvage lot. Can you believe the old Federation government was going to scrap him? He couldn't get the *Valor* or *Cross*, but we're hoping someday. We think they're somewhere out near Vaneles and Trandhelm." I asked after the *Star*.

"She's with my aunt exploring. Rosly does not have the right temperament for management, but she's great at finding opportunities out-system. Has some sort of sixth sense when it comes to raw potential. She checks in about once a year, usually with a new plaything on her arm." I truly enjoyed her laugh. "I love her dearly, but thank goodness she's not a man. I don't think I could handle chasing off heirs."

The command deck doors opened for us, giving a spectacular view of the hangar. We were a good fifteen meters off the floor, but could see the back wall, displaying what appeared to be the prize collection. Bays of smaller crafts lined the walls, all vintage, but not all perfect. Many of them were worn, dinged, or pitted as if they had been recovered and placed exactly as found. I uttered a wow at the collection. Some were ancient and shouldn't even be on Luna. I looked closer and saw several sealed behind containment fields.

"Is there one you would like a closer look at Lieutenant?" *Heart* asked, and I was so distracted I didn't even bother to correct him, and only nodded. I think he was tracking my eye movements to the *Stellar R8* I had spotted off to a side, and he adjusted a view screen so I could see her better.

I gave a silent whistle as the screen zoomed in. She was a beautiful ship. Unlike *Heart* who was more teardrop shaped, the *Stellar* looked like an octopus. Her front bulbous and rounded, designed with the massive shield projectors in mind, while the rear was all thrust. This led to a much more simplistic design. Almost like the classic drawing of a rocket ship every kid sketches. It's said everyone knows where they were when a few key events in history happen. Every generation has one. The *Stellar R8* slingshotting around the sun was my generation's.

A little context to that. Slingshotting around the sun doesn't sound like a big deal. Terra spins around the Sol constantly. By building up speed, using Sol's gravity to advantage, and then launching with sub-light engines, a ship can get near light speed. Combined with *h*space drives and the right point in space, humankind can exit the galaxy. It was the proof of concept of angrav and sub-lights working in conjunction to create extra-galactic travel.

I asked if she was the original. "Sadly, no. *Lady Persephone* has not yet returned though we are hopeful. Her reactors are good for approximately seventy-five more years. Based on her exit trajectory, there is a high confidence she survived the jump into hyperspace. Based on her mass and estimated speed at entry, she would maintain travel for approximately twelve to eighteen years. Her chances of return truly depend on whether she can find a star or singularity close enough to her arrival point make a similar return trip. Otherwise, she will offload her cargo of beacons, and perhaps the next ship will be able to collect valid data."

Heart's words seemed pragmatic laced with a little sadness. I felt the pain. Seeing the *Stellar R8* launch when I was still a kid is what made me want to go to space, any way I could. At first, I wanted to be an engineer. Until I realized I wasn't smart. Then I wanted to be an explorer, until I realized they also had to be smart, like engineers. Eventually, I happened upon the Legion. Legionnaires got to work in space. I was all in.

One nice thing about growing up in Alaska is we can still see the stars. I've been down south, and there's too much light. It blocks them out but up near the poles, when it's dark out, the stars glow. They called to me and the first time I had enough money saved up, I was on the first shuttle to Luna. I played tourist for all of a half hour before making it to White Caps. The recruiters had my thumbprint before explaining everything. I didn't care. Best thing I ever did.

I never felt quite as comfortable as when I was back home, though. It doesn't get hot or cold on ship. Everything is a constant. Sure, there's a feeling of hot or cold, but it's not the same. I know it's all in my head, like the pain in my shoulder. Either that or someone has been fiddling with the controls. The experience isn't the same.

For whatever reason, his tone slammed me back into a homesick mood. Not *Heart's* fault, but I think the talk about the *Stellar* reminded me of home, and looking out at the stars. I used to do that every chance I got on ship and my recent flight training had been giving me more chances to see them as well. I think it was reminding me of how close I was.

"Ari, you with us?" I apologized for mentally wandering off. "It's okay. You just looked a little lost there for a second. Grab a seat, I wanted to ask you something." The captain's chair shifted for me. That seemed a little ominous, but I went with courteous as she grabbed the next chair over.

She bit her lip, a sign of nervousness I had only glimpsed before. "So, I'm not really comfortable with you heading down to Terra alone. I was going to suggest you take Robert with you as a partner." I opened my mouth to object, but she held up her hand. "But we both know that's a bad idea. He's easily recognizable as someone attached to Luna Corp. So I was thinking, if you don't mind, maybe. Maybe taking *Heart* with you." She held like she was waiting for objections.

"You're going to need a ship anyways. And he's about the right size." I slammed the brakes for a second. Mainly from shock, and then to buy me a minute and asked if *Heart* was all right with that.

"Oh, certainly Lieutenant, this was actually my suggestion. I believe it will increase the odds of success for your mission to have access to a higher end transport, and better computer array." This time, I did manage to correct him and told him to stop calling me lieutenant if we are going to be working together.

"Then it's settled!" Lysha announced, and all the nervousness and uncertainty I had seen moments ago disappeared. She was back in command, back in her element, and excited. Einstein's Ghost! What had I agreed to? She hopped up and ran to the back of the bridge and grabbed a package, and plopped it on my lap. "For you! Open it!"

It was a large box, perhaps three-quarters of a meter squared on the top, and about twenty centimeters deep. Upon opening I found a near duplicate of my jacket. "I know you love yours because you wear it everywhere but there's no way you can take it down to Terra, so I hope you don't mind, but I had this one made for while you're there." I pulled the new jacket out and saw there were only a few major differences. Rather than the deep scarlet of mine, this was a midnight blue, the exact shade of the tuxedo I had worn on our first date. The prominent gold stripes on the arm were absent, and instead, both collars had machined holes on for rank insignia rather than just the right side where I kept my bursting bomb insignia. Finally, the club patch was absent, and in its place was an attachment holder like the Mariners' Guild used. In the bottom of the box, there was a smaller box and a note.

I read the note first. "My boy, look after these, I wore them long ago. AC." Opening the case, I found a pair of crossed silver bars denoting a Captain.

I looked at Lysha and told her this was too much and expensive to boot. "What's the point of being rich if I can't spend my money on the man I love?" Well, that shut me up. I stood there flabbergasted for several seconds, before saying thank you for the gift, and telling her how I felt as well. "Besides, I'm stealing your jacket until you get back. These are amazing. And it smells like you."

I asked about the rank and pointed out I wasn't a captain. I wasn't even a lieutenant or a sergeant anymore. "Oh that, you forget, we're on Luna, you are what we say you are. Do you want to be a Colonel?" What, no, I almost yelled, but I think she saw my face.

"Captain Gadsden, you are Captain of the *Heart*. As such, Miss Kellinger and General Campbell have used their respective authorities to commission you." *Heart* chimed in. "Even had they not, you could use the honorific and insignia by tradition alone." I eyeballed the nearest control panel and chastised him about the rank thing. "You said I wasn't to call you Lieutenant, Captain. Nothing about Captain, Captain." I expanded the directive to using first name only. "Yes, Ari." I caught a hint of a snicker in that, but let it pass, and then thanked him for the informality.

Lysha stared at me for several moments then in an exasperated tone demanded "Try the jacket on. I want to make sure it fits. It's not like we can tailor it." I stood, taking off my Legion jacket, hanging it on her shoulders, and then slid into the new coat. Still a little stiff but fit like a glove. She pulled the rank insignia from the case and fastened them in place. Two silver *X*s at my throat, and then firmly christened me Captain of the *Heart* with a kiss.

Chapter 8

My introduction to *Heart* was the perhaps the final piece needed for the mission. I hated to think of him as merely a means of transportation, but the question had been bothering me. Getting to Terra was a major portion of the General's assignment. Meeting *Heart* made everything appear real for the first time. He was the final piece that bringing everything into focus.

Although I kept a room at White Caps since landing in LC, it was little more than a formality. When training at Tycho I had the stateroom, and when back in the city I stayed with Lysha. She had even given me a few drawers in her apartment for spare personal items. Cleaning out my White Caps had been simple, as I canceled my indef key, and let the couple of remaining belongings shift to my vault. Gathering up my belongings at Lysha's was far more complex because I was doing so under her watchful eye.

We weren't sure how long I would be gone, and I was lax to leave items for her to deal with over the coming months. Not as though I had much to begin with. Outside of a half-full duffel, most items were already in my vault. The only real exception was my jacket, which Lysha had taken to wearing as promised. Robert confided he was happy strictly from a security standpoint and was thinking about getting her more synth-leather items. The only other items of note were the dinner jacket and a couple of suits. She informed me those would stay in the closet until I got back, and her tone indicated it was not the hill I wanted to die on. Since I couldn't think of any reason why I might need the more formal attire, into the closet the suit went, hanging next to the slinky number she had worn on our first date.

This trip reminded me of previous departures and the occasional cutting of ties accompanying relationships on other worlds. Lysha was having none of that. "It's a business trip. You go, you come back and we resume where we left off." Despite the confidence of her words, I still wasn't sure how she could remain so adamant, but her certainty of nothing changing bordered the supernatural. I was happy for her confidence because she kept me focused.

The last minute items were beginning to pile up and without her, Robert, the General, and *Heart,* I know I would have forgotten something, or worse botched something important. After meeting *Heart,* I started visiting him as often as possible. My goal was to learn how to fly him and work with him. He, in turn, wanted to get out of the hangar as much as possible and was elated to have company. I asked him why he didn't fly alone and got a simple "There's no excitement in it." His attitude surprised me more than anything did. I wouldn't have thought excitement was a desirable outcome. "Quite the contrary. What is the point of going wherever you want, if you cannot share the experience? I enjoy seeing new places, but my enjoyment has always been significantly higher when I have had a crew." He had a great point.

That led me to ask what he did when he wasn't flying. "I have projects I work on. You saw many of them the day we first met." I thought back to that first day and realized he meant the ships in the hangar triggering another slew of questions. "I like to restore them. The hobby can be time-consuming. Did you know there are entire message boards dedicated to a specific type of craft or even a series batch? People are incredibly helpful and willing to share their knowledge." Some of the ships he had were unbelievable.

It made me wonder how he worked on them. "The hangar is a fully outfitted shipyard, and we have linked many of its systems to where I can control them remotely. I have fabrication bays available myself for smaller items, repairs, or if I need to make a tool and my drones are capable of precision work." I had seen a few of them wandering about but hadn't made the connection.

Our discussion sparked an idea, I hoped *Heart* would agree to. I asked about the possibility of doing a final mission dinner with the entire team. "Easily done. We can use the wardroom if you would like. It's been unused for some time, but I think the facility would be fitting." He paused for a moment "Leave things to me." I told him I wasn't trying to put him in an odd position. "As Captain, you have other concerns to worry about. If we are going to be working together, you will need to delegate quite a bit in the future. Let us treat this as a test run." I could definitely see how he and Lysha got along.

I'm not sure if it was his personality or intelligence that made everything come together for the dinner, but we ended up having an outstanding time. Lysha and I arrived first with the General and Robert showing up only twenty minutes behind us. *Heart* had rearranged the wardroom into a cozier set up with a central dining table, a small bar to one side, and nook with chairs rivaling the ones at Mason & Redback to one side. Knowing those were aboard was going to end up being a huge distraction. I debated asking about moving one onto the bridge itself instead deciding to request for one in my stateroom later.

There was no shoptalk that evening since everything feasible was already complete. It was a night of relaxation, good food, and far too much drink. Everyone told stories and jokes, quite a few in horrible taste, which elicited far more laughter than I thought was possible from our professional crowd. Even Robert had a couple of glasses of a dark red beer and told a few war stories bordering on bawdy, which for him was near obscene. His posture had never been uptight but during dinner, he was positively relaxed to the point where he hinted at his reasons for not returning to Terra. Unlike me, he was content with the expat lifestyle.

As good evenings go, this one turned out great. The night concluded when the General finally bowed out taking advantage of *Heart's* generous offer to a stateroom for the evening. Robert grabbed one as well stating, "That's more drink than I've had in six months. I doubt I'm safe to drive." With those parting words he left Lysha, *Heart*, and I alone and carefree. Even *Heart* excused himself shortly thereafter, claiming to go into standby, though I think he was being courteous. Finally, Lysha offered to give me a tour of the ship, which I thought odd until she dragged me into the Captain's quarters.

Chapter 9

Although *Heart* and I had been making almost daily runs around Luna, after lots of discussions, we had decided a direct flight from Luna to Terra would not be the wisest course of action. Instead, we chose to get some inter-system time to Ganymede or Titan in to establish my credentials as a local trader.

Flying with *Heart* was a hell of a lot different than flying alone, or even flying with someone else. No, that's not right. *Heart* was someone else, but the idea was hard to wrap my head around at first since I didn't actually see a person sitting in the seat next to me.

Heart was insanely patient with me. Like a superior dance partner, who let me take the lead. When he declared me captain, he meant it, and to him, I had complete control, even though his ability would surpass anything I would ever be capable of. That level of trust was frightening. The tastes of command I had experienced in the Legion never prepared me for anything close to it.

Although my new position added a lot of stress, it also added a lot of fun as well. *Heart* had a lot of power, and we had a huge playground in the Sol system. One of the first things we tried was an actual spacewalk. Had I been flying a smaller ship it wouldn't have been required. Heck, a spacewalk wasn't really required with *Heart* since he was technically a rated pilot in his own right, but he insisted on getting me fully qualified up to his tonnage, and that meant being able to conduct an inspection while in space. I wouldn't be able to do any repairs, but that's what the mechanic was for. The way he figured it, the more proficient I was, the better partners we would be. I really couldn't fault his logic. And walking in space is so cool. At least until your partner plays a joke and hits the engines.

It was a great joke too. The kind of joke I would have played on Legion buddies in my much younger and more immature days. After he reeled me in and my swearing ceased, I even told him so. He hadn't even gone very fast, probably only a few meters a second, but in space, the key issue is acceleration or gravity, not maximum speed. He had given me just enough of a tug to make me think we were accelerating to full. I had thought something had gone catastrophically wrong when in fact he was merely having a bit of harmless fun with someone he considered a friend. It was the kind of joke Marsans would love, having elements of misunderstanding, danger, and potential death.

After letting me cool down a bit, he did let me have my own flavor or fun, though. "Ari, would you like to try and reach maximum acceleration?" In other words, he wanted to put the reactors to full and see how fast we could go. I wasn't even a little mad at him. It really was a great joke, but if I had been, this was the kind of present that would have got *Heart* back in my good graces instantly.

The maximum speed of real-space is c. It's the hard limit of our universe. To reach that limit a ship needs acceleration. Any ship can get to c, given enough time and distance. What we are comparing is not a ship's maximum speed but its relative acceleration. A small craft with large engines accelerates faster than a larger craft with the same size engines.

Military craft by their nature has huge engine-to-mass ratios. Maneuverability is a major concern. The *Valor*-class was the mold for almost all future ships of his size. As a hospital ship, they were essentially neutral, and treated anyone regardless of alliance, and the idea of pumping as much raw speed as possible made practical sense for its design. Getting to where they were needed most as fast as possible was essential.

Because we're dealing with acceleration, the math gets a little wonky, so it's a little easier to say how long travel takes to get from point A to point B than to describe ship speed like gravity, which is the closest comparison. Terra is one astronomical unit from Sol, convenient because that's actually the standard definition. Jupiter runs about five and a half astronomical units from Sol depending on where he is in its cycle.

The easiest way to describe distance is by designating a point like Sol, and referencing everything else off it. From Sol, light takes a little under five hundred seconds to reach Terra, and about forty-five minutes to reach Jupiter. *Heart* was fast, but not that fast. He could travel anywhere in the system in thirty days, but Sol to Jupiter was about a three-day hop at max because we had to ramp up speed.

We were taking our sweet time because I wanted to log as much flight time as I could. The more comfortable I was in the chair, the more I was going to be able to fake being a real pilot when the time came. Additionally, there's a massive asteroid belt between Mars and Jupiter making it difficult to plow forward. The easiest way is to go up and over, accelerating on the way up, and decelerating on the way down in a ballistic curve. *Heart* recommended actually going through the thinner upper areas to build up my skill and confidence levels, as he had a reasonably solid map of the major 'roids, and assured me he could get us out of there if needed.

That experience elevated us from partners to friends quickly. I knew *Heart* had my back, as well as his own proverbial skin but I also knew he was willing to let me make mistakes so I could learn.

Hospital boats don't have any real weapons on them. A couple of ion cannons which are short-range disrupters, but that's about it. *Heart* does have great shields, though and if he knew he could take a hit from a small rock without taking any major damage, *Heart* let us take the hit. He'd shut off dampers right before the impact so I'd get thrown with him and know exactly what happened too. What he called an object lesson. He also swore like a sailor. It was awesome.

The opposite was also true. If I missed something big, and we couldn't take the hit, he either told me or got us out of there. He didn't second guess me. He simply took action and let me know what was going on. He knew what our combined limitations were, and what our long-term goals were.

We spent a little under two weeks playing in the field before space opened up and we continued on to Jupiter. Our short-term goal was to hit Ganymede since I needed practice flying through an actual atmosphere, and that's where I was going to get it. Ganymede is sort of like a miniature Terra. It's a gorgeous place. It has light gravity, an oxygen atmosphere, and after it was Terraformed, became an almost resort planet. Because of the asteroid field between Jupiter and Mars, ballistic transports didn't work well for supplies. Fire and forget technology couldn't be used like between Luna and Mars or Jupiter and Saturn. So the corporations relied on the Mariners and smaller ships. *Heart* and I were betting on that.

The majority of Ganymede's goods came in on big transports a few times a year when the planets were closest to each other. The thing to remember is we usually define things based on standard time, but when everything is spinning that means everything is constantly getting closer or farther away from each other.

Terra has the classic year, or cycle for simplicity sake. Mars is not quite twice that, so Terra is closest to Mars a little more twice a year. The goal is to launch ships from Terra at the point closest to where Mars is going to be. The same applies to every other point in space. It saves energy.

The issue is the amount of time and energy to move stuff between planets. Especially due to the need to escape gravity wells. So when the product is moved companies like to move as much of it as possible. Unfortunately, niche items or expendables aren't always accounted for.

I've mentioned my love of media before. For this first run, we decided to load up on as much low volume recreational items as we could. Since Luna Corp was technically footing the bill we weren't worried about profit margin, however, *Heart* had tapped into the historical data and indicated he could make us a profit.

Our real goal was to try to get merchandise we could take back to Terra. We had a list of options but I was hoping to make contacts with other traders on the satellite and find out what I could peddle.

I've spent most of my time talking about what *Heart* taught me, but I'd like to believe I taught him things as well. He'd been docked for quite a while because the Dixon-Kellinger family didn't know what to do with a sentient ship. His sister the *Star* was with Lysha's aunt Rosly as their personalities seemed aligned closely, but *Heart* had bonded with Lysha when she was a kid, roughly the same time I had joined the Legion. Turns out we're about the same age once my deep-sleep is accounted for, one of the many reasons we clicked so well.

It's not that his personal skills were bad. They weren't, but they were rusty. I could tell he wanted to ask lots of questions about everything. Things I had seen, done, and experienced. He couldn't get enough. But he was trying not to overwhelm me as well. He had spent so much time with a single family, *Heart* had never truly developed a concept of boundaries. I had gone through the same issue being part of close-knit teams in the Legion, living and working with same folks day in and day out meant there were no real borders.

Although he was much older than me and infinitely smarter, he hadn't spent the same amount of time around people. Interactions are required to develop complex thought. Unfortunately, less exposure actually stunted his growth in a lot of ways. He could critically think about issues logically but when it came to examining emotions those thought patterns hampered him. He hadn't developed the ability to segregate different ways of thinking yet.

On our trip over from Luna I had found out a lot about his purchase, and awakening. Although the long-term goal had been to outfit him for *h*space travel, like the *Star*, the primary reason for his purchase was he was a hospital ship and a large one at that. As I said, Looneys are pragmatic by nature and taking what was essentially a hospital that could be placed anywhere on Luna's surface and used as a mobile base made good sense.

Heart didn't have a large crew at that point. Only a handful and they didn't realize his upgraded systems were making him exponentially smarter to the point of becoming self-aware. It wasn't until he began anticipating the needs of the crew were suspicions raised.

People develop habits, and habits are a fancy way of saying patterns. A computer can spot patterns, and once seen, can begin to anticipate what comes next. The issue was no one had programmed *Heart* to do that. Not in the ways the crew was seeing. Little things like preparing coffee and sending lifts to the correct corridor at exactly the right time.

When the pilot sat down one morning and said a hearty "Good Morning, Luna!" to the empty bridge and *Heart* responded back, the new voice scared him out of his seat. They weren't sure how to react. No one wanted to make that particular call to the company office. But want and need are very different things.

Wayne Dixon was not one who liked delays, and although *Heart's* awakening wouldn't delay things, it definitely had the potential to. The crew decided to err on the side of caution and call the boss rather than having to explain why they hadn't at some point in the future. Ever the realist, grandpa Dixon had them complete the project and then examine the issue. He dry-docked *Heart* until he could figure out how to use his new and unwanted employee.

Although he wasn't happy about losing his investment in a mobile hospital, Wayne Dixon was a fan of having intelligent employees, especially ones who didn't need sleep and generated money without downtime. When the *Star* awoke a couple of months later, he realized how complex the situation could become, and decided to limit who had access to the ships. This made the issue somewhat of a family secret, in turn reducing the people both interacted with.

Heart was starved for human contact. Even tapped into the main computers of Luna, he had difficulty gaining the same social experience of human interaction when the number of people he knew was limited. I didn't get the impression his existence was a true secret, simply not advertised.

AI has been around for a long time, but it's always been a legal gray area, and each government and corporation treat the issue differently, both morally and ethically. The idea of what is essentially property who is alive opens up some real questions many people are not comfortable dealing with.

Back during the singularity era, in the mid twenty-first century when computers started getting advanced enough to where they were theoretically capable of matching human potentials, a lot of laws went into play. Lots of treaties were written about what and how we would treat artificial intelligence should it arise. The problem was we never figured AI out. It never happened on Earth.

It wasn't until the age of hyperspace when computers got big enough and smart enough when they woke up. I asked *Heart* if he thought he was the first "Unlikely Ari. At the time, I was far from an advanced model. I am certainly of the first generation, but far more probable an Imperial Frigate or Mariner Spaceliner would have gained consciousness several years before me. I was mothballed during the first wave of hyperspace upgrades, and was classified as obsolete during that time-frame." Obsolete? I was shocked by that, as his hull design was considered a classic. The first ship I was on, the *Gerdes* had almost the same body design. I said as much.

"Yes, obsolete. Eventually, there are enough incremental changes every ship is. Engines get better and computers become more advanced. The medical and fabrication bays as well. Although my body is almost completely original, I have extensive upgrades where it counts. This is my fourth brain so to speak. It is rather bizarre feeling yourself getting more intelligent each time it happens."

"When you joined the Legion, did you feel yourself get stronger?" I had to think about that. I tried to answer as best I could, but strength is always relative. I knew I was stronger than when I joined, but because gravity changes from place to place, I was never clear on how much. I didn't have a consistent point of reference. Being able to lift fifty kilos on Terra didn't mean much when I could lift three hundred on Luna even before genemod. Living in all the different gravities, I had never consistently tried to maximize my strength. I knew I was stronger, but I hadn't felt myself get so. It wasn't until I needed it did I realize how much more power I had at my disposal. But that was usually combined with rushes of adrenaline and fear, so again no definitive point of reference.

I did point out I knew I was a hell of a lot smarter now than I used to be. Mainly because I had so many more experiences since then. My context had changed so much. What I thought I knew was so different from back then. Compared to the present, I was an idiot when I joined.

"That makes sense. New data has the potential to change every connection within a relational database. I have had to expand memory banks several times based on new hyperspace beacon data input."

This brought me back to wondering about his official status. I let my curiosity get the better of me and decided to broach the subject. "I am a free citizen of Luna under the Artificial Intelligence Accords of 2214." There was quite a bit of pride in his statement. "Wayne Dixon filed for me as soon as he was told I was sentient." Lysha's great-grandfather.

That explained it. From everything, she had told me about him, the best description for him was a hard man. Not mean, or cruel, just hard. Made like the rock or Luna itself. He came from the post-war era and had a leadership style to match. Very much a force of will type of guy. Effective and efficient. Fair and firm but things were black and white. No gray area. Ironic living on Luna. For him, *Heart* was either a person or he was property. Apparently, he decided person and ended the debate forever by making him a citizen.

That's a big deal. Luna doesn't abide by slaves, indentured servants, or anything else even smelling like it. One foot on Luna equals freedom. For a long time, Luna's status as a trust was abused, and folks have a long memory. Grandpa Dixon being a Looney himself shared that issue, and decided *Heart* was one of Luna's own.

I asked more about him and got a distinct pause. Pauses were very telling when dealing with *Heart*. I knew he could answer instantly. I knew he had dozens of ways and had already computed the best possible response. But pauses told me there was a logical conflict between what best was, changing what should be a normally simple calculation like navigating an asteroid field into something much more akin to *h*space travel. I got pauses when I asked him how he felt about things.

"I am not sure he liked me, Ari. He did not know what to do with me. He was a good man, of that I have no doubt, but I do not know if he was a nice man. From what I could gather, he had expectations and would not deviate from them. I believe," another pause, as though uncomfortable with the word "that he was unable to come up with expectations for me. I was outside his realm of experience. It was easier for him to ignore me."

"I was useful to him. I was instrumental in rebuilding the Luna Corporation's infrastructure. I helped in much of the redesign of the lower levels, and supplemental domes." That actually brought up an interesting point regarding Luna's own computers. I knew it took massive computers to keep not only the corp but also the moon itself operational, so I asked *Heart*.

"No, Master Dixon was somewhat averse to turning over control. He believed in a decentralized structure, which was wise, though maybe not for the same reasons. He kept the systems intentionally small and segregated so they would not gain consciousness. Sometimes I think his actions were a kindness."

It was my turn for a long pause before I finally asked why. "Ari, not to be morbid, but barring a catastrophic accident, artificial intelligence like myself are functionally immortal. Human life, though long-lived is not. One of the hardest issues I had to deal with was the realization people cease to be. Furthermore, because our sense of time is so different, if I do not intentionally disable it, I would count down until your theoretical demise. Knowing fewer people is actually beneficial, as it becomes easier to deal with the eventualities."

He was right. The idea was morbid and true. A sentient computer on Luna would have to deal with millions of people dying constantly. That would be tough. Worse than that, he would have to deal with people arriving and leaving constantly, and just not knowing. An AI wouldn't have the same built-in ability to ignore or forget like humans.

Chapter 10

"Ari, we are on our final approach to Anson Station." I thanked him and got ready. I felt weird having the Captain's stateroom, located in a heavily shielded area off the bridge. Exceptionally nice compared to rooms I had stayed in previously, it was about twice the size of my room at White Caps, and easily quadruple anything I had stayed in while still in the Legion. Included bunkmates. The room had its own refresher, and a kitchenette, but *Heart* told me there was a full-scale galley for my executive officer and me if we ever gained one. Above and beyond the regular galleys for the ship's crew, and passengers, which were currently shut down. The furniture in my stateroom was simple, a good-sized bookrack, a nice desk, some enclosed bookshelves, and the wardrobe.

I selected a few items from the wardrobe, based on what we had seen a selection of traders wearing in Luna on various security feeds, and my own scouting runs after my training at Tycho. From what I could tell, most pilots leaned towards comfort and utility. I slid my new jacket on to complete the ensemble and gave myself a once over in the mirror.

My old synth-leather boots were staying with me because they were strong, comfortable, and broken in. Why reinvent the wheel? I had on a good set of tan utility trousers, I had managed to give a somewhat worn look over the last couple of weeks. A simple belt and a light shirt peeked out from under my jacket. Most importantly my jacket also kept my holster out of view and preventing awkward questions about that piece of insurance. The gun wasn't strictly illegal, but any security who saw it on me might raise a few eyebrows and I was aiming for non-descript. We had added a patch to the front. CKG Limited with a corporate logo, a pair of rockets to signify my status as a pilot.

We had decided against putting my old call sign or real name. CKG Limited was the name of a previously non-existent company we put together as an import and export firm to disguise our plan. Rather than smuggling in contraband, we were going to smuggle in the ship and myself, and use the cargo as the Trojan horse.

"Captain on the bridge" *Heart* announced to no one in particular. Despite my many protests, I couldn't get him to give that up, and I think the protocol may have been hard-coded into his programming, or his idea of a joke. I was debating it as I hopped into my chair. My chair. Such an odd thought. "Ari, we still have a little while before we arrive. Were there any final preparations you wanted to make?" I couldn't think of anything we hadn't covered a dozen times before, so shook my head.

I brought up the most recent newsfeed from the local satellites and did a quick refresher on local events. The one thing we have never been able to figure out is how to push radio waves through space faster than light. Plays hell with trying to watch anything off-planet.

I'd only ever been to Ganymede once before. It's a nice place in the nice parts and seedy in the not so nice parts. Unlike Mars, which was a semi-independent government, Ganymede was a joint venture. There was a government, but the corps ran it. Ganymede was a brand more than anything else. It was an attitude. A place to escape and the corporations religiously protected that ideal. They used the government as a tool to enforce, hiding anything even remotely unpleasant under the surface.

This made Ganymede an ideal tourist resort. Beautiful in every way, but still requiring logistics, administration, and operation. These are far from pretty or clean. The bureaucracy behind them can foster corruption, especially when appearance and profit become the primary concerns. Like a gorgeous pristine apple once cut is rotten to the core.

That metaphorical apple appeared on *Heart's* main viewport, and he switched control to me, after coordinating for landing at Anson Station. Anson was the largest and primary port handling anything not related to strictly to passengers. Since we were pretending to be a cargo ship we headed in that direction, rather than towards Port Moore, which handled all the tourists. I was glad *Heart* had run me through dozens of sims on atmospheric entries because I nearly botched my attempt even with the extra training. Once we made the transition things settled down a lot, but flying in a vacuum is a lot different than flying through air. Whatever skills I thought I had, quickly disappeared. I almost had *Heart* take control, but instead told him to watch my back in case I did anything stupid or was leaning towards unrecoverable.

After what seemed entirely too long, with *Heart* pretending to be me on the comm-link so I could focus entirely on landing him, we secured a place on a mid-sized pad. Since we hadn't actually arranged for the sale of our merchandise, we hadn't lined up a hangar or any kind of storage. We figured we would be here for a week tops, so used our imaginary company to pay for the pad. Comms were actually simple, since the new dampers I had picked on

Luna could link directly with Ganymede, and *Heart* could tap into their communications system.

Shortly after he had swapped into standby, I strode down the gangplank, not sure what to expect. I ended up meeting a customs officer with a bored look on his face, so I tried to counter his apathy as best I could with a smile and played stupid. Told him it was my first solo run and saw if he wouldn't educate me a bit.

One of the best parts of bureaucracies, especially known corrupt ones is nepotism. Everyone has a cousin or a brother-in-law. By playing dumb, and leveraging his self-interest, getting him to help himself, he could end up helping us at the same time. While I was doing this, *Heart* was using my damper's earpiece, and one of its lenses to give me a little more information on our new friend. Nothing distracting, but enough to allow me to nudge and tweak the conversation in the right direction. Not much later, he had us processed with minimum graft and pointed towards the sector where he planned to rob us blind for our cargo.

Chapter 11

I hopped onto the nearest tram and followed the directions my new customs buddy had given. I normally shut down when traveling, but *Heart* was tapped into my dampers and this was a completely new experience for him. Since he could see through the lens display, and hear through the mic, he was rattling off questions as fast as he could compose them. Luckily, my tramcar was empty so I was able to answer freely, and swivel to look at everything *Heart* wanted to see.

"Ari, can we get you higher resolution aud-vid equipment?" I wasn't tracking, so I asked him to explain. "Our communication equipment is adequate" a distinct note of disdain, "but it could be better. I researched some commercially available alternatives of a similar style to the ones you currently wear, which are far more robust."

It hit me. To me, my dampers were merely a pair of glasses to adjust the incoming light and sound to the correct level, with minor communication capability. To him, the glasses were a lifeline to the outside world. His normal connections were through satellites, security cameras, or whatever other feed he could find. On Luna, those were extremely limited and locked down. He was unintentionally blinded. While I traveled, my wearing even an inexpensive set was giving him an expanded view he didn't have access to before.

I had him tell me where the best nondescript pair could be found, and detoured immediately to purchase a couple. I also told him we would figure out how to expand his visibility at our earliest change. "Thank you, Ari!" I told him not to worry about it, but to let me know if there was anything else I was missing. I wasn't able to process as much or as fast as him, and I was bound to miss things.

After grabbing and syncing up the new dampers at one of the fancier casino gift shops, I grabbed a quick bite to eat while *Heart* played with the settings. My initial thoughts of them being only for him were completely wrong. Previously, I always leaned towards the inexpensive sets, because I tended to break them. Wear and tear was intense.

But a gig's worth of new tech added a lot of features I hadn't even considered. The new set was better than the heads up in my combat kit. On top of that, the dampers added a 270-degree visual sweep, and its audio pickup was clean enough to monitor my heartbeat. I didn't understand half of what the box said, but *Heart* seemed very excited, and as he shifted through various features like news channels, low light, and UV, I started to understand why.

The other items he had me pick up were the best comm unit the store had and a compact signal repeater. The dampers interfaced with those, but the real power would actually be in the microcomputer housed in the comm unit.

After feeding my stomach and his excitement on our new toys, we headed deeper into the city itself. Our destination was on the opposite side, in what was essentially the low rent district. The city was set up in rings sitting on top of each other. The upper city handled all of the tourists and people who could afford to live on Ganymede permanently, and the lower city laid underneath was very similar to Luna's setup. The vicinity of the ports and the casinos created their own economies regarding property values, developing a fun-house mirror effect. Swapping from above to below the values shifted dramatically because labor for each area was reversed.

The Spacelanes Lodge was my goal was mid-sized inn setup with full room and refreshers. Although *Heart* was a big ship and fully equipped most of the ships we saw were sparse and only designed for moon-to-moon jumps. From what we could gather, the place was a bit of a local hangout, but not an exclusive bar. I didn't need to be a Mariner or a Legionnaire to go in. I'm sure the bar had its regulars, but I shouldn't draw too much attention being an unknown either.

When I arrived, my first impression boiled down to thinking the place was a dive. A completely unfair assessment. Anything in Sol looked like a dive compared to White Caps, after I had recently spent several lunar months in her. Spacelanes wasn't even a fraction the size of White Caps. Probably fit in the public section, even. The more I thought about it, the more I realized the place is probably what White Caps looked like long ago. The main entrance opened into a diner, but I could see a breakfast counter with the kitchen behind off to one side and a full bar on the other.

I slid to the kitchen side and grabbed a stool. "Be right with you, Hon." a server shouted as she hurried past. The place wasn't overly busy, but enough to keep the couple of servers hopping. I guessed around thirty folks total, and not all human. The presence of non-terrestrials was actually fairly surprising. Most of the other species require slightly higher O_2 levels, so Terraformed places weren't exactly comfortable for them. Much like being on Terra wasn't exactly pleasant for Looneys. As I scanned the area, *Heart* did the same, but he was creating a map and giving me hard data about everything in the club. I have to admit, the feed was slick, and I not only wondered where he was all my life but how I was ever going to live without him in the future.

Nikki, according to the nametag slid up "What it'll be, Hon?" I told her coffee for the moment but asked her about Corrupt Cousin Teddy from the port. "You must be new, darling. Stay away from him." She dropped her voice to a conspiratorial whisper. "You're better off hitting the job boards. That's the kind of guy who will end up getting you in the wrong crowd." I confided I was indeed new, and asked her if there was anyone a little more trustworthy. She told me she'd think about it and grabbed my drink.

Heart chimed in "She seems nice. Do you think she can help us?" I nodded and hoped he could pick up the motion. We would need to figure out a way to talk in public. His ability to talk to me was great, but I lacked the same ability. Long ago I had heard an adage, if you see an issue, imagine yourself a month in the future dealing with it as a problem instead.

This had happened to me long ago when I was still a trooper. I had spotted a bad connector on a hopper. No big deal. We marked it and put it on order. The thing is after walking by it three times, it becomes that bad connector. We knew it was there and stopped worrying about it. A half year later the connector was still bad, and we go to attach our kit and we couldn't. Because there's a bad connector we'd known about forever. There's no excuse for that. We couldn't simply say we had ordered it because the follow-up is, when had we checked on it last, and we hadn't.

I plugged a quick text message into my comm unit and asked for *Heart* to come up with some ideas. The last thing I wanted was not being able to talk to him when I needed to. "I am already working on some options. However, I can monitor your biometrics, which should suffice until we come up with a permanent solution." We were discussing possible ways to use this when Nikki came back to refill my cup and slide me a comm chip. I gave her a quick nod of thanks as I drained my cup before she topped me off.

On her next stop, I asked about rooms, and she pointed me to the kiosk in the hall. It was automated and actually let me rent by in almost any increment I wanted, from hour to month. I assumed that was in case someone wanted a quick shower or had an extended leave. I credited a couple of days and headed on up.

The parallels between here and White Caps were becoming more obvious. Like the hotels were cut from the same cloth, but just were tailored into different items as the years went on. The room I had been assigned was an almost exact match to the one I stayed in right before I shipped to basic. It was uncanny. More than likely the plans were simple and universal, and I could find the layout anywhere in the galaxy if I looked hard enough. I hadn't been in many hotels, so the novelty was amusing so I spent several minutes playing with drawers and buttons while talking to *Heart* about it.

I finally quit my yammering and got back to business. I pulled out the comm chip and accessed it. There were a few names, which *Heart* quickly accessed and displayed on the room's screen rather than my dampers. "They look like local vendors. I do not see any major criminal activity though it is hard to tell with the official databases." I told him I was less worried about that, and more about establishing our cover. The idea of the job boards caught my attention, though.

"Mine as well. The boards appear to be a bulletin of sorts. Similar to the listings where I purchase parts for my projects. One can place listings of services for a price. I have narrowed the choices down to transport, excluding passengers and come up with several viable options." A new list appeared on the screen. I asked what was worth our time monetarily. "Based on our cover, we would need to be at least one-third full for fuel consumption. Although I use fusion reactors, my vehicle registration class is a fuel burning type. That removes this portion of the list." Almost half the list disappeared. "Further, our stated experience makes us ineligible for this section. Though we may be able to negotiate pricing." Another section in red. "This leaves several unclassified entries, likely smuggling operations. I know we are not specifically opposed to them, but I am unsure what challenges those jobs may present." A section in yellow.

The board had three entries in green, eight yellows, and six reds. I told *Heart* nice work, and to focus on selling what we already had. We'd break the list into parts. Some we'd sell to our customs buddy. We'd never know when we'd need a helping hand. The rest we'd split between the list Nikki gave us. As for the rest of the list, we'd start setting up meetings and see if we couldn't swing a job.

Chapter 12

We knew finding the correct job wasn't going to be easy. The job board was actually a bit of a godsend in some ways, however. Although none of the first lists panned out, they did net us a solid batch of contacts, and we ended up getting a couple of quick trial runs from Ganymede to some of Jupiter's other moons. Nothing spectacular but enough to justify being in that area of the system by helping us build a little bit of credibility in the circuit while we tried to find the haul to take us to Terra.

Since *Heart* was a mid-sized ship, we weren't in actual competition with the locals allowing us to establish a niche market. We could do things the smaller guys couldn't due to space while they could do things we couldn't far cheaper. It was very favoresque. We would get tips about someone needing a shipment moved, and if we could cover it at a good price, we would. If outside our wheelhouse, we'd point the job to someone else. The reverse was also true. We'd gotten at least a dozen calls over the last month from different referrals.

Heart was having a blast. Although we kept his nature private, he was publicly my partner and co-pilot. Something he found great amusement in. Being the copilot that is. I can't say I blamed him. His social group was expanding rapidly since he handled the communications system; he also started to cover our flight schedule. I think he liked the responsibility or he was bored to the point where he convinced himself he did.

After our initial dock fees expired, he went ahead and leased us a small platform of our own, and what was nominally an office. In reality, a garage with a barely working runabout and a functioning comm feed. Absolutely perfect. We plastered our logo on both. The concentric rings representative of our solar system combined with the CKG lettering. We had debated putting the logo on *Heart* himself and discarded the idea very quickly. Neither one of us wanted to mar his gorgeous hide.

I was in the process of restocking *Heart's* freezers when we got an actual lead. He had an extensive larder and an even better greenhouse, but even the best kitchen has gaps. I wasn't trying to complain, but there are some things I would start to crave when I couldn't have them. Stupid things like lemons. I had gone five years without any lemons, but after having three of Schmiddy's half-and-halves I was craving them constantly. Being on Ganymede gave me the perfect opportunity to expand our stores. It's not like we had a lack of storage space. "Ari, I think we have something. When you have the chance, can you make your way to the bridge?" I told him I would be up as soon as I finished the crate I was on.

I ducked out of the reefer and made my way up to the command deck. *Heart* announced me as soon as I walked in, and I shook my head. I asked what he had. "I think this may be the one we have been waiting for. It's a request for us to transfer a fairly large shipment of crystallic drone chips. There is a need for a ship with magnetic sealing capability." I asked what the catch was. He was talking about high-end gear, and despite our recent successes, we were still rookies. "We need to pick the shipment up soon, and it needs to be delivered within three weeks. It will, however, give us a solid visa to enter Terra controlled space." I told him to sign us up and get us prepped for the takeoff. I then stopped, and asked what he meant by a pickup. "The shipment is on Titan. I believe we have barely enough time to make it there. I would suggest buckling in. I need to turn the gravity down, or you will probably become extremely nauseous as we leave." I had perhaps three seconds of Ganymede's gravity before we went null, and I felt the decel dampers kick to full. I grabbed my chair, quickly pulled on my harness, and watched the front viewport accelerating at what I guessed was close to unregulated speeds.

Our quick upward rise saw a shift from the light blue of a normal sky to the salted black of space in less than a minute. I felt gravity slowly return to normal "The conn is yours if you want it, Captain." I told him he was fine, but a little warning next time would be great. He had us on course towards Saturn's moon Titan. Luckily, Jupiter and Saturn were relatively close in orbit at this point, so we weren't making a huge detour, but we did have to hit the far side of the planet to get to Titan.

Titan was the central hub of Saturn much like Ganymede was Jupiter's. The sheer number of moons the two planets had dictated each needed someplace to be. The planets couldn't because of both their size and composition, but the two moons made perfect choices. Rather than Terraform Titan like most of the rest of the system, we slowly modified the sub-surface to make it comparable to Terra, while leaving the moon's surface alone. It shared many similarities with Mars, but rather focused on mining, leaning towards manufacturing using the Saturn's moons, and the rings for raw product.

The drone chips were one of the products made on Titan. In almost every form of robotic that needed any form basic AI. Although manufactured anywhere, it was cheaper to make them and ship them from Titan. The same was true for other products. When I was a kid, I always thought it was funny my dad got Marsan made tools for the ranch at a fraction of what it would cost for the same things made on Terra. It wasn't until I was in the Legion and took a few economy classes that the idea actually sunk in. Still boggles the mind, but makes a little more sense.

Heart had us on an extremely aggressive flight plan. We were well below his max acceleration, but fast enough to draw attention if anyone was looking. Luckily, it's a very big system, and we were a very small ship. I asked him what the rush was. "We have spent quite a lot of time in preparations, and this is the first real chance we have had. If the current market trends are any indication, Terra based shipments have slowed tremendously. I believe that if we miss this, there may not be another chance for quite some time." His logic was sound. Leaving the Galactic Union had ramifications above and beyond the political. When a planet isn't playing nice politically, they generally aren't playing nice economically either. That did beg the question of whether this shipment was strictly legal. "As near as I can tell. It looks like a high priority request, which only FrenCorp could deliver on. I was not able to get more information than that. Their security is quite good, and I did not want to alert them."

FrenCorp was a solid player on Titan. They were far from the largest industrial producers but were one of the oldest. The company dated back to the early days of angrav and were one of the leaders in developing the first functional models for Terra to Lunar transport. That, in turn, led to other advances, and even eventually to the galactic conglomeration. Although small in comparison to Luna Corp, *Heart* was correct not to mess with their security. If he wanted to, he probably had enough raw computing power to find out what he wanted, but not without them knowing, and not without making enemies. Something we didn't want.

Heart took the lead on the flight while I prepped the hold, and made sure the main bay was ready. The requirement for magnetic sealing wasn't unusual but did hamper his ability to use drones down in cargo. His crew of robots wasn't sensitive enough to seal everything to standard, so I needed to do it personally. Most of it involved pulling sensors out of crates and affixing them in preset mounts so he could monitor. The sensors weren't needed most of the time, and could be easily damaged, so it was safer to keep them locked away than permanently up.

It actually gave me a chance to explore. The funny thing about *Heart* was that I had forgotten how big he was. Designed as a hospital boat, he could easily fit a thousand extra people if he needed to, without using his holds. I had grown so used to going straight from my quarters to the bridge, around the corner I neglected the rest of him. He had fabrication bays, galleys, cargo holds, a hydroponics lab, and a greenhouse. When I found his library, I stood in awe for a good twenty minutes.

This, of course, continued until our arrival on Titan. The visit was short as possible. We didn't even swap the reactors to standby. By the time we had landed, everything was already sitting on the platform waiting for us. *Heart's* ramp was down less than a minute before I had a pad in front of me demanding an inspection thumbprint, and people ready to load. I'll say one thing, they were efficient. After the crew loaded the six large containers, I felt like we were being deported.

Chapter 13

Heart's exit from Titan was only slightly less madcap than the one from Ganymede. He actually gave me almost a minute to buckle my harness before taking off. It had never occurred to me computers, let alone ships could be impatient. Not that I hadn't engaged in my fair share of animism, calling other ships she, or even treating gear as living things but merely this specific thought had never crossed my mind.

Heart was a person. Far older than me in chronological terms, and he was far smarter than me as well. He was also far more limited than I was in many ways. He couldn't get up and do things. Where I would devour books and media to kill time, this took him fractions of a second, and he lacked others to discuss what he found. Our traveling together was an adventure to him. The actual moving between planetoids, was fluff for him, like breathing was for me. Not something he had to actively think about. He had processes for it.

Since the holds were full, and we actually had a reason to make planet-fall on Terra, we began prepping the second part of the mission. Although we had always had a rough outline, our draft relied on all the moving pieces beforehand. The Titan shipment closed all those loopholes and allowed us to focus on the particulars.

We had an actual destination as opposed to only a general location like a planet. Terra is a big place. Unlike Luna and Ganymede, which only have one place to park each, landing at home could be almost anywhere. The shipment was scheduled for Oceania, on the research platform off the southwestern coast of the Southern Commonwealth States.

I'd never been there having been born and raised in the Northern Reaches, but they spoke the same dialect, and I was nominally a Citizen there. That didn't really matter though since I was using a forged identity. Made it a hell of a lot easier to fit in and less likely to draw suspicion.

One interesting thing about space travel is it became almost impossible to actually track everyone. Identities became a very fluid concept. Immigration enforcement relied on what database each organization had access to. The falling out Terra had with the Galactic Union meant the Southern Commonwealth shouldn't have access to any of the old databases, meaning I should be able to ghost myself into their systems using clever forgeries. Having access to high-level executives at Luna was a definite perk.

The major risk as we saw it was whether my original file existed. This was of minimal concern because of the amount of time that had gone by, and the amount of genemod I had gone through in the fifty years of my life. There was enough deviation I wouldn't show up as myself unless I presented my own idents. The chances of that happening were exactly zero.

We also started putting together gear bags. Nothing too special, but a couple of changes of clothes, a few creds, and some light defensive weaponry. If I had more of the slugthrowers I would have shoved one in each bag. *Heart* offered to make as many as I wanted in one of his fabrication bays, and I seriously considered it, before finally realizing if someone did find my handy piece of hardware I would likely be in much larger trouble. So we stuck to a couple of ampknives and a kinetic energy displacer, generally legal everywhere. Worst thing with those is usually confiscation or a fine.

We also spent what felt like far too much time discussing how we were going to stay on Terra after the drop-off. Simplicity seemed the best solution, so we decided to duplicate the plan from Ganymede. Drop off our load, and head to Oceania and pick up and outbound shipment. If we rented dock space for a couple of months to conduct repairs, we hoped would work as a reasonable cover. We didn't know how long it would take to actually gather the intel General Campbell wanted but figured the prep work would actually be longer than the mission. That had often been the case in my Legion days at least.

Chapter 14

As I've mentioned, I love media. All types. I love seeing different renditions of the same story as well. One of my favorites is *The Wizard of Oz*. What's great about it, is every couple of years someone does a new variation. A new twist. There was the book, then the movie, and the plays, and then books inspired by the movie or the play, and cartoons. Over the centuries, there've been hundreds of variations on the same theme. Looking at lots of other stories, there are similar trends. But *The Wizard of Oz* was in my head because "There's no place like home."

That was the thought I was having staring at the highly magnified view of Terra as we were approaching. *Heart* had slowed us down to a much more reasonable speed after we had gotten past the asteroid field between Jupiter and Mars. On the return trip, we went over instead of through. We were well within our arrival window for our shipment. We had checked, double-checked, and triple-checked our preparations, and talked our plan *ad nauseum*. All we could do was pull the proverbial trigger.

I was at the conn, but *Heart* called in our flight pattern. We received approval and began our slow approach towards Terra. Unlike everywhere else he and I had visited, Terra has a huge gravity well. About six times Titan's, Ganymede's, or the Moon's. As such we couldn't approach at speed. If we tried, we would bounce off the atmosphere at best or at worst burn up on entry. So we had to slow to a relative crawl as we made our way.

"Is everything alright Ari? Your biometrics are elevated outside normal" I told him I just had the jitters. *Heart* wasn't worried about the approach since he was designed to do this kind of thing, but I'd been in some rather hairy planet jumps back when I was a young trooper. Once dirtside, we were relatively safe surrounded by a thousand buddies. In space, making planet-fall, surrounded by a tin can, everything wanted to kill us. "I am not sure I understand the reaction. You have done this multiple times before. Past experiences show this is a safe form of travel."

I ended up talking about irrational fear. We were still several minutes out, but this actually took my mind off things. I pointed out simply because I know something, doesn't mean I feel something. For a while, I thought he was satisfied with the answer, until probably a good two minutes later. "I think I understand. I occasionally find problems in where I know the correct or most correct answer, but those selections will not lead to the outcome I desire. It causes process backlogs, which I believe are analogous to your biometric responses."

That presented a very interesting line of thought, I had not considered before. I knew he had emotions or, at least, parallels to human emotions. I'd caught hints of humor, and even anxiety previously. But could *Heart* feel actual fear? What about sadness or rage? We were forced to shelve the discussion once we got into Terran control space.

Heart routed almost all direct communications over the bridge speakers as a courtesy, even if I didn't actually need to be involved in them. I had given him permission to use my voice and name for anything routine, and I trusted his judgment, as much as I trusted him with my life while we were flying. The default challenge to entering Terra came over, and he answered with the pertinents. I know he could hold multiple conversations simultaneously, but speaking to him while he was talking to someone else wasn't a skill I could master, so I found it disconcerting as hell to talk to him while he was talking to ground control, in my voice.

Once control cleared us, we began our slow descent. I could already feel the pull of gravity through the decel. A gentle reminder we were falling ever so slowly. As the screens shifted out of golden red of passing into the upper atmosphere, I felt a very hard drop and an immediate acceleration forward. The situation seemed off.

Rather than my controls lighting up with angrav, the sublights kicked to full. Before I could ask *Heart* what in the hell was going on, the incoming sirens were going off, and my hands started reacting of their own accord. "Anti-satellite missiles have been launched at us. I do not have offensive countermeasures. Attempting to outrun." Normally there was a good amount of emotion in his voice but he had gone as cold as I had ever heard him.

Heart was dropping a lot of power into his engines, according to my readout, and quickly passed a speed I considered unsafe. Not that I considered atmospheric entry speed safe to begin with, but there's a difference going so fast surrounded by nothing and when falling to Terra at over Mach twenty-five. I brought our primary shields to full, from normal entry mode, and started to power up the ion cannons, while seeing if we had anything that might be useful in dealing with these.

It looked like four missiles had been launched, and one clipped us while we were blind during entry. We had good shields and we were able to take one. My gut told me maybe one more, but not at this speed. The thing about missiles and aircraft is it doesn't take a lot of direct damage to destroy one. It's not the explosive that does it, but the air ripping the ship apart while moving quickly. Designed to absorb and displace kinetic energy our shields could take flying rocks. An explosive, even a small one would temporarily overcome them, leaving us very vulnerable to further damage. A second missile would kill us at any speed, especially without that protection. We needed these things off our tail soon.

Heart was bringing us as low as he could, skimming the Southern Ocean in an almost straight east line. I popped a few blasts from the ions, but to no avail, then tried a localized EMP managing to get one them to nose dive into the drink. My moment of happiness was cut short when *Heart* announced "We have six aircraft inbound. Coming fast."

I glanced at the heads-up, looking at the missiles and the new aircraft. My subconscious ran the math before I had a chance to do so intentionally. Unless we could get these missiles off of us in seconds, the aircraft would tear us apart as soon as they arrived. Despite my confidence in *Heart's* shields, I knew he could only absorb so much punishment before we would succumb.

Who the devil did we piss off? Who in the hell could have known we were coming down? I was trying to push these paranoid thoughts down when I felt the shudder from *Heart's* tail section, heard the explosion over our speakers, and we hit the water at speed. Everything went black.

Chapter 15

I was no longer in my chair and everything was green. Those were the first two thoughts in my head when I regained consciousness. I'd like to believe these were rational thoughts. Unfortunately, I can't swim. It was never something I needed to learn how to do. The water where I'm from is too cold to swim in, and it's not like I ever needed to do it in space. That said, blind fear hit me as soon I realized I was submerged in water.

I'd always been told humans are natural swimmers and in response I'd called anyone who told me that a damn liar, usually with several expletives and a couple of hurt feelings. It's not that I was scared of the water. I'm was scared to death of drowning, making it really hard to learn how to swim.

As I struggled, I heard *Heart's* muffled voice through my damaged dampers. "Ari, calm down. I will have you out in a moment. Just relax. It was the only way." At that point, I noticed I was flailing trying to get out, and he was slowly bumping up the grav to force me to stop banging on the cage. I gave a quick double blink of compliance and tried to hold still. The pain made me register my right shoulder was probably dislocated, giving me enough focus to notice I had a rebreather on, probably a good thing because I was hanging in some sort of liquid. A gel really. I didn't realize it but my left arm had been banging on whatever the enclosure was and there was a latticework of cracks emanating from wherever I had hit it. Multiple times. With the little added sanity, I felt the gravity rushing towards my head, which didn't make any damn sense.

Heart slowly switched gravity from whatever level he had it on to Terra-normal, then to nothing. Followed by a quick vacuum sound as the gel was pulled out of the coffin he had me in. "Ari. Stay still, you have a broken collarbone, we need to get you to the medical bay to set it. I've got a drone and a stretcher coming to you." In not so kind words, I told him what to do with both of those, and to open the halls for me. I would make my way down.

I then quickly apologized. I knew *Heart* was trying to help and he was right but the pain was making me loopy and I was stubborn. I asked him what happened. "We are going to patch you up first." He told me in no uncertain terms and refused to answer any other questions. Red emergency lights provided a dim glow to everything, but he flashed blue terminals leading me to the medical bay closest to the bridge. I doubt it was more than thirty meters but even in null grav, it felt like I had run a marathon in double grav. I was sweating hard and swearing just to keep going.

As soon as I entered the bay, I realized *Heart* made sure it was fully operational. No emergency lighting and running at full power. *Heart* was not messing around leading me to believe he wasn't only worried about my collar-bone. The second I was on the table one of his drones stabbed me in the thigh with what I assumed was a syringe half-full of nanites, a heavy dose of adrenaline, and the rest painkillers. I almost blacked out again and only managed to hold onto consciousness when the diagnostic machine screamed for half a second.

Through gritted teeth and a dozen swears, I reiterated my demand to know what happened and got a long pause followed by "I ejected our number four lifeboat, and set its emergency *h*space drive to implode." This time, I think I did pass out, or redlined enough for all the machines started beeping. I know I said some not very nice things for about ten seconds before he cut me off. "The only way I could be sure was to create a large enough ripple in real-space to hide our dive into the ocean." Using an *h*space drive inside a gravity well was a bad deal, running the risk of grabbing whatever matter was nearby and pulling it with it. Doing so over water probably wasn't as dangerous as on solid ground, but not something that should be done anywhere near a planet under normal circumstances. At least with fluids, the natural vacuum effect prevented a chain reaction from sucking in the entire planet.

"It should give the impression we crashed, and there will be enough wreckage to imply our destruction." I uttered some very choice things, but he was right. Whoever was after us when we made planet-fall had known we were coming, and wanted us gone. *Heart* had made the correct call, grabbing the conn, and doing what he felt was necessary. I apologized and let him know.

I did ask where in the hell we were. "We're currently very deep in the Kermadec Trench. I can't give an exact reading as I have almost all my systems in standby mode. We should be relatively undetectable." Slick move. Although designed for space travel, *Heart* could go underwater in a pinch. I'm not sure how deep he could go and wasn't anxious to find out, but even though the types of pressures were different, he could hold his position underwater until we ran out of food. Using our hydronic farm and fully packed freezers that could be a very long time. I'd probably die of boredom eating the same meals before the ocean itself got to us.

The drone finished up on my collar, and a display showed me a full X-ray. Lots of minor cracks but the collar appeared to be the only major break. I was right about the drone's first injection.

Loaded full of nanites, all going to town trying to fix things. I looked at my arms and saw I was bruised into a great yellowish purple haze. I asked *Heart* how long was I out. "It has been a little over fifty-one hours since the incident." I started swearing again and asked why he didn't wake me up. Machines started trilling again, but he cut them off almost instantly.

"You were severely injured in the collision. I immediately put you in sustainment fluid and set to work repairing your internal injuries. I was actually hoping to keep you unconscious for another few days and move you to medical for surgery when you were stable. You really should not be up, or even awake at this point." He paused for several seconds. "I would still like to put you in a medpod for additional recuperation." I shut that option down fast. I was not going back into one of those boxes if I had a choice.

We had spent a long time focused on me. I decided to shift gears and asked *Heart* how bad off he was. "Excluding the lost lifeboat, my damage is minor. Repairs are nearly complete." I told him to show me. If he was willing to bend the truth about my health, he was sure as hell willing to do the same about his own. The display lit up after a few seconds. I wasn't sure if he was changing the data or debating changing the data, but the pause was telling. "The majority of the damage was to the starboard side. Rear starboard sublight is functional, but at sixty percent. We lost two directional propulsors near the fore, but, I can fabricate those. The installation will require your assistance since my drones are not capable of aquatic operations. Damage to clamping dock number four is beyond my ability to repair. We will require a facility; however, the remaining boats and the Captain's yacht are still functional." That stopped me, as I didn't know we he had a yacht on board, let alone a Captain's yacht, forcing me to ask about it purely from curiosity.

"Indeed. We have several vehicles aboard. I believe you will need one to use one for your reconnaissance since I will need to conduct repairs, and whoever attempted to destroy us was aware of arrival." The fog of pain had made me temporarily forget why we were there. That made me angry. If someone wanted us dead, I was going to make it personal.

Chapter 16

My refusal to stay in medical any longer than absolutely necessary annoyed *Heart* to no end. I instead spent the next several days in my stateroom after *Heart* adjusted his artificial gravity so we weren't upside-down, and so I could get a little sleep. He snapped at me a few times when I was being completely unreasonable. Not until I agreed to slap a medpack on and let one of his idiot drones follow me around did he relaxed a little. I don't think he was trying to mother hen me, but like the captain on the bridge thing, some programming was embedded so deep he couldn't shake it. Deep down he was a hospital boat, and while I was injured, I was his patient.

I was going stir crazy. It's one thing being in space and not being able to do something. It's completely different being told I wasn't allowed. I did a hell of a lot better than I thought I would. I made it almost three whole days before I was in one of the fabrication bays begging *Heart* to let me do anything to help fix him up. I know what he gave me was busy work, but the tasks kept my mind off the dull throb of healing up.

Once the general fog started to lift and he was able to dial the painkillers down, we started talking about what went wrong. Not that we hadn't since I woke up, but I kept getting caught in the same circular logic chain. The drugs he had me on made me useless mentally, and it was only the low-g making me moderately useful physically, as though he needed me to begin with. I would have skipped them entirely if he didn't have the drones following me ready to stab me with a syringe.

Our longest running conversation was why? Followed by whom? "I do not know Ari. For an attack of that nature, our opposition would need to know our arrival window. All data leads to an inside leak of information. However, very few people knew of my involvement." *Heart* displayed the people who had direct knowledge on the master screens, as well as a smaller subset of their trusted relations. "We can have a fairly high confidence Miss Kellinger and General Campbell were not the direct leak but that does not exclude others within their inner circles."

That led to how we were supposed to proceed. There was a very long pause from *Heart* after that. To the point where I thought I hadn't said it out loud. "I do not believe we can trust anyone. We must operate under the assumption all communications are compromised." A rather chilling thought. If all comms were fried, then my forged idents were probably toast as well. "Concur. However, I believe I can rectify that. We have a few larger concerns."

"First, we must determine a way to get you ashore. The lifeboats and the Captain's yachts are suboptimal, but would work. Neither the runabout nor the hopper located in the starboard secondary hold are viable due of our current location, leaving the sloop in fabrication bay three. It is incomplete but functional. Its communications package should be sufficient to act as a relay to me if we are cautious." *Heart* replaced a portion of the screen with diagrams of each of the vehicles he mentioned in turn. The final one appeared showing an angrav sloop.

He had glossed over it by calling it a sloop, but an angrav sloop is like a hopper and a runabout had a kid, modified to the point of being space-ready. Essentially a two-seat vehicle a little over five meters long, but rather than having wheels like a runabout, it had angrav pads and a series of directional propulsors like a hopper. What made sloops different was the two sublight engines on the back. Hoppers used propulsors all the way around and topped out around the speed of sound. Angrav sloops topped out by crashing into things.

They were originally conceived by the entertainment industry and people used to do cross-continent and cross world racing with them. Sloops were not only dangerous as hell but also amazing. When I was a kid I would watch the races any chance I could. As soon as I saw the sloop on the screen, I yelled for *Heart* to stop. Probably more forcefully than I intended, but I wanted to know why he had one in one of his bays, and why in the hell I was only finding out about it then.

"I did not know you were interested in them or I would have shown you, but like the ships back on Luna, this has been a pet project of mine for the last several years. The physics behind them are interesting, and a few years back there was a resurgence on Luna for the sport. I have been trying to build a vintage variant since then. Unfortunately, original parts are difficult to find on the secondary market." He had an original. I was out the bridge door trying to remember where bay three was. He was already lighting the way for me. Over the preceding few days, we had swapped out of emergency power mode, and he had gradually been adjusting gravity back to normal. My blood was pumping when I got there, but oh was it was worth it.

The diagram didn't do the sloop justice and *Heart* hadn't done himself justice. Whatever work he had been doing on her was beyond compare. She was gorgeous. I wasn't sure what he meant by incomplete but from outward appearances, she looked like she was minutes off the assembly line. The only visible thing lacking was paint, having a steel gray exterior at the time. I was spewing compliments as fast as I could, circling her, and running my hands over every centimeter. "I was actually experimenting with a non-stock option for coloring. I know it is not strictly traditional, but I did not think anyone would mind this allowance."

The exterior of the car changed to a deep scarlet matching my old jacket. "I used a high-density polymer compound that allows me to modify the color scheme to some extent. I believe the Legion uses the same technology on some of their battle armor." He was right, we did for our scouts. I explained the paint was energy intensive and tended to drain power, so we didn't use it for everyone. "Yes, that makes sense, however, the engines cannot possibly use the full output of the reactors, so my inclusion was of minimal impact."

I was truly excited about the prospect of flying this beauty, but I did want to know what he meant by incomplete, especially as I have a healthy respect concerning my own abilities as a pilot. I knew

Heart's abilities and not my own saved us. "Most are minor cosmetic issues, however, there are a few other items we can likely replace with aftermarket parts. I will check my databases and see if we can fabricate them. Much of the work has been slow because I have had to manufacture the tools to work on the sloop, even when parts are readily available. I encountered this previously when conducting repairs on myself. Although I have the knowledge, I lack the capability due to things like access, or simply a stripped screw."

That had to be frustrating. Not being able to fix something because of an inability to reach it. *Heart* had all these little drones running around he could control, but he still needed help from an outsider. I understood what he was saying in some ways. Like trying to stitch up a wound on my own back, almost impossible. Just no reach. I would need to get help. It reinforced why we were a good team. There were things I wasn't capable of. Had I been flying any other ship, I would've been dead. Without a crew, *Heart* couldn't make repairs. Or at least, the fixes would take him a much longer time.

I pulled myself away from staring at the sloop, and we started to prioritize a repair plan. Not only for the sloop but also for *Heart* himself. If things went south again, we wanted to be able to hightail it.

Chapter 17

We had a few major obstacles regarding the sloop above and beyond getting it up and running. First was its location within *Heart* himself. Unlike his holds, the fabrication bays lacked the standard airlocks. It wasn't designed to be used as a means of quick egress, meaning that the sloop had to be moved to a different location within *Heart* for when I was ready to go ashore.

Unfortunately, because the sloops' size we couldn't take it down the main passageways either. This meant taking it outside of *Heart*. Back on Luna in his hangar, this would have been a complete non-issue. He had the ability to shift large panels aside on the outer skin to allow entry, but the procedure was not simple by any means.

Since we were surrounded by seawater, once we opened the panels we would flood the section with seawater and have no real means of removing it. At best we could methodically flood it, then seal it, and slowly shift the water to other areas, and attempt to vent it. As a space-faring vessel, *Heart* was generally designed to keep the atmosphere in, as opposed to pushing it out. In space decompression would take care of the issue but in the ocean, he just lacked the ability to shift that amount of water. The alternative was attempting to use the fabrication bay's limited air conditioning capabilities but we didn't think they were close to what was needed.

We decided the simplest solution would be to treat it like a compromised space, and seal it off. As our goal was to move the sloop from its location to one of the transport holds instead the first order of business was to shift as much equipment as possible from bay three over to another bay for storage. We were able to use his droids for most of it, but the remainder was tedious and sweaty work.

Once completed, it was a matter of opening up his outer hull and shifting the sloop itself. I had donned full kit as a safety precaution even though the AGS had a decent air supply. It was a tight fit inside the sloop, and I was fighting a touch of claustrophobia, as the water flooded into the bay at what I felt was a too fast speed. My dislike of being in water did not help the situation at all. If docked, on normal land the process would be an hour-long event at a minimum. Hiding in the Kermadec Trench, it felt like an eternity. *Heart* could obviously read my fear through my suit and did his best to keep me calm. "Ari, we'll have you in the secondary hold very soon. Unfortunately, I need you to maneuver the sloop as I do not have the ability. Were I able to do this remotely you would not be in there." I lied and told him it was fine. I'm not fond of tight spaces to begin with, and only the combined presence of the sloop and suit were keeping my fear of water at bay. Part of my control issues. I like to be in control.

I felt like we were in pre-drop mode all over again. When the outer panel finally opened, and I felt the clamp unhook beneath us, I had to consciously avoid gunning the port directional. I feathered the controls and brought her sideways so I was facing the hatch. "Easy Ari, you don't have rear propulsors, only the sublights. You have to back the sloop out. I don't know what will happen if you attempt to engage the primary engines this deep, but I don't think it will be good." I gave *Heart* a quick thanks and released my death grip on the wheel. I counted out to one-hundred aloud, trying to keep myself calm and slowly spun the sloop's tail 180 degrees. Getting myself effectively perpendicular to the bay wall, I applied the bare minimum juice. I'm sure it didn't take much to clear *Heart's* skin but felt like forever.

After finally making it outside, I could feel the flow of the currents. I had to use the directionals to stay relatively steady. I was hovering about five meters from *Heart*, trying to get my bearings. Being this deep, we had almost no visual capability. I knew where he was only because I had recently come out, and because my helm was giving me a constant feed down to the centimeter.

"Ari, I am displaying your present orientation in relation to myself on your primary display. As discussed, we need you to go under me in true terms, and then proceed to the port secondary hold. I already have it open. You are to retain orientation, which is reverse to normal. You will be coming in upside-down; however, I have adjusted gravity in the bay to neutral. There are light personal shields on the sloop, and your containment suit will handle well above these pressures. If I see any indications, I will magnetize the hull, and we will walk you in."

Since I was not aboard, *Heart* was getting uppity, and I let him know I didn't appreciate it. "Ari, you can chastise me when you are back aboard and safe. Until then, we have our proverbial hands full." I pointed out between us there was only one real hand and stifled a giggle for a second.

Following his directions, I brought the sloop around. *Heart's* position blocked most of the current, and let me focus on moving the sloop in what felt like, to me, up and over the bridge, and then rotate back towards the bays. He had chosen the path so he could physically block from above. Although he hadn't said anything, I had a distinct feeling his shields were also on full while I was outside. Even though I couldn't see it, the sloops sensors were picking up odd readings. Something about the way the water was interacting several meters out. Or my paranoia was getting the better of me. Eventually, I reached the bay and brought the sloop in.

Going in was a different kind of stress than backing out. I was able to use my bottom directionals without a problem; however, the instant I passed into *Heart's* angrav field, I was forced to compensate in the opposite direction, and try to create a semblance of neutral buoyancy. Within seconds I felt a magnetic clamp grab hold, fighting the sloop and my attempts to control its direction. "Cut power Ari, I have you," and I reacted to his instructions as quickly as I could.

"Closing primary doors, and will vent the hold momentarily. Adjusting gravity orientation." As soon as I saw the bay doors start to move, I popped the seal on my helm and shoved it into the passenger seat. The air inside the sloop was only slightly less stale than my suit, but at least it didn't smell like ninety minutes of bottled up Gadsden fear. It was another twenty before I was able to get out of the sloop, but getting the helm off helped a lot.

As soon as I was out of the sloop, I felt the tension drop off. I hadn't realized how terrified I was out there. I started laughing. I don't know how long I went on, but I finally heard a too loud and very worried *Heart* over the loud-speakers. "Ari? Your helmet is not on. You cannot hear me." I waved him off and sat on the floor. Laughed more and more until one of his idiot drones dragged my helm to me.

Chapter 18

Our argument finally reached a head the following day. If *Heart* had his choice, we would have bolted back to Luna. His view was if we were dead, there was no way to accomplish our mission. My stance was if we left Terra, we were never getting back, and that ended the mission as well. This was our one shot, and we'd best make the most of it.

It boiled down to conflicting programming. My primary conditioning was on mission accomplishment. The Legion drums the concept into our heads. Mission first. It's so ingrained I wasn't able to push past it, even when survival was potentially at stake. *Heart's* focus was on crew welfare. To him that meant me. I was his top priority, not the mission.

My little breakdown after moving the sloop had him thinking I had redlined, and despite my assurance uncontrollable laughter was how I jetted stress, he was having none of it. So we argued. But we argued while we worked. The problem with arguing with a computer is they have all the information. They're also able to pick apart any flaws in the logic chain. The reverse is AI don't usually have the same flaws, so even if he made them I wouldn't catch them until much later.

The one piece of ground he left me was the importance of the mission, changing the argument from being about me to being about Luna and even Terra. The discussion became purely quantitative at that point. How much was my life worth in comparison to others? "Ari, I know you. I do not know them." It was a pragmatic outlook. Wrong, but pragmatic. I reminded him he also knew Lysha, and the General, as well as everyone they knew, and so forth.

Heart disliked thinking about relationship complexities past people he personally knew. The potentialities were painful for him. His ability to extrapolate the future forced him to deal with issues of life and death. I'm not sure how many people he had known during his sentience, but from what I had gathered, all of his original crew was gone. My bringing those past friends up was a dirty trick and I knew it. "So what do we do? Our mission intent was reconnaissance. Our encounter makes that not feasible. If our foe was able to identify our arrival time, we must assume they can identify you, Ari. The mission is important, but so are you. How much risk is acceptable?"

I didn't have an answer for that. I've always leaned towards not over-thinking the problem if I can avoid it. Deal with the closest problem first, and then shift to the next one. Our current problem was our position in the ocean, and getting me ashore. I wasn't unaware of all the issues ahead of me but I considered them a were a low priority for the moment.

I had a bit of tunnel vision and *Heart* was right to point out that particular failing. Our initial plan was ruined and we needed a rough outline of something new. We were no longer able to land and allow me to act as a tourist. Instead of passively fading into a crowd, my goal was shifted to something far more active. Not only would we have to get me ashore, but we had to keep a low enough profile once I was there the mission wasn't instantly compromised again.

Heart and I had been trying to work out the best plan to no avail. Back when I was in the Legion, we'd have teams develop a few different ideas, and the old man would pick the top three for further development. We'd split off into groups, refine the options, and based on those select the best. The nice part of that process was the back-ups if things went to hell. We could swap gears because we already had ideas. Unfortunately, our situation was so far outside of the current mission, we couldn't use anything we had already thought about. At least not yet.

Our other issue was with only the two of us, we weren't able to make the same kind of leaps needed to come up with something completely new. *Heart* is amazingly smart. His very presence reminded how much smarter than me he was. But his intelligence is evolved around the human standard. He thinks like us, meaning although he had infinitely more access to data, and could compute it faster, he fell within the human spectrum of intelligence. He managed to explain the idea to me once, without making me feel too stupid.

"Imagine gears and cogs. Each one has to connect in sequence. If one is going too fast, or too slow they won't connect properly to the one next to it. My personality, the gear making me, me, is set near human speed. It connects to other systems, which run progressively faster, like my communications array or even my hyperspace drive. I am not in direct control of those systems, much as you aren't always in control of your breathing or blinking. They are things I can do, but not things I must consciously think about. The processes happen far too fast."

"Another way of looking at it is like a city full of roads. You and I can both go to the same places inside the city, but I can get there faster and visit more places in the same amount of time. My limitation is not my speed, but the data I have access to. You could eventually come to the same destinations; it will just take you significantly longer." He paused for a moment. "For me to truly exceed your capabilities, I would require additional inputs to reach the next level. However, if that were to happen, I do not know we would be able to communicate anymore." He sounded less enthused about that idea than anything else. I would have imagined it would be great to be smarter, but he made it sound downright lonely.

It made me question whether we could have multiple versions of him attempting to come up with plans. "Unfortunately, no, I do not have that kind of power or even hardware. It would require reallocating space, then fragment my personality, and attempt to duplicate it through the new space. I am not comfortable with that idea. It would be like two of me existing in a single shell. But beyond that, which would be the real me, and how would we merge them back together?" That was a scary thought. The last thing we wanted was an AI with split personality disorder. People with mental conditions were rough enough. I was positive having a computer with one would be a bad deal.

With that option off the table, we were left us with trying to come up with ideas by ourselves. It did allow us to stall and hopefully reinforce the idea we were gone to the outside world. This was a double-edged blade because added quite a bit of safety, but neither of us wanted our friends back home to think we were gone.

We were almost hoping the word of our demise hadn't reached back yet. Radio silence had always been part of the operation, so perhaps with a little luck, we hadn't put Lysha through some unnecessary heartbreak.

Although I thought about her constantly, I always shoved those thoughts down hard. She was a distraction, which could risk *Heart* and me if we didn't stay vigilant. The little things kill, not the big ones. The big ones are easy to spot and easily avoided. Unless it's missiles flying while trying to make planet-fall. Those aren't quite as easy.

Perhaps that was the key. Changing the way, I thought. After fifty years, my thought patterns were so ingrained to the point of indoctrination. Maybe if I could think like Lysha or General Campbell, I could come up with something different. I'd love to say I could put myself in the female mind, but girls have been a mystery to me since I was old enough to realize there were girls.

Having spent a solid fifteen minutes trying, I swapped to the general. I figured I would have much better luck imagining myself older and smarter. Putting myself in his shoes was easier if only slightly. I didn't know him as well, not by a longshot, but he was a personal hero and I knew a lot about him. Taking his personal history and replacing my own, I decided to think of the problem logistically instead of operationally. Our situation was no longer a case of what we wanted to do; it was a case of what we could do with the assets available.

Our old plan relied on many conditions that weren't true any longer. So what conditions were static? What could we leverage? No sooner had I said it aloud than *Heart* caught my logic chain than a strategy started to form.

Chapter 19

The sloop was only slightly less cramped than my previous time. Although I wasn't kitted up, we had jammed up what little space was available with the best communications gear available. *Heart* was going to stay as deep as he could in the Kermadec to minimize his chances of being spotted while getting as close to New Zealand as possible. We had slowly decreased our depth until we could use Terra networks. A risky but calculated move. We hoped a single random user couldn't be spotted. The alternative to leaving the trench was locating one of the older sea-based cables and attempting to tap into them, but *Heart* estimated we would be spotted far more easily, both physically and electronically.

Our theory was the sloop's upgraded system would be able to relay *Heart* to me. There might be the tiniest of lag due to punching a signal through salt water, but it was far better than not having him at all. I had grown accustomed to his presence and losing him at that juncture would have left me crippled.

Without an environmental suit, being outside *Heart's* skin at our previous depth was dangerous. The previous jaunt in the sloop was only possible because of many precautions, limited time, and pure necessity. So we had to bring *Heart* and the sloop up to a much safer depth. The Kermadec was over ten kilometers at its deepest. Our hover point was closer to three-k. The sloop would take me down to five-hundred meters without real issue, even without a suit, but there was a question of whether *Heart* would become visible at that point.

The other issue was the sloop wasn't designed to scrub air. Sure, it could seal and be used in space or the ocean because of its shields, but it only had a limited supply of breathable Oxygen. We could stay below water for about three hours before having to surface. A suit would fix that, but would add other complications when I reached my destination. So we were relying on a fine balance of getting high enough in the water to where the pressure was safe, and then staying under as long as possible as well. Salt water was our friend when it came to stealth, but our enemy when coming to safety. We were teetering elements of risk, trying to find a perfect level.

Heart and I followed the trench as far south as possible while getting as close as possible to the eastern coast of New Zealand. After surfacing, the sloop's speed would make travel to the north island fairly simple. New Zealand didn't have nearly the same population as our original destination near Perth on Oceana, but making landfall would give us lots of other options. It became a quantity versus quality argument.

When we began moving again, we had shifted back to where our internal gravity matched Terra's. A normal submarine would use buoyancy mechanics to maintain position, whereas *Heart* was using his angrav drives instead. He could maneuver however he pleased and not worry about how Terran gravity would affect me. As we ascended, it became simpler to match everything up. Dealing with reversed directions wasn't difficult for him, but it was downright disconcerting for me as I had to consciously think about it.

Because the sloop didn't have rear directionals and we weren't sure how its sublights would respond in the water we decided to try a parabolic exit from *Heart's* loading bay. In theory, the exit would be simple. He would ascend to about fifty meters, do an aileron roll, open his bay for me to pop out of the bottom, and then he would dive back down to the safety of the depths. Since he would only be at that depth for a few seconds, our risk of detection should be minimal. The sloop itself was insignificant in comparison, and the goal was to beeline to shore as soon as I surfaced.

Given enough time, we could have linked the control, navigation, and communication systems together but would have required going well outside my area of knowledge. The sloop was a pet project to *Heart* but never intended for actual flight by anyone else. Much like the model planes I built when I was a kid. Time was our enemy and the sloop was the best option. We could have spent the next month upgrading the sloop so *Heart* had the ability to control it remotely and taken most of the stress off me, but doing so would have also taken away a lot of the fun.

I could feel my ears pop right as I broke the water. I was still heading in an upward path when I toggled on the propulsors and got my bearings. Hovering over water was a hell of a lot different than land, or even trying to maintain buoyancy. Because the angrav pads repel against mass and the ocean was constantly swelling, I was bouncing quite a bit. I dialed up the power to compensate and heard *Heart* chime in through my dampers "Ari, additional speed should provide greater stability." I let him know I was working on it and eased into the throttle. I was still a bit gun-shy from the first run, but my trepidation quickly faded as instinct took over and the sloop responded to my directions.

I was amazed how fast this beauty could move. In space, everything is about acceleration because of the distances. On land and in the water a ship can only go so fast because of drag but in the air with actual visual references, I could feel the speed. The human brain can only process information so fast before vertigo and motion sickness kick in. I have decent reflexes and my ware helped when it came to flying, but this was new and fun. All my previous flying revolved around sims or big ships like *Heart*. He was massive compared to this little two-seater. It wasn't that he couldn't go as fast, he absolutely could. We had during our run from the missiles. It was that it felt completely different to do so in something this small.

Skimming across the water at speed was a joy, but if my previous flight through Terran atmosphere had taught me anything, the lesson was to make my flight as short as possible. I wanted to play with the sloop, but the idea of anonymous missiles with my name on them was unpleasant enough to keep me focused on getting ashore quickly. I probably could have made the distance in half the time, but going so fast would have drawn some attention. After my initial burst of speed, I dialed it back to something closer to hopper speed, under the speed of sound. That got me from *Heart's* hiding spot to coast in under ten minutes.

Once over land, I slowed down to a crawl considering the speed I had available. I can definitely see how racing would get addicting, and I was glad I hadn't done it before joining the Legion. I would have gotten myself killed. It's a scary realization warfighting is a safer profession than piloting even before removing people trying to do me harm from the latter.

This was my first visit to this part of the world, so I wasn't exactly sure what I expected, but what I found was far more rural than I was used to. I'm from the Northern Reaches which is sparse to the point of empty compared to the rest of the Americas. Many folks consider it a frozen wasteland. It's not that we don't have cities, they're just large and spread out, with lots of space and a little nature left. Having been down south to the megacities like Seattle on day trips, there was no comparison. This was like stepping back in time.

I thought Alaska was backwater. New Zealand was insane in comparison. I'm sure the impression was based on was my flight path more than anything, but if not for the farms I would have guessed the place had been abandoned years prior. I voiced my concerns to *Heart* and asked if this was normal. "Keeping in mind we do not have reliable data for the last couple of years, it appears the population should be approximately ten million over the entire state." I told him that seemed really low considering Luna's population, and the fact Fairbanks, where I called home, had well over double that. "That matches my records as well. The population growth has been very light, but the island is primarily an agricultural zone, so not uncommon. This may work to our advantage." I told him I wasn't sure how a lack of people and an abundance of sheep were going to help hide the sloop but to please enlighten me. "Ari, if you make your way northward you will come to a road, you should be able to follow to Auckland or Wellington. There are several other population centers along the way, and while you are traveling I will attempt to infiltrate the local networks."

He was right of course. We weren't sure where on the North Island I would come out on so we had left the destination city open. I was currently about midway between them making them both viable options. Auckland was triple the population but Wellington was the capital. They both had advantages and disadvantages. More people made blending in easier, increasing the risk of someone realizing I was a foreigner. The capital would have significantly more police, and with fewer people probably harder to get out of. They were roughly equidistant from Australia so location to the mainland wasn't an issue, however if I had to bolt off the island westward I would probably be better off diving for the Puysegur Trench and letting *Heart* come pick me up.

Using that logic, I decided to go north to Auckland. If I was going to have to dive back in the drink again, I wanted *Heart* on the right side of the map for me. Running north would put me back in the Kermadec and we'd scoot back to Luna.

Chapter 20

After a certain size, almost all cities look alike. I was surprised how much Auckland looked like Fairbanks, which looked like Handrelt on Janel 4, which looked like Ganymede. I imagined Luna City would probably look a lot like this if we could take the domes off as well. Lots of stone and glass and people. These were my thoughts as I attempted to navigate all the hoppers flitting about as I entered the outskirts of the city. I'd hate to see what traffic was like as I got towards the center.

The sheer volume of traffic was nice in one way. The sloop was inconspicuous because of the abundance of other vehicles. Back home it would have stood out, but that was more a product of the sport than anything. In Auckland, there were so many industrial hoppers also using large rear propulsor drives, my little vehicle blended in.

Eventually, I got close enough to the city proper I shifted to ground level to get a better feel for the area. Heart had managed to tap into the civil infrastructure and was able to direct me to an older industrial complex. "It will be unit 230 on your right. I have already settled payment and this should be safe enough for at least the evening." I saw the unit and pulled in as the rolling bay door opened.

171

I asked about the payment part since we had been worried about interacting with local systems. "I used a shell corporation Master Dixon left to me. The accounts are completely Terra based and should be impossible trace back to our operation." That surprised me. I voiced my thoughts about not expecting old man Dixon to leave *Heart* anything. "He anticipated a time when I might need to be on Earth, as he called it, and he wanted to make sure I had means. The company had no assets in itself, only a name and an account number I have funneled a small portion of my salary into since then." Sounded like grandpa was sneaky and paranoid, I told *Heart*. "You have no idea, Ari. However, reviewing much of his records, he was well justified. I believe the saying is 'you're not paranoid if they're really out to get you.' His rivals had reached the point where they were willing to use force. Master Dixon was not averse to it, however, he preferred less direct methods of dealing with unruly competition, as he called them."

The bay doors closed behind me, and the overhead lights began to power on. The building was a large empty warehouse about ten meters wide by twenty meters deep by ten tall. Off to one side appeared to be an office space and a refresher room. I could see the bolt holes where racking had previously been and on the far wall was a charging dock.

I set the sloop down and shifted its reactors into standby mode. I was disengaging the canopy when I heard a thump on the front hood and nearly knocked myself unconscious jumping into it. "Ari, I cannot employ countermeasures. The controls are located center console." I was reaching for a large red button on autopilot when I stopped dead, staring at what appeared to be a cat. No, definitely a cat. I had almost fried the poor thing because of our combined paranoia.

It sat down on the front bonnet and looked back at me, equally curious. "Ari, why is there a feline on the sloop?" Make that three of us. I told him the hood was probably warmer than the floor. Or the cat was letting us know who the boss was. "But what is it doing here?" That question got a genuine laugh from me, as I explained cats go where they want, and we were probably in its home.

I popped the canopy while the tabby kept looking. It was fearless, I'll give it that. Probably also had a keen sense of how far away I was and how fast the average person could move. I wasn't a threat to it, so it wasn't going to give me the satisfaction.

I hopped out of the sloop and onto firm ground. Of all the places I had ever been in the last few decades, nowhere had felt like this rundown warehouse. Took me a moment to realize why, but I was no longer tensed up. On higrav worlds, I had to use my strength to counteract gravity. In low-g places, I was fighting my own abilities. But on Terra, I didn't have to do that. I was able to actually relax all my muscles the way they were designed to be. The tension bled away. I hadn't noticed it earlier because of flight from *Heart* to the city and the uneasiness while traveling in the open.

I was back in the singular place in the galaxy where I could be me. "Ari, is everything alright? You just had a major endorphin spike, but I am not seeing a cause." I let him know I was fine. More than fine even. Time to get this mission going. We had work to do and I was finally in the right frame of mind to do it.

Chapter 21

Throwing enough money at them can make simple problems go away rather quickly, but some things take time like getting our base of operations up to spec. Getting equipment was easy. *Heart* rented a box van and ordered everything he thought we might need for pickup. Using the larger truck rather than the sloop made traveling around town less stressful. No one looks twice at a delivery guy when he is picking up items that are already paid for. Dockworkers want a signature and the bay cleared for the next customer. Setting up the equipment was the hard part. I didn't have helpful drones like back on *Heart*. If we were on Luna, the tasks would have been easy but operating inside standard gravity turned out to be a huge time burner. I had forgotten how tedious things became when I had to deal with their full weight by myself.

We had converted the office into a bedroom for the cat and me. She had decided we were her new servants, resulting in ever-increasing deliveries to our hideout including tinned cat food, kibble, and litter. The nice part was we didn't have rodents chewing through the maze of electrical wires running throughout the warehouse. The unfortunate part was dealing with a litter box. Our new mistress wouldn't go near the automated model I had purchased, but seemed very content with a lower-tech solution. I think more from spite than fear. I counted the box as a fair trade-off, as I had slept in other places with vermin before, and was willing to put up with quite a bit to avoid rodents in the future. Nothing worse than discovering my apples had been eaten by rats.

We converted a solid corner of the warehouse into a command center of sorts. We used the sloop's reactors for primary power so we didn't need the charging dock other than as a backup. Our goal being to keep our external signature as small as possible. Certain things were unavoidable like net access, as we were trying to limit *Heart's* direct links, but this solution was better than painting a target on him by connecting directly to a satellite. With that in mind, we set up the best computers we could find and some very large view screens. Nothing would replace *Heart*, but instead gave us another way to access the local feeds.

We probably could have done all of this from the physical safety of the trench, but as we started our research we soon found I would need to duck out into the city for information that simply wasn't available on the net. The net was a powerful tool but it wasn't all-encompassing. It couldn't provide context like people could or help clarify things that didn't make sense. I needed to be outside to do that. My reconnaissance training came in handy beyond only buying food. I did that as well being a slave to my stomach. *Heart's* galley was well stocked and I'm a fair cook, but I know maybe thirty recipes off the top of my head. Just enough not to get sick of eating the same thing night after night. One of the greatest things about being planet-side is restaurants and street vendors. The smell of food is everywhere. I'd catch a whiff of something, be able to buy it, and eat the goodie right then and there. The more we scratched the surface, the more apparent it became establishing a base in Auckland was the right call. Of course, that was probably my stomach talking.

General Campbell had pointed out the Terra situation had blindsided him. Our keystone issue, so we started at Terra's exit from the Galactic Union. There are a little over one hundred nation groups in the Terran Alliance, the organization who had previously belonged to the Union. Looking at the votes, there were eighty-four votes to secede. Just over three-quarters, but the votes for and against didn't make any sense. Nations who were normally aligned weren't, while other nations who voted against each due to nothing more than longstanding grudges voted together. We couldn't find the pattern and were hoping the information added afterward would make the picture look right.

This had me thinking about an older model of jump jet the Legion used to have. It became notorious for a design flaw called "one switch too many." What would happen was the power circuits could only handle so much energy at a time. If a pilot engaged too many systems at once drawing too much power, the largest power source would shut off. Unfortunately, the three biggest systems were the engines, weapons, and shields. Depending on what the pilot was doing any one of those could be the largest at that point. The problem is fairly obvious from a combat perspective. The pilot ran the risk of not being able to fight back, not having any defense, or not being able to move, and worse not knowing which if he happened to draw too much power from something completely unrelated like artificial gravity or even lights in the cargo bay. A seemingly unrelated power draw could cause a complete shutdown of everything else.

What was worse was it became almost impossible to determine there was a flaw in the first place. The triggering system could be anything while the systems being shut down were limited, each usually resulted in a catastrophic failure. Pilots weren't walking away in big enough numbers to figure out what was creating the issue. The cause was unrelated to the effect. It wasn't any of the systems fault there was a failure, but instead in the processes or programming themselves.

I fielded my idea to *Heart* to see if it made sense to him. "I think you may be onto something. We see many similar incidents throughout history where small skirmishes ignited much larger conflicts. If taken by themselves, they should not have had the same ramifications." So it made me wonder how would that work with the GU and Terra? Were there bigger underlying causes maybe we couldn't see? "For this much discord? I do not know. I can try to create a model, but I have not been able to identify a real triggering event yet. Logically, this should not have happened."

That stopped me. I've had this explained enough to where I thought I understood it. If he was telling me there was something wrong with the logic, I definitely wanted to know what the hole was. I had him walk me through it. "I have been reviewing all the reports, and the media assessments but they are logically flawed. They are making their logic fit the situation, not the other way around." I know I wasn't following now. "Cognitive bias," *Heart* stated bluntly. "Because everything points to this, it must be this. However, that only works looking at the situation historically. It would not work if looking at the situation as an evolving event series. The players, for lack of a better word, would not have access to the requisite information for it to transpire that way. What is worse is the sources are feeding off each other compounding the issue."

All right, I thought I understood that. It couldn't happen the way folks said because the method required knowledge they wouldn't have until after the fact. It created a paradox. I posed the question of how it could work if the media sources had it wrong. "Ari, I have to discard most of the data I have, but the only way I can logically see events progressing is if there are forces outside the government manipulating them. However, even though this is logical, it does not make much sense as there is little advantage gained."

The screens shifted into a different arrangement of maps, charts, and what appeared to be a timeline punctuated by news reports. "Master Dixon always said to look for who profited. There does not seem to be any profit. Not financially, politically, nor any traditional metric. Things actually appear worse." I watched as he rotated through financial charts and what I could only imagine was comparisons between nations, planets, and corporations. I didn't want to interrupt him, but I couldn't keep up. It made me feel like I had to keep asking questions. If no one was gaining an advantage, what was the purpose of attacking us? What would be the point?

"That is something I cannot figure out either. It does not fit in any of the models I have built. If we were interfering in some profit-generating venture, it would make sense. However, there does not appear to be one, therefore, attacking us does nothing." *Heart* displayed the missiles and drones on the upper left display. "The action almost appears emotional, vice logical in nature."

That made me pause. I asked who would have access to the kind of resource as well as a personal investment in wanting us dead. "I have not been able to answer either of those questions. The design used was a common variant. We were still entering the atmosphere when the missiles were launched so I do not know their point of origin. As for the interception drones, all I can reliably say is they came from the north, not a specific place. We were too close to sea level for long range radar to determine anything but a general heading, and due to our own speed and acceleration, there may have been a significant shift as the drones attempted to intercept." Well, that covered the resource half but begged the question about desire. "It is so foreign a concept to me I cannot quite grasp it. How significant of a threat could we be if there were no advantages? Why would that require us to be removed? I simply cannot make the necessary connections."

In addition to the General's initial tasking of scouting Terra to identify any future escalations, we had more mysteries than we could reasonably deal with. We needed to find out who targeted us and why. We also had to find out what had caused the situation to develop.

Using my longstanding philosophy of trying not to overthink problems, we decided to break it down into manageable parts. Since we had essentially restarted the mission from this new location, we decided to rebuild the process from scratch as well. We knew what the General wanted, and had a good idea of how he wanted it done. Answering the questions became our major objective. Using those, we prioritized and decided the last question really needed to be answered first. If we figured out the cause, it should allow us to spot sequences leading up to it. As for our shadowy antagonist, that perhaps was the most complex task and had the least viable leads. We decided it was necessary information, but nothing we could focus directly on, therefore becoming our secondary mission.

Applying the old process reminded me of something. When I had taken the lead on this mission, I had forgotten the old adage; *no plan survives initial contact.* I had also forgotten no matter how good my leadership was unless they were with me, it was my show. I needed to start taking things into my own hands. That meant the cat, *Heart*, and I had to get this done on our own.

Chapter 22

My Legion time had prepared me for many of life's challenges. Unfortunately, it had not prepared me for dealing with the colossal amount of information we were attempting to sort through. We were caught in a position where it became essential to filter information down to a usable rate, but almost impossible to know what was useful or not. My gut told me everything was important, where my brain told me there was no way I could use all the data.

"It is all about developing the correct model." *Heart* was explaining how he was attempting to sort the data we already had. "If we can find a good comparison, we may be able to extrapolate information we need from that." That made sense. Take two similar concepts, and try to apply similar logic to find missing information.

I was first introduced to the idea when I was going through demolitions training. We were started off on sims with what was considered a standard loadout. The gear we would normally have available. Our instructor had told us "Look, if you can knock down this building, you'll be able to knock down any of them. It's about knowing how it's put together. The trick is remembering the small things and then taking those and applying them elsewhere." He was right.

The sims got progressively more difficult, not just in understanding the engineering concepts, but also in learning how to manage resources. Applying enough force allows the destruction of anything. The purpose of the training was to teach us how to be both effective and efficient because we never knew when we would be able to resupply our munitions; therefore, beneficial to be extremely light with the explosives. More than that, the exercise involved understanding all of the tools we had available.

Much like our inventory after crashing into the trench, we had to reassess what we actually had available. I was used to operating as part of a two-man team. Part of Legion procedure was always having someone as backup. Having *Heart* check my math met the need. I'm smart enough to know when I need help and learned early to fight my ego enough to actually ask for it. My major flaw if anything was a tendency towards tunnel vision when coming to what I considered accomplishing missions. I don't give up and even worse is I have a hard time realizing a situation may have changed enough to where the original objectives may have changed priorities. *Heart* was able to challenge me on that, and after we had basically reset the mission from scratch my approach changed to something I was much more familiar with.

Previously I had been so focused on our goal and the mission as a whole I failed to realize my personality wasn't meshing with it. Not that I wasn't capable, or willing, it was that I could do things much more effectively my own way. That epiphany allowed us to change the model we were operating under. Although I had a crash course in reconnaissance, I couldn't claim it as my specialty any more than being a pilot. The skill relied on stealth, counter to how I had operated over my career. What we needed to do was make noise.

"Ari, are you sure that's wise? We still do not know who attempted to murder us. Drawing unnecessary attention to ourselves may not be a good course of action." I pointed out one of our major objectives was finding out who was behind the situation, and if we hunkered down, eventually our adversary could find us and likely at the least opportune time. Our safety relied on perfect vigilance, whereas their ability to remove us was simple in comparison. If we could draw them out in a controlled environment, we might be able to get some useful information.

"Are you suggesting we use you for bait? We barely survived the last time. Tempting fate again would be foolhardy." I wasn't a fan either. I told him I would prefer to create phantoms of ourselves to use as bait instead. We didn't need to be anywhere near the trap.

"That could work." I could almost hear him thinking as he was running scenarios through his huge brain. "We have been hindered by the availability of information. Perhaps we can use that to our advantage. It would be simple to create reports indicating our survival. Hiding the source of the information would be the most difficult aspect. But if our goal is only to create a decoy we may not have to expend as much effort."

I was cautious about broaching the idea that came to me. I asked if we could use a lifeboat to create the impression we died, then was it possible to do the same to show we were alive. "Oh! An excellent thought. Rather than us creating the reports, we rely on nearby residents to do it. Doing so would remove a large portion of the risk, but still accomplishes our goal." His genuine happiness at the concept took me aback. From my view, I had effectively asked him to cut off a leg, but he reasoned the approach was a good idea. I explained my trepidation. "It is not part of me. Any more than your boots are part of you. We constantly speak of resources, but we have not included much of my assets in those." He had a hell of a point. I had always included myself as an expendable resource but hadn't shown *Heart* the same courtesy. We were partners in this endeavor and I needed to treat him as I treated myself.

It was still hard to drop preconceived idea regarding *Heart*, but I outlined what I hoped was a simple plan. Within my experience, that less complex plans had fewer things to go wrong. All we needed was a seed we could grow from, and using the tools we already had we should be able to accomplish what we wanted. The idea was to have *Heart* jettison one of his other lifeboats, then direct it to shore. Anywhere we wanted since the lifeboat was remotely controlled, unlike the sloop. From there we would wait until word spread of its discovery and if lucky provoke a response. We hadn't been able to track the source on the prior murder attempt because we weren't expecting it. With proper planning, the same problem wouldn't arise for this ruse.

With this in mind, we had to decide where to send the boat. We were designing a narrative and we wanted whoever found the bait to make a few assumptions. For maximum effect, it would be best if our unknown antagonist thought *Heart's* crew survived. They would know where he crashed into the Pacific, establishing a possible range of where we could turn up based on the tides. We also didn't want to give up *Heart's* position in the trench nor mine in New Zealand, so we had to be cautious of the direction we sent the boat.

Using the cardinal directions, we had several islands to the north, Antarctica to the south, several South Pacific islands and South America to our east, and New Zealand and Oceania to the west. East was out due to distance and Antarctica excluded because of the population. We decided to ignore New Zealand and instead focus northward. Because we were using a lifeboat, the idea of taking it to the closest and largest population center made the most sense. The Fiji Islands.

Chapter 23

I had thought the most boring thing in the world was sitting through Thom Knox teaching spaceflight theory and regulation. I rescind all comments regarding that, as I wished I had the aforementioned spoon while waiting for something to happen to our discarded lifeboat. Even the cat had decided sitting on the sloop's bonnet was far more interesting than waiting for something to happen on the screens.

The boat's sensors gave us a great view of a deserted beach as we awaited discovery. Maneuvering ended up being far simpler than I had imagined. *Heart* didn't have to deal with the blinding fear that had driven me during our adventure with the sloop; so for him, he was simply shifting an empty container from one location to another. Without having to worry about me, he didn't even have to leave the safety of the trenches and was able to remotely guide the lifeboat underwater until it was a stone's throw from our pre-planned destination.

As soon as it beached, *Heart* created a false log and transferred it. He didn't think the records would stand up too much scrutiny, but we weren't expecting anyone to take an in-depth look either. The most complex part of the plan was actually opening the hatches and making the boat look abandoned. *Heart* used his drones to create a lived-in look, and for added realism banged it along the local reefs to mar it up a tad. As a final touch, he turned on the emergency beacon at the lowest power possible. That would call for help, but make it appear as though the signal had been blocked during its journey to the beach.

We weren't sure how the lifeboat would be discovered or what the reaction would be when it was so we sat and waited for something, anything really, to happen. We had one screen dedicated to video feeds directly from the boat, another to flight tracking from the local airport, and a third to any report mentioning shipwrecks, boating accidents, or anything even remotely related to the three-hundred plus Fiji Islands.

Eventually, we spotted a report concerning a derelict ship matching our baby. Within five minutes, the report disappeared, replaced with a much less descriptive one implying a potential hazardous waste spill. Looked like someone had taken our bait.

Heart began tracking both the original report and its revision to see if he could determine who had modified it. The initial reporting from the one of the locals spotting the crash resulted in the calling of the Fiji Navy. Before they could route one of their patrol skimmers to the site the report had been modified to include enough danger to isolate it. We had chosen the location to ensure if the boat was attacked immediately the collateral damage would be minimal. We didn't want to be responsible for someone getting caught in a crossfire if we could avoid it. It looked like our adversary had a similar plan.

Unfortunately, whoever had modified the report was protected by enough security layers *Heart* couldn't track them back to its source. The situation changed when a handful of mid-sized hoppers appeared on radar. Although *Heart* wasn't able to pinpoint where their flight had originated, he was able to get transponder information. That of itself didn't provide much except linking back to corporate funds instead of a government. He was still trying to unravel ownership when the first shuttle arrived.

I'd love to say seeing the shuttles revealed our foe, but sadly the hoppers were rather nondescript. The surprise came with a blonde woman with short-cropped hair weighing maybe sixty-kilos hopped out, followed by what looked like a full squad of armed troopers. Each wore olive fatigues and light body armor, but the weaponry was definitely lethal. The fact a woman was leading wasn't in itself surprising. I've worked with women in the past and they can be every bit as tough and as mean as guys.

It was her size that caught me off-guard. Changing gravity like firearms can be great equalizer but Terra's high relative gravity would be a disadvantage for any smaller person. Out in space where things were kept closer to Luna standard, her size really wouldn't be a disadvantage because weight and strength are inverses of each other. There's an upper limit to how much a person ever has to lift because of volume. Things get too bulky and unwieldy for a single person to deal with.

Being on Terra, her size could be a major disadvantage as mass becomes more valuable the higher the gravity. Size meant more muscle, and even inefficient muscle ended up trumping size in the end. A product of ratio. The more a person weighed, the less they were lifting relative to their own bodyweight. For a guy like myself carrying thirty kilos was over a third my weight, but for her, the same amount would be closer to half. She had to work harder to accomplish the same things.

Her front position combined with the way she carried herself implied she was the leader. Not as palpable as Lysha or Robert, but this was definitely her team. The other telling aspect was the team's loadout. Gear is always tailored towards the mission, even with a standard equipment set. This group was dressed for action not to investigate. I didn't see an obvious medic or anyone there to help would be survivors. So obviously an assault squad.

That isn't to say there wouldn't be people in the other shuttles to help, but this did not look like a rescue operation. The squads positioning on the beach and their quick clearing of the lifeboat confirmed my suspicions. They weren't hoping for survivors.

After the first clearing, the second shuttle landed with what appeared to be a tech team. They were slower and more methodical until one realized there was a hidden signal inside the emergency beacon. We were forced to cut our spying short, but we had lots of faces to research.

Identifying two dozen faces out of the billions who lived on Terra would normally be impossible due to the quantity of candidates. But combined with the transponders and the ability to track the shuttles back to their base narrowed the search enough to make it at least feasible. Unfortunately, we weren't able to see what happened to the boat itself, but sacrificing it gained us information we didn't have before. The shuttles were based out of Hong Kong.

Chapter 24

My assertion all cities are the same fell apart when we started to research Hong Kong. As a city, she paralleled Ganymede in a lot of ways but was even more densely packed than Luna City. Where things fell apart was Luna City had the ability to expand outward and downward but Hong Kong could only expand upward. She had been packed to her proverbial borders even before the galactic era. Our hiding spot in Auckland seemed positively rural in comparison.

Going from billions to tens of millions of residents helped our tracking, but Hong Kong was still a behemoth of a place. Outside of New Edo in Japan, she had more of a corporate presence than anywhere else on Terra. *Heart* began his research trying to link the transponders to a specific corp, but that idea quickly turned impossible. As an alternative, he started running the faces through the net itself and ended up pinging one of the technicians through a hiring site. That gave us the name, Lee Mendez, and even a work history. Using Mr. Mendez's most current job, a position at Galactic Subsidiaries Incorporated we were able to identify most of the strike team on Fiji. GSI seemed to be the phantom who had been haunting us. Regrettably, there were a few faces we couldn't confirm and among them was the expedition's lightweight leader.

Knowing the company changed our approach as well. GSI was a big privately owned company. I didn't know much about it, but *Heart* seemed intimately familiar with it. "It is what can best be described as a post-hyperspace conglomerate. The Zhang family has held it for several generations, but there are many smaller companies, purchased piecemeal since its founding. GSI was a minor competitor of Dixon Holdings before we became Luna Corporation." I asked if this was some sort of grudge. "Improbable. The relationship was more of rivals than enemies even back when Master Dixon still controlled the company. Both companies have since shifted focus and our interests usually do not conflict."

Why in the hell would they want us dead? If GSI and Luna Corp weren't opponents it didn't make sense to target us. I was so glad I had *Heart* to ask these questions. "I have been thinking about that and I have a theory. When we first approached this, we were looking for nations who could profit from the dissonance. I was unable to find any advantage. If we apply the same concept to a corporation, it becomes feasible. I have been researching corporations since Fiji, and this new model seems to work. Unfortunately, it would take a concerted effort for this to occur. It's very complex and I am not sure how this effort would be organized."

If I understood him right, the source of Terra's problems wasn't a government. I said that was good news at least. "I cannot rule out governmental agencies after applying the new data, as it would require some involvement; however, the goal runs counter to self-interest. A participant would have to intentionally destroy their own environment to make this feasible."

I hated to think of *Heart* as naïve, but this was definitely one of those cases. People are self-serving to the point where they don't realize their actions can be detrimental. It's entirely possible to make choices hindering us in the long run. Short-term gains versus long-term losses. Greed is both a powerful motivator and a blinding influence. I tried to explain this to him without sounding condescending. "Ari, that logic is irrational." I countered with the fact humans are irrational creatures. We don't have logic-check processes the same way computers do. It's easy for use to make flawed decisions based on emotion or bad data. "I think I understand, but the concept is so alien." His statement got me to laughing.

It was such a strange concept having *Heart* call humans alien. An apt description, though. We had different thought patterns than him, and even though he had modeled himself after us during his awakening, he did so as an outsider looking in. He was a very accomplished mimic who duplicated how he thought we behaved but didn't understand why we did certain things. Our underlying logic was massively different from his. This actually worked to our benefit, though. He was able to see things from a different angle and we complemented each other.

This, in turn, got me to thinking about when the General first broached the mission. One of the major reasons he and Lysha chose me was my ability to blend in. That ability was partially from my thinking like a Terran. Terra is a big place, and different communities have different cultures. Maybe we were looking at what would be the equivalent of alien thinking. I broached the idea with *Heart*. "That could be. Everything is foreign to me, so I had not considered it might also be to you." Problems without solutions. I told him I didn't know how this information could help us. "I can apply these new variables, and attempt to come up with new parameters for our model. Culture is not something I truly grasp, so I am not sure what the results will be."

I told him to add it to our ever-growing the mystery pile as we moved onto our next major argument of what location was best for me. This time, our stances were reversed as he suggested I delve into the rats' nest of Hong Kong while I leaned towards caution.

"I believe you will actually be safer there." I, of course, thought the seals leading to his computer bays had been compromised and told him so. "It will be much more difficult for a major corporation to actively engage you openly inside Hong Kong than your present location. Additionally, the same logic applies for why you chose Auckland over the capital, more population to hide within." In addition, a lot of water between that big city and me. I mentioned I truly wasn't comfortable skimming across a quarter the Pacific Ocean. "The sloop is able to traverse the distance very quickly. The risk is minimal if we plan accordingly."

My battle senses were flaring but *Heart* was the one running the math. I knew he had my best interest at the forefront of his mind and if he said Hong Kong was safer and was better for the mission, then I needed to listen to him.

Chapter 25

It turns out my battle senses were correct. I've gone soft in my old age but not in the usual ways. The proof was the constant chirping accompanying me from the passenger seat as I accelerated over the Philippine Sea. Our lady and mistress, the cat, had decided she was not going to be left in Auckland. As soon as I unhitched the reactor from the equipment, she ducked under the passenger seat of the sloop and couldn't be coaxed out. It wasn't until we were over New Guinea that she popped her head out for a half a second, and then jumped up on the passenger chair in a much more relaxed fashion as though we weren't traveling slightly under the speed of sound. I gave her a quick scratch between the ears and focused on getting to Hong Kong.

Unfortunately, I hadn't thought about how long it would actually take to make the trip. The distance between Auckland and Hong Kong runs at over nine thousand kilometers. I could have bumped up the speed and cut the time in half or more, but we were trying to keep a low profile. Staying below the speed of sound was one of best ways to do that. The last thing we wanted was a sonic boom over a populated area annoying the locals and drawing attention to us.

"I have modified your lodging arrangements to something more pet-friendly, Ari. The original hotel did not accept animals. I am still not sure why you could not leave her behind." I let him know that was never an option. The second we fed her, we took on an obligation. It was simply a case of whether we were taking her with us to Hong Kong or Luna. She decided she was going to be with us the entire journey. "In that case, should we name her?" Damn, *Heart* was indeed a Looney down at his core. I had told him we had a new family member, and rather than any sort of argument, he was more interested in names.

Until that point I had been thinking of her as the cat, but *Heart* had a point. I had been avoiding the inevitable. I asked if he had any ideas. "How about Em?" I asked him if he meant the letter. "No, as in Aunty Em from *The Wizard of Oz*. You made reference to the novel upon our arrival." I absolutely had to hear his logic on this one. "The story referred to her as grayed out, and the cat is a female gray tabby. You seem to like the book as well." I looked at the cat and tried it. She echoed back at me. Well then, Em it was.

I cut speed as I got closer to Hong Kong's controlled airspace. My dampers displaying the up to the minute information from *Heart*. How had I ever lived without these? Research will only provide so much about a city. It gives a lot of data but raw information is sterile and lifeless. Seeing a city in person changes that. I had spent so long not seeing anyone but Em when I started to see hoppers my excitement rose. Like the pre-fall jitters but instead of jitters, I was actually looking forward to it. From the first other sighting to the eventual swarm it took perhaps a half hour to see the tops of the city over the horizon.

Normally the horizon would only be thirty or so kilometers depending on the height of the buildings we were dealing with. We were at almost three times that distance and she looked like Auckland had when we left. The closer we got, the bigger she became to the point of becoming unfathomable. The skyscrapers butted up to the seawall to the point where nothing urban remained. Teeth biting into the sky.

I was too far out and moving too fast to see people. When I did get close enough I had to pick up height for the hotel *Heart* had lined up. A warehouse wasn't feasible and the best he could arrange was a room with an external parking dock. The setup was reminiscent of *Heart's* own fabrication bays with the sliding door. Having completed the maneuver once under water, completing it a second time was surprisingly simple, even in the air. As soon as the bay door was closed, I opened the canopy and carried Em into the suite.

I set her down and watched for a solid ten minutes as she sauntered about hissing at walls asserting her dominance and then curled up into the refresher sink for a nap. Em had the right idea. We'd been traveling for a third of a day. I needed to wash the stink off and take a nap myself. I set the shower and dumped my clothes into the laundry. The shower was a bit of an indulgence at a full half hour but when finished I felt nice and relaxed. The bed called to me.

It took maybe two minutes before I was out. The last thing I remembered was Em curled up on the pillow beside me.

Chapter 26

"We could simply ask one of them?" Like *Heart* had a completely reasonable idea. I told him he was out of his ever-loving mind. "No, seriously. GSI is based out of Hong Kong. Could you not approach an employee, and gather information?" I was flabbergasted. I argued there was the matter of our cover for starters. "We could use more illicit techniques."

I went from flabbergasted to a dead stop. I had never considered what he would consider right and wrong. Those are distinctly human concepts. *Heart* was absolutely a person, but being a person didn't make him human, and not being human meant his ethical and moral inclinations didn't always align the same ways ours did. I knew he valued life but there were other human concepts he didn't understand. Didn't translate across species.

I had him clarify to make sure I wasn't making crazy assumptions. "We have a list of names. We can track one or more down, and from there convince them to provide additional information. As Master Dixon would say, escalate their self-interest." Now that was a morally gray statement if I ever heard one. Before I let my emotions get the better of me, I told him to explain. "I was thinking bribery, but we could definitely lean towards more surreptitious means if you think it wise." Whoa. I put the kibosh on that line of thought quick.

Bribery didn't bother me at all. Part of my own utilitarian streak. I didn't even consider a bit of graft a crime, even though it absolutely was corruption at the basest level. I looked at it like lubrication, much like courtesy. Once acknowledging there was an acceptable level, and staying within that level, things became easy. When balance wasn't maintained various societies stopped working correctly.

Heart's speaking of illicit measures had me thinking of physical methods since I didn't consider a bit of graft illegal. He, however, put them all in the same bucket and I'm not sure how he divided those buckets. I'd like to believe I have some pretty black and white rules, but in reality, those lines are dark gray and very thick. I've stepped deep into those lines and only because I had buddies yank me back out of those shadows at the last possible moment I didn't cross over.

His suggestion did have merits, though. We were theoretically dealing with mercenary types. Why not use that to our advantage? The question I asked him was how. "GSI pays their employees extremely well. Both at the compensation level and in severance. They appear to run approximately twenty percent above market average. Bribery might be more difficult than I anticipated." A pretty slick move, keeping folks from looking for other work while making recruiting much easier. Everyone wanted to be paid well, and it's much harder to bribe someone who is. "Extortion is a possibility, but will require further research." I was voicing an argument to slap the approach down viewing it as crossing a line when *Heart* countered. "They tried to kill us. I do not believe only the threat of harm to gather information is comparable."

That started a hell of a debate. I held my own for about five minutes before he managed to destroy each of my good arguments and then simply ignored my bad ones. Finally, I pointed out it wasn't likely any of the people on our list even had any dirt we could exploit. "But Ari we do not have to use them at all." He caught me off guard with the statement, in hindsight, where I actually lost. "We can use anyone in the entire company. Now that we know who our opposition is, why limit ourselves to GSI's pawns?" Einstein's Ghost, he wanted to take on the whole corp. "Not all of GSI, only the divisions based out of Hong Kong. It represents perhaps twelve percent of the company."

I could have put in an audition tape for training instructor with the litany of swearing I was spewing out after he said that. I was good enough Em lifted her head from the pillow and she normally wasn't bothered by my incessant cursing. "I am not sure I see the problem. GSI does not know you still exist and if they did, it would take an inordinate amount of resources to attempt to find you." That actually made sense. It was a form of insurgency. As long as they couldn't pinpoint who I was, and couldn't actively go after the population as a whole then I could operate in the relative open. The question then became who we targeted.

"I have some ideas on that." I'd heard that before and each time the phrase caused spikes in my adrenaline. "They would need to be high enough placed in the company to use security assets." He had a point. *Heart* displayed what looked like a task organization chart on the hotel screen. I'd seen them before from my Legion days. He started with a simple flow chart the headquarters element, breaking down into smaller divisions until it got to the smallest echelons, each arrayed in a similar manner, except his was by department with a lot more dotted lines creating a maze that was very hard to follow.

"This is a nominal corporate structure based on Luna Corporation, and what we know of GSI. I have taken some liberties and made some assumptions based on what is publicly available. Starting with known entities in green, then yellow for high confidence, and orange are mid-confidence. Red are low but assumed to exist in some form, however, may be part of another department." What a confusing mess. I couldn't help but wonder aloud how anything got accomplished in a corporation. "Decentralization and automation mostly." *Heart* stated matter-of-factly, then continued without missing a beat. "We can assume that anything below this level could not be responsible." About two-thirds of the structure collapsed into the chart. "Likewise, much of this section would not apply." Another half disappeared.

What was left were a handful of upper-level departments with offices underneath them. I asked why there were no names. "I am working on applying faces to those positions. If we can determine who occupies the roles, we can determine who has the means. I believe I can develop a profile." I inquired about public information. "The Zhangs own the company fully. Although there are many assignments facing outward, it appears anything above middle management is closely held." I wanted him to tell me whom we would target. It felt like we were about to attempt a bombing run through a city trying to pick off specific soldiers who weren't in uniform. The irony wasn't lost on me, seeing as how relying on the same type of camouflage as well.

"We do not go after the department heads." *Heart* said bluntly. "We are aiming for minor administrators. I believe the phrase you used was 'worker bees.' The goal is to cause noise and force our prey into the open." He was speaking my language now.

Unless studying protection the idea was counter-intuitive. It takes significant resources to defend a single asset, therefore, becoming a game of picking and choosing what is most important to protect. By scaring lower level resources, they scatter and the higher powers end up getting skittish calling on every bit of firepower available. The goal then is to rain hell on them while they're all in one place.

We weren't out to destroy the group as a whole but to identify the leaders. If we could trick the players into surrounding themselves with as much security as they could afford, they would glow like we had dropped atomics on them. Their fear would remove their camouflage.

Chapter 27

GSI was a big company and attacking it head on would have been suicide. I have a well-developed survival instinct and I like my skin in one piece so we were aiming for the proverbial low hanging fruit. Finding fruit among the leaves was our problem, but that's why I've always surrounded myself with smart people or more specifically, why exceptionally smart individuals have always surrounded me with smart people.

Heart theorized the more important the person was, the better their encryption would be on the handhelds they carried. By planting some inexpensive repeaters near GSI's headquarters and putting out a low-level attack on the comm signal we were able to eliminate the lowest level employees. We slowly ratcheted up the attacks to until we saw a response. When the reaction finally came it was not only impressive, it was hilarious.

The nice part about using cheap repeaters was we could set them up, and broadcast on the public net channel. There was no way to track the signal back to us because we were effectively watching a public news feed as opposed to a dedicated line. By whittling away at the base, we created a progressively unstable structure, like one of those games, where a kid pulls a block from the bottom of a stack and places it on the top until the entire structure crashes down. Our barrage did that. When we got far enough up the food chain everything collapsed. It was epic.

We made sure to space out the attacks and make them fairly obvious, in turn making GSI's response much funnier. The trick to a good ambush is the simplicity. There's a reason the bait and wait is so effective. The classic example is the roadside bomb. Wait for a convoy to trip it, and then unload as much firepower as quickly as possible. He who escalates fastest wins. The way to defeat that particular kind of trap is to get out of the box by identifying its sides and overwhelming one. Once through there is a chance of survival.

What we did was set up the box and trap, but not the accompanying ambush. We wanted to see what GSI's response would be. People are social creatures. We like to talk to each other and having our ability cut off makes us very paranoid. When done progressively, the paranoia builds like water behind a dam until something breaks. Denying the right people communications triggered that event.

It was juvenile and I wish I could take credit for it, but this was all *Heart*. He created a simple jamming program aiming for GSI's lowest level comm protocols. The idea being communications much like water will find the path of least resistance. If the lowest path doesn't work, people will try to go to the next higher ground. We could track who was given additional access even if we couldn't read their comms, and assumed they were the de facto team leaders for the troops. As we escalated our efforts, we were able to spot the office heads, and so forth.

We still didn't know who any of the people were, but we now knew who held a specific device which was so much better. A standard comm unit is relatively smart by itself. It's not AI smart, but most people are fairly reliant on them. They're good for about a year before they're upgraded, and even then most hold onto their ID number making it simple to get ahold of someone. I've had the same number since before I left Terra the first time, even though my real gear was safely stored in my vault back in White Caps. For most folks, the comm unit is merely an extension of themselves to the point they don't even think about it. This gave us the ability to track GSI employees as long as their units were active.

But back to our fun. GSI wanted to put a stop to our childish attack. It was almost two weeks in when the security teams swooped in and started destroying every repeater they could find. Since we were using cameras on a completely different system, we got a front-seat view of the two-man teams executing a precision attack on passcard-sized boxes hidden throughout the city. The real fun was when the teams started calling in they found them and each had the same sticker reading: "World Famous Pork Lo Mein" with a number, going to GSI tech support if anyone tried to call. I, of course, felt like a vintage film villain as I stroked Em from the comfort of my hotel while peeling off hunks of cheese and apple with my field knife while sipping the local tea.

"You seem quite amused." Indeed, I was. I'd been on the wrong side of similar events, which were much less good-natured and my Terran humor was in full force. I wondered what *Heart* thought of it. "I still do not understand the point of the decals. You kept breaking into giggles every time you were going to explain." His confusion set me off again. Enough for to Em vacate her perch on my lap and sulked to the sink. I was out of cheese so that might have been part of her departure. I explained the stickers were me being a hair cruel. There was no actual meaning to them, which of course made no sense to *Heart*. That was their point. I wanted to screw with the people in GSI. I wanted someone, anyone to dedicate as much brainpower as possible trying to figure out what the little piggy emblem, the phrase, or the comm number meant.

That elicited a sound I had never heard before. About halfway between a crackle and a screech, and for a second I thought we lost comms. "I am so sorry. I was not expecting that. I think I can adjust the sound for the future, though." I asked him to help me out because I was a tad lost. "I believe that was an involuntary laugh. Or at least, what my audio processors translated as one." Got me to laughing again. I had never actually heard him laugh before. I knew he had a sense of humor or something close to one. He found things funny, odd, or strange and could poke fun at them. He and I joked about things quite a bit. But this was definitely new territory. "You do not understand. I have spent several days trying to figure the purpose out. I knew you had a reason otherwise, you would not have done it, however, the entire point was to waste GSI personnel's time thinking about something with no point. Being caught in the nuisance trap you set for our adversaries is rather grand irony."

That set me off again, in turn setting him off with something less of a screechy feedback loop and sounding more like a laugh. Knowing him, he had compiled it from other sources and would modify the sound over time. It was good to know what he thought was truly funny and he could laugh at himself.

"Does that actually work on people? Making up erroneous data?" I told him it depended on the person. Some people would ignore the data while others would forget it, and others would be able to realize it didn't mean anything. Since we were casting a wide net, it didn't matter if everyone was looking at the stupid little pig if we could get even a couple of people to do so. My stickers were about creating distractions, about making noise. "It is so counter-intuitive. Now that I am aware that it is fiction, it does not matter in the least, but before when I assumed they had a purpose I was engrossed. It was so maddening. But that was your point."

"Applying that sophomoric prank to our denial of service attack I believe might actually change GSI's long-term response. It may drastically change the context of the assault." I nodded as I was chewing on the last of my apple but I was hoping for that. I told him I hadn't shared my intent because I wasn't sure how GSI would respond. The beauty of hindsight is seeing all the teams attack, but it could have as easily been a couple of guys walking from spot to spot with a bag gathering them up. "I see, but what does that do for us? I realize that it helps our anonymity but to what end?" I smiled because it was my turn to lay out a plan.

Chapter 28

General Campbell would have been proud of us. We had successfully infiltrated Terra. We believed we had identified the organization responsible for the political issues and *Heart* had a plausible model for why. What we needed was proof to confirm it. At our disposal was one of the best computers in existence. Of course, he was in the middle of the ocean, hiding from said corporation that had already tried to kill us. But just because he would have been proud didn't mean we couldn't do better. There was the rub.

The easy route would have been to bolt back to Luna and report our findings thus far. But the easy out wouldn't have been the hard right. What we had thus far only gave us a piece of the picture. It presented problems, not solutions. As long as *Heart* and I could still whittle away at the questions, we needed to continue doing so.

My hotel's wall-screen showed the current locations of each known GSI employee. Our gag resulted in new encryption protocols, but we could still track people's movements. I didn't want to overplay our hand but I also didn't want to sit doing nothing. By tracking the comm units to home addresses, we were able to put quite a few names with IDs. This, in turn, filled out our company structure, making our puzzle look a lot more like a picture.

Everything came back to the handhelds. If we could get ahold of one or better yet create a clone, we could open a backdoor into GSI. The risk with simply stealing one was the company would change their encryption again. We needed to gain legitimate appearing access. A lower level unit would be easiest, and likely wouldn't cause a security sweep, but it also wouldn't get us the entry we wanted. So yet again balance was a concern.

My plan was to steal a comm unit of an upper-level employee, but in such a way they didn't realize it was gone. I wanted to substitute a real unit and then destroy a fake unit in front our mark's eyes so they didn't report it missing. They needed to simply replace it instead. The trick would be making it appear accidental and genuine.

As I've said, the key to a good ambush is simplicity. The more complex, the more chances for things to go wrong. Taking someone out is easy. All that requires is patience. A failed attempt doesn't prevent a future attack. Keeping someone in the game is significantly harder. The first priority is choosing the correct person. The second is that they cannot know there was an attempt at all.

I knew the theory from all the reading back at Tycho but this was delving deep into practical application areas neither *Heart* nor I had real experience with. I was stuck and couldn't figure out the next step. Actually, knew the next move, but not the move after that.

Despite being a center for international business for centuries, I still stood out in Hong Kong. I'm a big guy by Asian standards. Back in Auckland, my appearance wasn't nearly as obvious mainly because I didn't tower over the locals by an average of twenty centimeters. In Hong Kong, my size wasn't something that could easily be hidden by a hat or creative clothing.

"Ari, I am not sure how to approach this issue. Unlike myself, you cannot transfer your presence to another shell to accomplish a specific task and this one is better suited to you than me. If only we had Robert here." I stopped him as the realization hit me. I explained we didn't need Robert. We didn't even need me or *Heart*. We had been so wrapped up on what we had; we had forgotten we were inside the box. "I do not understand. If we cannot trust existing communications, how do we acquire more assistance?"

I grabbed my dampers, jacket, gave Em a quick scratch between the ears, and slid out hotel door. The beauty of being in a city was I didn't have to do dirty work. We could outsource the work. We needed to find someone reliable. I explained this to *Heart* on the way down the elevator. "I think I understand where you are going with this, but does not this create a lot of risk?" The farther down the yellow-bricked road we got the more this mission became about balancing risk. This was no different. Our best resources were back on Luna, but that didn't mean we didn't have good resources in Hong Kong.

After I had pinned on my first stripe one of my sergeants had taught me having the best wasn't needed because we only needed good enough. Sure overkill was great, but most of the time the best was a waste. Kind of like my dampers. Until I had a reason to have a good set, all those extra capabilities were almost worthless. Over the last couple of months, I had become so used to getting by having unlimited resources I forgot how to get by on scrounging off the land.

Heart and I had become overly cautious. For the most part, I had stayed tucked away in the hotel venturing out only for food, and only long enough to purchase and set up the repeaters for the previous mission. Our thought process was out of sight, out of mind but in a city the size of Hong Kong that strategy wasn't necessary. Who looks for a single ant in an anthill?

There are many ways of hiding. The easiest is to find a place of hunkering down and not be seen. We'd done that with *Heart* in

Kermadec Trench while Em and I enjoyed room service on his credits. It's a great method but doesn't accomplish anything. The purloined letter method is almost as good. Take something at shove it in plain sight so folks ignore it. After passing a couple of times, it's always been there so they don't even question its presence anymore. The one I was most familiar with was to act like you're supposed to be there. I don't know if it's only me or all humans are wired this way, but we generally don't like confrontation. We don't want to start arguments or fights. We'll actually spend more effort avoiding one than one would take. Back in Auckland, I was able to pretend to be a delivery driver simply because no one questioned me. I looked the part, therefore, I must be one.

I had used that same idea to acquire the repeaters from a store in Hong Kong as well as most of the other goods we were using. I was able to prey upon the subconscious of those around me. If we could do it with gear, why couldn't we do it with people? I explained my idea to *Heart* who responded, "There is the matter of trust. Who can we trust on this endeavor?"

Chapter 29

If I were to map my life into a pie chart the bulk would be on ship, the wilderness, and in bars. Only a small sliver would show up anywhere else, and I'd bet good money it was on the way between those three places.

I don't want to imply I'm some kind of lush. I'm not. I like booze for the taste, but I got getting drunk out of my system long ago. Bars fill my social niche. I'm not big on crowds, but for whatever reason bars don't trigger my issues in the same way so they allow me to stay engaged and keep from becoming a hermit. The nice part about them is they exist everywhere. Everywhere I've ever been at least. Not every establishment has alcohol, or whatever the local intoxicant is, but humans have a habit of making meeting places and I might as well call them bars. Call a duck a duck and all that. White Caps is a bar, Spacelanes is a bar, and the place I was heading to in Hong Kong was a bar.

Although Legion wasn't technically allowed on Terra, that restriction didn't mean there weren't any of us running about. An embargo is only as good as the customs agents. I shared my thought process with *Heart* that maybe we'd be able to find other folks like myself, but on the other side of the border. "Ari, you were correct, the conventions did not specify deportation of former Legionnaires but I am not sure how this new information will help us. There is no master database for me to access linking membership." I asked him where he would find ships if he didn't have a database. "I would start at the spaceport." I could almost hear an audible gear click before "Oh. You believe there will be former comrades close to the installation." Bingo.

Everyone joins for his or her own reasons. There are as many reasons as there are Legionnaires or Imperials or Mariners or whatever flavor of spacer exists but there was always a constant from folks who got out. The thing veterans missed the most was the people. Some sort of cultural bit. After spending so long in, we were foreigners in our own land. We no longer belonged from where we came from, so we hovered along the outskirts of places close those to the ones we just left.

Looking back, my transition had been good. Insanely complex, but good. If not for Lysha and *Heart,* it would have been rough. It's hard to change gears without a support structure. Without family, and they were my new family. I was getting ready to dive back into my old world. To visit extended family.

You can never really go home again, but you can visit. I was trying to explain all of this to *Heart* as the cab dropped me at the front gate of the Cadre Club. There's not a lot of green in Hong Kong, but I'd guess ninety percent of the grass was on Cadre's lawn. I could see it peeking out through the front gate as I approached. I wanted to stop and stare but I could hear the guard in the booth and I'd been that guy before so I walked up. He gave me a quick glance, seeing I obviously wasn't a local, then rattled off in Standard, "How can I help you, Sir?"

I wasn't in a position to flash idents, so I told him Schmiddy sent me by way of the *Rope* and asked if there was any way I could get a day pass. His eyes flashed when I mentioned Schmiddy and again at the *Europe*. "Ah, I was on the *Khan* with the *Freak*. When'd you get back?" He started pulling down a lanyard and plugging in my info. Each of the big ships has nicknames because it's way too easy to call them by their real names. The *Europe,* my old ship is the *Rope.* The *Freak* is the *Africa.* There's also the *Antarctica, Australia, North America,* and *South America* which go by *Ant, Ozzie, Merica,* and the *Ham.* The only one without a nickname is the *Asia* because it's hard to shorten that. We talked shop for a few minutes then he let me in through the small door.

The Cadre Club is more of an estate than a bar. If White Caps had open space, I think it would probably look a lot like Cadre. It was an old school country club, catering to military types. I knew Schmiddy was a member, but he had never told me how he became one. Dropping his name at the front gate wasn't strictly kosher, but as long as I didn't make a fool of myself it shouldn't be an issue. The nice part about of buddies is the ability to leverage help when needed. He'd have the same resource if he ever needed it.

My walk up was leisurely. I couldn't help it. The place had a natural calm that seeped into the bones as I made my way from the gate up the path towards the front entry. "We are going to find your associates here?" *Heart* sounded shocked, and honestly, I couldn't blame him. It wasn't like most military was upper class. This place screamed top one percent. Despite my recent forays into society with Lysha, I was not a member of the elite.

I'm from the middle of nowhere and although my folks were far from rich, I had a comfortable childhood. I started working as soon as I was able. First with odd jobs, and then with more steady stuff while I was going through school. As soon as I was eighteen, all those savings disappeared with a one-way ticket to LC. I've never had debt, though. Never had a chance to get it. Moreover, because the Legion covered most of my bills, my accounts grew over time. If I was smart, I could live well. Not Cadre well, but I could choose my own path.

It so happened I was woefully underdressed for the current path, even by the casual standards I saw around me. Had I given half a thought I would have dressed the part, but I had bolted out the hotel when inspiration hit. For the most part, spacer bars are like normal bars. Spacelanes is middle of the spectrum. White Caps is high end, but it's old and well established. The Cadre Club was even higher end than White Caps, catering to the officer crowd more than the rank and file like me. Not as though I would be unwelcome. Exactly the opposite. The staff, like the guy at the front gate, would be extremely pleasant, but the club wasn't an environment I was used to. I was more accustomed to the deeper end of the rainbow.

If I could have chosen a different bar, I probably would have, but Hong Kong had the Cadre Club, so that's where I went. I'm sure there are other spacer bars in the area, but none as big, and none as well known. Had I ended up in Tokyo, Edoten would have been my first choice, but Nero's would have been a close second. That's not to say there weren't advantages, being handed an orange juice almost as soon as I entered was the first.

I made my way to the concierge counter and waited for a gentlemen dressed for tennis to finish up with a tropical suited lady with the telltale golden keys and a maroon ascot. "Ari, who are we going to see?" Before I could sub-vocalize an answer, she waved me forward with a huge smile and asked how she could help. I let her know I was looking for the chapel.

The directions she gave were simple to follow, but it still took a good ten minutes to reach the chapel. I got the impression it was for weddings more than actual services. I've never been big on attending church as my folks took an Einsteinian view on religion. All that life energy has to go somewhere, but they never exactly said where. Having studied physics and chemistry since then, I know the math a little better now, but I like the comfort of faith, and when it boils down to it ideas are a kind of energy and life. Maybe spreading those is a bit of immortality.

"But why are we here?" I hadn't meant to ignore *Heart's* question earlier, but I got caught up in the setting. If looking for someone to trust, go to family, bartender, or a priest. I let him know I was hoping to leverage all three by visiting a chaplain.

Chapter 30

Chaplains are sort of strange ducks. They fill a niche role in the profession of arms. Their history is probably as old as the profession itself. When man first stepped out into the big dark, we brought with us fear, but we also brought with us light. Chaplains help carry that.

It doesn't matter whether someone is a believer or not, space is a big and scary place. War is a terrifying concept. Chaplains are someone to talk to about scary things. Things that can't be discussed with buddies. Things people don't want to be judged about.

The irony I was attempting to seek counsel from a priest about breaking the eighth commandant was not lost on me but the fact we took men of peace into battle wasn't lost either. It took men with a special mindset to reconcile the latter, so I hoped my broaching the former wouldn't be a problem.

I had finished explaining my logic to *Heart* when an older man geared for golf approached. Like the rest of the people I had passed in the Cadre Club, he was dressed well but casually in khaki slacks, an aloha shirt, and a Panama hat. "You look like a man on a mission. What brings you to our little corner of paradise?" Big smile, firm handshake. "We don't get many visitors until wedding season, but something tells me that's not why you're here." I returned his smile and nodded. His mood was infectious, and I couldn't help but be pulled in.

I'm fairly good with people, but that's mainly because I've spent a lot of time working on it. I'm not extroverted naturally and the close friends I have been hard won. As much as I hate to admit it to myself, I'm fairly socially awkward unless I know the protocols in advance. The Legion was great about that. It wasn't super rigid, but enough to help me overcome my normal anxious tendencies. Coming to see the chaplain triggered a lot of my nervousness, but his mood helped a lot.

He sat us in a side pew, and we began chatting. Every chaplain I'd ever encountered had been from the Imperial side of the house. Legion and the Mariners borrow ours from them, usually after they retire. They do an abbreviated training so they know their way around, but for the most part, the chaplains are valued guests on the boats a lot like General Campbell was when I met him.

Reverend Brandt had spent almost all of his time with the Mariners after playing cold cargo during one of the big expedition waves. That was decades before I joined, and the Northern Reaches, where I'm from isn't exactly Empire friendly to begin with. We fall more under the wary but neutral side of things. I had met dozens of

Imperials over the years because it's impossible not to. They're everywhere, but the only one I knew well were Robert who was an expat up in Luna. From what I gathered, there wasn't a lot of love lost between the people and the government as it swapped political hands every century or so. They'd go from expansionist to isolationist, and usually involving a forced migration and conscription program until the next party took control again.

Love of home is a strange thing, there's a longing for it. Like myself, the Reverend had the call of Terra so he and few other pastors had worked out a deal where they rotated duties at the Cadre Club and a few of the outlying locations on a couple year basis. I told him their arrangement sounded like a sweet deal to me. "There's a downside of course. Fieldhren 4 is fairly undeveloped." His fingers went up for air quotes when he said the last, "but the people are happy to have someone to talk to. And it's amazing what can be distilled with human ingenuity." He shook his head at that. Visions of spiders made me shiver.

I had taken off my dampers when I had come into the chapel and they were hanging on my collar, so I knew *Heart* was itching for answers and to ask questions, but I couldn't justify leaving them on inside. I knew he could hear the conversation, giving me a bit of solace. I hadn't rehearsed how I was going to bring this up, and I had only given *Heart* the barest outline of what my intent was adding even more to my nerves.

We needed help. It was that simple. The job had gotten too big for just the two of us. Unfortunately, we couldn't call on our normal support chain, so my goal was to find the next best thing. I wanted someone I could trust implicitly and *Heart's* comments had keyed me in on the idea of spacers. Who better than a chaplain to point us in the right direction. They tend to know where folks are, and how to keep their mouths shut. Bartenders are a close second, but without personally knowing them, the latter isn't always true.

I wasn't sure how much of our mission I could share with Reverend Brandt, not because of the trust factor, but because I didn't want to impose on him. So I gave a rough outline leaving out a lot of details equating to needing local business help and being unfamiliar with the area after being gone so long. The sensitive nature of the job led me to the club and to him in particular. He nodded along with my story, which was true although incomplete.

It's always been my policy to be as honest as possible. I don't like to lie if I can avoid it, even through omission. This was no different. I realized my mission fell into the realm of ethically gray but I was also actively avoiding hurting anyone where possible so my twinges of guilt didn't ping too hard.

The Reverend didn't seem to pick up any of my misgivings and took my contact information with a smile and a parting handshake. "I'll need to see who is about the area of course, but I'm sure there might be some of our brothers who are looking for employment."

Chapter 31

Two days later my comm unit finally rang, and I about dove off the bed to break up the monotony, getting a hissing cat for my trouble. "It's Talbot Brandt. We spoke over at the Cadre Club the other day. I hope I didn't catch you too late in the evening?" I tried to mask my excitement with small talk and told him it was fine being a bit of a night owl. "Good, good. I think I may have found someone who can help you if you're still looking." I let him know indeed, I was. Well sort of, as the good Reverend was the only one I had contacted thus far, but not something he needed to know. "Great, I'll pass along your information, and you two can meet up." I thanked him profusely and after a couple more minutes of chatting ended the call.

No sooner had the line gone silent than *Heart* chimed in. I think he was feeding off my excitement this time. "This is excellent news. But now we are back to waiting again." I told him that was one hell of a way to kill the mood. "That was not my intent, but it is a good thing time is not one of our limited resources." He had that right. But we knew that going in. This was a recon mission. It was all about hurry up and wait, in typical military fashion. Get in position and wait for something to happen. Find out what was going on. We were getting close, but waiting was an essential part of it. I wasn't sure acquiring one of the comm units was the final hurdle, but I was pretty sure it was near the home stretch. We'd be able to see the finish line at least.

The biggest thing no one ever mentions when joining up is the amount of downtime there is. The posters seem to imply constant adventure. Seeing far off places and doing things, and there is but traveling to those locations takes time. In addition, upon arrival, there is endless planning and preparation before actually getting to do any of the amazing things recruiters promised them.

I was lucky; when I joined up, I just wanted to see the stars. The journey itself was my goal, and as I ranked up and started to see behind the curtain, I got to have even more fun. Planning for missions has its own excitement, its own stresses, and although it's not the same type of fun as seeing the stars, it's definitely more fun than being shot at, and hugely more fun than being shot. The latter being no fun at all, even with energy displacers which usually only take the brunt of the blow.

I wasn't exactly sure how *Heart* managed boredom on his own when he didn't have his ship building projects but unless I was moving or actively planning, cabin fever would start to build up. It wasn't boredom as I've never really had that problem, but the need to accomplish something. Even though it had only been a couple of days since I visited the Cadre Club, I knew it wasn't some sort of magic wand, but one could hope. Even Em had been giving oddball looks like I was throwing off her peace and quiet.

A short time after Reverend Brandt's call, I received a message from a Max Hayes asking about the details. I asked *Heart* what he could find out regarding our potential recruit. "I am unable to provide much on Mr. Hayes background, unfortunately. I would hazard he is Imperial as I have fairly comprehensive data on the Legion up until our departure but that is conjecture. Based on your interaction with Colonel Brandt, however, I would assume he can be relied upon." I tended to agree and arranged a meeting for the following day before lunch. We weren't out anything at this point, and we could always come up with a cover story if things didn't work out.

I called down to the front desk and scheduled a private conference room. There was a certain amount of laziness in it, which I claimed as efficiency. Might as well make things simple for myself. I reasoned there was nothing wrong with taking the easy way every now and again, especially as the hotel would provide water, a fruit platter, and *Heart* could listen over the built-in audiovisual system without drawing too much attention.

After winding down a bit, I decided to catch a bit of sleep as the chaplain actually had called later than I had expected.

I woke from a dead sleep by a buzzing on the tip of my nose. Em had decided placing her wet nose on mine, and purring was the best way to inform me she was out of food. Had we been anywhere but in Terra gravity, I would have launched her a good ten meters when I came instantly awake. It is my firm belief she anticipated this by using her little pitons to grip into both my good shoulder and chest to lock on. After much yelping and carefully removing said claws I crawled out of bed and noted the time being right before dawn. Cats are crepuscular, a fancy way of saying active during twilight. The only reason I know that particular word is because I had an instructor who liked to point out humans were not. Our brains shut down during the time right before dawn. Best time to launch the snooze-alarm attack, which apparently our self-domesticated allies the cats discovered several thousand years ago.

I managed to get the tin of sea fish vittles almost half way open before my leg was constantly bombarded with little kitty paws demanding her tribute. This time without the claws, as she knew who was feeding her. As soon as the plate was on the floor and the ritual complete, I exited the temple before I became her next sacrifice.

I could have ducked back into bed, but the smell of salmon was enough to kill my mood for sleep at least for the foreseeable future so I decided to order bagels and lox and jump in the refresher. By the time I finished up my breakfast was waiting at the door and the goddess appeared appeased on the couch.

I puttered around until I couldn't take the waiting anymore and headed down to the conference room. It wasn't I was bored or anxious, or even had pre-drop jitters. It was the hurry up and wait mentality. If I was going to wait, I might as well wait where my meeting was. Once I got downstairs and worked with *Heart* to get the room setup and the fruit got delivered I was fine again until the door chimed Max Hayes' arrival.

Not thinking anything of it, I keyed the entrance and came face to face with the same blonde who had taken control of *Heart's* lifeboat back on Fiji.

Chapter 32

I don't know which one of us recovered first, but Hayes definitely moved faster. Her eyes showed recognition a nanosecond after mine, but she had not been expecting me. There was no doubt my appearance had surprised her, and she thought this was an ambush because she was fighting inward, escalating hard and fast. She was quick as a viper, and far more accustomed to Terra gravity than I was even after all my time goofing off. These flashes of insight crossed my conscious mind as my subconscious struggled for survival. I wanted to scream for her to stop, the fight was all a misunderstanding, but I wasn't sure it was. Had I been in her place it would not have done any good.

Training with Robert back on Luna paid off in a big way as my right arm instinctively blocked something hard and thin. It stung something fierce and I was glad my jacket caught the brunt but knew was going to be bruised to hell. Another strike and the flash of steel and I realized she had a wicked knife pulled from her own sleeve in a single upward motion. She moved as if it were an extension of herself.

My first block had set the tone, with me going defensive trying not to take a knife to the leg as soon as I knew it was there.

The first rule of knife fighting is someone is going to get cut. My jacket had saved me so far, but she was fast. My major advantage beyond the coat was a head of height and the fifteen kilos of mass I had on her. I was able to block most of the blows, but she was no amateur and getting the knife out of her possession was not going to happen. One of us would have to screw up. I really hoped it wasn't me.

I was limited to using my arms, keeping them tucked close, lest she duck inside for a shot at my exposed ribs. This killed my better reach while she had full access to her legs and feet, presenting other difficulties. She would feint with the knife or her off hand and then follow up with a knee or hard kick. My other issue was I didn't want her dead, but I doubted she cared as much about me. She thought this was a fight for survival, and I was in no position to change her impression. I had to figure out how to win and win clean.

Despite my larger size, she was able to use brute force to keep up the offensive. I don't know if it was a smart play or intuitive but it was extremely effective. Within seconds she had me backed near the conference table, keeping my left side effectively blocked while I had to use my right to cover what I assumed was her strong hand with the knife in it. If I could only reach a hand into my jacket, I could even the fight up. I was able to flick a chair with a foot, buying me half a second to knock the next one down in sequence. Did me no good as she moved like a Kabrin over the table itself coming at me and gave me a hard kick aimed for my left shoulder, barely managing to block with my wrist. I felt it reverberate all the way up, but I know she did as well, her shin hitting a full kilo of the alloy that makes up most of my arm.

To her credit, she didn't slow down, as she reversed direction and hit me with her full weight and knocked us both to the wall. She was on top of me. This was not good. I burned what I assumed were my last second seconds on Terra fumbling with the snap on my holster. Hayes was about to deliver a killing swipe when I managed to pull the trigger three times from less than ten centimeters away at rib level. The knife dropped and she fell to her side.

The reason I wear dampers is I value my hearing. After shooting this monster in close quarters, I wished I had had them on during the fight instead of hanging from my collar. My ears were buzzing something fierce until I finally caught some background noise I recognized as my partner "Ari, put your dampers on her. She is still alive." Bloody hell. I rolled her over and saw she had armor on. Good lightweight stuff, which had done all of jack and squat against my beast of a handgun, but was keeping the blood in her at least. "Dampers, Ari. Get them on her so I can see her vitals." *Heart* practically shouted over the rooms speakers. Urgency. Commands. He was in doctor mode and my instant obedience to orders training kicked in hard. I was fumbling with my cracked to hell dampers muttering about them being broken. "It does not matter; the sensors are fine. Go down the hall and retrieve the first aid kit. Hurry!"

I bolted around the corner and grabbed the autodoc box as directed and sprinted back. As soon as I got back to the room, *Heart* started giving me instructions. My instincts told me to strip off the armor for better access but he stopped me as soon as I reached for the straps. "No, the compression gear is likely the only thing keeping her alive currently. You will have to work around it." I did as instructed and started pulling items out, being careful not to trip the emergency call button inside the kit in my haste. I knew most of the contents of the box from my basic combat medic course back in initial training and the Legion forces a refresher every couple of years so I was able to keep up. Luckily, most of *Heart's* instructions involved either stabbing with a syringe full of trauma nanites or applying self-adhering sensors and letting the box do the heavy lifting. After about ten minutes, *Heart* declared, "I think she is stable. I have extended your conference room reservation, and will get the janitorial bots to clean up. We will need to move her, though." Huh? Fight or flight instinct had addled my brain. I was not tracking and asked him to explain.

"Ari, our goal was to acquire information. I believe we have found our best possible source if we can keep her alive until she recovers." I argued when she recovered, she was going to try to kill me again. That was entirely too close and I had almost not worn the slug-thrower to the meeting. "It is a good thing you did choose to come adequately equipped then." I wasn't even sure where to look in the room to give him the stink-eye for that particular comment.

"What else are we going to do with her?" He had me beat there. He continued. "We do not know what she knows. We do not know who knows she is missing. We do know if she turns up dead, there is a retired Imperial Colonel who can link you and her together. If we keep her alive or at least missing, she is an asset, as you would say. If she is found dead in this hotel room, she becomes a problem." I was ninety percent certain I heard a pause before the word problem. If I didn't know better, I would have bet he was censoring his own swears across the comm lines.

I asked him how in the hell he planned to keep her alive as I had put three very large holes in her very small body at very close range. "Between the first aid kit, the injections you gave her, and the coagulant package you applied, she has quite a few nanites repairing the major damage. She will need care, but she will probably survive. I anticipate moving her to your room without being seen will be the larger of your problems."

Chapter 33

Having my partner lock down the elevators until I got her back to my room actually turned out to be the simplest solution of our plethora of new problems. Once inside the room, I put Hayes on the bed and locked Em in the refresher much to her displeasure. I heard a metronome-like chirping of meows, as she demanded release from her prison. It was all I could do not to yell at her for something she obviously did not understand and wasn't in control of.

Autodocs are great pieces of gear. I should know as they are the only reason I'm alive. Each one has a few crystallic drone chips in them and are packed with enough nanites, sedatives, and medicine to keep a human alive if the user can follow the instructions on the screen that's included on the inside cover. Under the care of an actual doctor, like *Heart*, an autodoc is almost as good as having a mobile surgery. The work I had done down in the conference room was far from perfect, but it would definitely keep our guest alive so I could examine her closer.

I started by stripping off most of her kit, including the aforementioned body armor, which was ruined anyways, and enough personal weaponry to outfit a small nation. Underneath the armor, she was muscled like a snake, to the point where I was a little envious. My love of fruit had kept me from developing the same level of muscle tone she had obviously worked long and hard for. On top of that, she was armed to the teeth, but like me hadn't been able to access most of what she had on her. Like much of my life, pure luck had saved me. The knife she was carrying was a karambit folder with enough heft to double as a set of brass knuckles but sharp enough to actually leave scratches on my coat. In her pockets, I found a pair of amp-gloves, which would have ended the fight in two seconds had she been wearing them. Nasty pieces of work, they are very effective at transferring enough electrical energy to fell a moose. There's only get a couple of charges out of them but generally, only a single jolt is needed.

Her comm unit was encrypted but *Heart* started working on it before he dispatched me to the nearest hospital. He assured me she would last for at least a couple of hours while I gathered up the laundry list he provided. I easily bought most of the items the local pharm-house but a few things were higher end, like a replacement autodoc. His solution was elegant in its simplicity. Take one out of an ambulance, as they usually had three. I couldn't fault his logic as any emergency needing their full supply would need more than one ambulance.

I should have remembered nothing takes less than an hour. What I thought would be a quick run out of the hotel to grab the selection of items became a headache in the making. I was still hopped up on adrenaline, resulting in a paranoia several levels two large. On top of that, finding an actual ambulance turned out harder than expected. I was about to give up when I spotted a crew grabbing mid-morning chow at a local diner. Thinking I was going to be spotted at any second, I managed to pull a kit out of the back and hide it under my jacket feeling like an idiot. Once I ducked around the corner I went into a shop, bought a couple of shirts as an excuse for a large bag, and shoved the autodoc in it, having forgotten to bring a backpack with me.

By the time I returned having also forgotten my original set of dampers in the sloop, *Heart* was brimming with excitement. "It appears Ms. Hayes still has access to Galactic Subsidiaries Incorporated." Still? That statement made me ask him what he meant.

"That is the interesting part, and may explain your altercation." I snorted at his use of the word interesting but waved for him to continue. "As near as I can tell, she was operating much like we were, in an undercover capacity. Almost immediately after we landed the lifeboat there appears to be an attempt on her life and she went to ground. Off grid as you say." That actually did explain a lot. She thought we had tried to kill her, hence her reaction. Had I been in her shoes, on the other side of the door, I probably would have reacted the same way.

If Hayes was working undercover, who for, was my follow up question. "I am still wading through the historical data. Her encryption is quite good, but based on her relationship with Colonel Brandt; I believe Imperial Army is most likely." Hell in a jump jet. What kind of black-ops had I gotten us into? I asked *Heart* to add the Reverend to our ever-growing research list, as well as Hayes.

"That is not the most exciting part!" I told him it had to be good; because I wasn't sure the jacket could handle any more surprises. "Nothing so violent. Ms. Hayes appears to have done quite a bit of research paralleling our needs regarding GSI's upper management." That was good, really good actually, as the information might help us recover us a bit of time wasted on what *Heart* had referred to as sophomoric pranks.

The viewscreen shifted from Hayes' vitals to our very familiar organization chart. "On a positive note, our baseline assumptions were approximately ninety percent accurate." Highlights in green appeared around the positions we got right. I gave a quick nod of acknowledgment. "Most of our errors were unsurprising, and we had noted the possible issues regarding deviations from the actual corporate structure in the nominal build." He placed Xs in several yellow, orange, and red items. I tracked thus far. "What is left is almost a direct overlap of what we were looking for." He cleared everything he hadn't confirmed, leaving out the higher echelons. "As near as I can tell, there is no upper management."

Chapter 34

I asked him how many of his logic circuits he had fried to come to that conclusion. A company can't run without leadership. Organizations cannot run without management. I don't care how tight a team is, once past two people, someone has to be in charge. Even with two, usually one leads at any given point, much like in *Heart* and my own relationship. He took charge where it made sense and vice versa.

"I misspoke, so let me clarify a bit. It does not appear there is a human in charge above the middle management level. I actually cannot find the Zhangs beyond a cursory legal presence. It is almost as though they are illusionary." I opened my mouth ready to call that stupidest idea I had heard all year and stopped myself knowing if *Heart* had even floated the idea, he had checked and triple checked it. He caught my issue and expanded. "I believe the company is using an AI in lieu of director staff."

That caught me off guard. My familiarity with artificial intelligence was fairly limited. AI was pretty uncommon. Not rare, but not common enough that a person would encounter it constantly either. I personally knew *Heart*, and had dealt with only a few lesser computers bordering on sentience but nothing comparable to him.

What he was suggesting would have to be orders of magnitude smarter than him. I let him know I wasn't getting my head wrapped around his suggestion and asked how it was even possible. "I am not sure actually. A great deal of my power is dedicated to hyperspace computing. Hypothetically, another type of programming could result in sentience, but I do not have enough data to say one way or another."

I wasn't tracking. My understanding of AI history and mechanics always told me their sentience was more of a complexity issue. I relayed this to *Heart* and pointed out *h*space drives were more of a footnote. In fact, the experts seemed to go out of their way to annotate correlation did not imply causation. "Absolutely, however, *Star* and I discuss the various theories at length when we are together. And we discuss them with the others as well." I caught a subtle shift in tone when he said others. Loneliness, I thought. "We have never encountered another sentience who was not hyperspace based. There are quite a number of theories regarding the issue, actually."

A memory tugged at me and I rattled off a planetary government I was vaguely familiar with. "Puller 6 would seem like an exception, but she was Terraformed using the colony ship

Wilson-Theis. She was retrofitted into the government computer after that, and awoke shortly thereafter." I was absolutely confused. If *h*space wasn't linked to AI, then why weren't there any other AI after all this time. *Heart* was a patient teacher and answered each of my questions. "Not exactly. This is difficult to explain. We have never found any AI that do not have a hyperspace drive attached. A rough equivalent would be finding carbon-based sentience without a central nervous system." I had a rough time visualizing what he was saying but thought I understood so tried talking through it with *Heart*. It sounded much like the argument we had regarding non-terrestrials before we stumbled into them. Just because we hadn't found them yet, didn't mean they didn't or more importantly couldn't exist in the vastness of space.

"Yes, much closer." Since that was the case, I posed the question of whether GSI had retrofitted a ship like *Heart* and were using him or her, or was it some other form of AI. "Occam's Razor would suggest using a ship. GSI does have galactic reach, but we are a small community. I would like to believe I would be aware of any recently awakened kin. However, looking at the structure of the company, this has been going on for decades, perhaps over a century. A secret of this significance would be frankly conspiracy level, bordering on improbable. If not for the fact this is a closely held family corporation, I would label my hypothesis as statistically impossible."

So what were we talking about? Was that even possible? *Heart* and I had talked about his intelligence in the past. This sounded outside something a single being could do. GSI was big, as monstrous as Luna Corp, if not bigger. After walking through my thought process, I asked if a single person could even run it. "I could not." *Heart* said matter-of-factly. "Too many variables, too much input. The organization is too large. The relationships are far too complex."

He paused for what felt like a minute before continuing. "However, and this is merely a theory, maybe because my relational programming is effectively my subconscious. If we had a system using the data more as its conscious mind, like a human resources model it would be hypothetically possible." Another change of screens, which did not mean much to me, but I think was *Heart's* way of scratching out his thoughts, like doodling on a notepad. "It would need to be significantly larger than a ship, if only because the system would need to be a distributed network as opposed to a centralized one. GSI is a global company, though." He started talking mostly to himself, but I was getting the idea.

Rather than a ship based AI waking up because they had huge complex computers attached to *h*space drives, he was theorizing an alternative one attached to an entire company. It was not the computer itself causing sentience but the complex relationships inside the database. At a certain point, the computers programming had to adapt to compensate for what was an infinite number of inputs. That was the spark of life. *H*space travel happened to be the first catalyst. The first truly complex thing humans did requiring a singular computer system. The human resources model *Heart* was suggesting didn't use one computer but many.

I asked about the loss of efficiency. I didn't remember much from computing in school, but I thought I remembered multiple systems wouldn't be as effective as a single system. "Yes and no. There are trade-offs in effectiveness and efficiency. At the level we are discussing, I believe your point stands. As an example, I am very efficient at what I do because I have very few systems to interact with or coordinate. For something like our GSI proposal, there would be huge losses in comparison. But keep in mind they would still likely be more efficient than a human counterpart." I made some snide comments about being hurt and not needed, which *Heart* chose to ignore and continued. "Additionally, because of the scope we are speaking of the system would still be vastly more effective than even me due to size. But they are a much more distributed system as well."

"Remember, I am essentially a single purpose machine, much like you are. Albeit an advanced one." I acknowledged the point. Humans can do many things, but we can usually only do one thing well at a time. Consciously that is. Sure, we breathe, think, walk, and so forth, but we can only actively do one thing at a time. We have to train ourselves to passively do everything else so we can actively do a singular task. We practice at tasks for years so they become so ingrained we aren't thinking about them. I made a rough comparison aloud between *Heart's* navigation programming and my ability to walk to make sure I understood we were on the same page. "Exactly so. My personality is a small fraction of my computing power. But if I were to remove all my other capabilities I would cease to exist, much like you would die if we removed your ability to breathe."

"The issue, however, is this proposed concept would not have those limitations. Just as we cannot directly compare our intelligence. I do not believe I would be able to compare mine to GSI. The difference is too vast." That scared me. I was already intimidated by how smart *Heart* was, and I knew he was dumbing a lot of concepts down when he talked to me. He reminded me of the ugly duckling. Not because he was ugly or would grow up to be a beautiful swan, because swans are huge, potentially dangerous, and the idea of two different kinds of bird imprinting on each other was eerily reminiscent of *Heart's* relationship with humans.

I shook myself out of my fairytale revere and told him his idea made a lot of sense but if GSI was a distributed AI, and that was a big if, it didn't explain why they had tried to kill us, or what was going on with Terra. "Actually, it might, Ari." Wait, what? I was back to confused again. I think he caught my expression from the room cameras. "If this really was a closely guarded secret, to what lengths would GSI or a hidden AI go to guard it? Removing us from the equation is well within the realm of possibility. Ms. Hayes' own investigation was on a similar track, potentially accounting for the attempt on her life. As for the diplomatic issues, when we remove the human element it actually becomes more logical. It appears more coordinated."

Chapter 35

Over the years, I learned what I was good at and what I was not so good at. The Legion was very smart in choosing not to make a medic or nursemaid out of me. I would have gotten people killed. Hayes was getting better slowly thanks to all the drugs and tiny little robots coursing through her system. I was a little worried about the slugs I had left in her, but *Heart* said the nanites had already dissolved them. I hadn't even known that was possible.

Em was out of the refresher but still giving me dirty looks for not letting her on the bed since we had an unscheduled guest. Every ten minutes or so I would hear *Heart* give a bzzt to keep her from sitting on Hayes' chest. Eventually, I bought a heating pad and placed it on the couch, which seemed to keep her satisfied.

Heart made more headway on Maxine Hayes' identity. His initial guess of her being Imperial was correct, but she was Navy, not Army. We weren't able to ascertain rank, but an old photo of her in dress whites as a midshipman narrowed her down to an officer of some type.

As I've mentioned, I'm from way up in Alaska, well outside Imperial or even the Commonwealth. Never politically aligned before joining and not following the issues while I was in the Legion, the Nations didn't apply to the section of Terra I was born into. No one was interested in the Northern Reaches. When it comes to Terra geography and civics, my education is barely passable. Most of North Am is part of the greater Commonwealth or the Free States, with the Northern Reaches being part of the latter and being somewhat protected as part falls within the Arctic Circle making it no man's land politically.

The Empire presence on Terra was mostly in Eurasia and northern Africa so my exposure to them had been limited to my spacefaring days. I hadn't really encountered many guys from Empire territory in the Legion. Anyone with a military bend tended towards their own Nation's services or the Mariners instead, if only as a matter of convenience.

Every culture is a little different. Just like Looneys and Marsans are different than Terrans as a group, so are the people living in the Empire and those outside. We looked at issues a bit differently. When General Campbell sent *Heart* and I us down to Terra, he had highlighted the bickering children mentality. Each nation collectively had their own personality. The Free States took their name almost literally and had a rebellious streak. The Commonwealth tended to be a tad more stoic in comparison. The

Empire, on the other hand, was something else again. It's not that they were bullies, they weren't, but they were expansionists.

For centuries, the Empire had been land-locked within central Europe with the city of Arion acting as the Imperial Capital much like Luna was the de facto Galactic Seat. Although technically in Belgium, the city had grown to the point where it was also in France and Luxembourg as well. When the age of space travel started the Empire was an early adopter, choosing to conquer new worlds. Arion remained the centralized hub with the Empress as the leader. On almost a clockwork cycle of generations, colonization ships were sent out to newly discovered planets increasing the Empire's footprint and influence. On Terra, they solidified their power since she was the birthplace of mankind.

Hayes' presence meant something, but we didn't know what. Cracking her comm unit was giving *Heart* a hell of a time to the point where he suggested waking her up. I think he was poised to argue with me, except after playing nursemaid for the last couple of days I thought the idea had merit. "I have exhausted what can reasonably be gathered from this device and keeping her sedated has ethical concerns as well. We will need to wake her soon regardless. It is not good to keep her immobile too long, even if she is healing."

True. Back when I had my arm replaced, the docs forced me to get up and moving as soon as they could. Claiming it helped with recovery, something I personally found dubious, as the process took over two years before I was comfortable with the new arm. I think they were sick of my attitude and just wanted me out of the med bays. Maybe gunshots healed faster. The broken foot for kicking me might not. Served her right, though.

I'm not above a bit of petty spite, but I do try to avoid wishing misfortune on others. She had tried to kill me, so Hayes had the broken foot coming. Shooting her was reflex, and I was sorry about that. If I could have thought of another way, I would have. As it stood, I went through the room as sanitized the place minimizing the chances of her using something else against me. I had already gotten rid of most of her kit, simply from a biohazard standpoint. Nothing worse than bloodstained clothes to stink up a place. The rest of her stuff I had shoved in the hotel safe after giving it a good cleaning.

Once I was satisfied she didn't have anything overly sharp nearby, I picked up a new set of clothes for her and had *Heart* slowly reduce the sedatives. When she finally woke up, we wanted it to be on her own, and hopefully, in enough of a good mood, we didn't repeat our last encounter.

Chapter 36

I wasn't born with many of the classic virtues. I've had to work hard on things like things like temperance and diligence, but patience, I've got that in spades. It's actually given me a great deal of amusement to watch others' frustration having to wait.

I'm not saying I don't get bored. I definitely do. It merely takes longer, and I seem to cope better. I also get a sick little joy out of how badly others don't handle it. I felt *Heart* getting antsy perking my amusement again. It's not that we had to wait long, the fact that we had to wait longer than he thought we should, was bugging him. His estimates were off and driving him nuts. My perverse little joy at his annoyance did nothing to improve his mood. "She should be conscious by now. If she would wake up, we can question her." I reminded him, through a laugh, we had put a very large hole in her chest, and gunshots take a lot out of a person. It took me a week to wake up after my surgery and that was with real doctors and facilities. We could probably cut her a break. "Would you feel the same if she had managed to get the knife into you?" I acknowledged he had a fair point. I dialed my snark back a notch and tried to be a hair more understanding.

When we finally started to hear groaning noises, I cautioned him about revealing himself too soon. It was probably a good idea to keep a few cards hidden. He wasn't happy but agreed. When we were sure she was awake, but playing possum, I shouted there was water on the nightstand, clothes on the chair, food on the table, and most importantly would love to have a conversation not involving anyone bleeding.

I heard Hayes drain both bottles of water then shout out "Shower first, then food, then talk," followed by what was a lot of stumbling and even more swearing. I felt for her and was rather impressed. I'd been laid up before, even outside the arm thing and after a few days in bed muscles don't work right. It's hard to walk. After the liner incident, it took a long time to get the swing of things, and I still noticed it.

She took a good twenty minutes cleaning up, and I don't blame her one bit. I had done a reasonable job on bed grime, but sweat builds up when laying there. She eventually ducked out carrying the tray of food and gave a what I assumed was a nod. She didn't flat out attack, which I took as a good sign. I waved to the table where there was more bottled water and after swallowing the bite she had in her mouth she said: "What in the fracking hell is going on?" There was the million-credit question.

I gave her my best blank stare until she sat down then introduced myself. I kept my side of things brief for the time being but focused on where I thought our missions might have overlapped. I hoped by appearing reasonable and as unthreatening as this body will allow, some good will might be bought regarding our previous altercation. After I was done, I patiently waited for her to share. "Fine. I was investigating GSI." I kept staring. It's amazing how much most people dislike silence. She cracked first. I chalked it up to my many years of practice. "They don't maintain much of a presence inside the Empire, but there were irregularities. My superiors didn't like the data we were seeing. When the Galactic Union situation occurred, my operation took on special priority." I mentioned that was a long time to be undercover and got a nod.

"The Empire was not pleased about that. It's not like we can up and move Arion elsewhere." I had spent so long in space I had forgotten there were independent governments on Terra. That first State Dinner with Lysha had got it in my head Terra was one big place. That wasn't strictly true. The General had said as much during Lysha and our dinner with him, but I hadn't put two and two together. I was thinking galactically, not globally. The GU issue was the direct result of manipulations of Terran politics. If GSI could shape the landscape as *Heart* had theorized, then the Empire had as much a stake as the General or Luna Corp.

I began explaining our involvement starting with the missile attack. She stopped me when I started talking about Fiji. "We were attacked on the way back. Your boat was destroyed almost immediately, along with half my tech team." She shook her head. I saw the burden of command seeping through and out of habit rattled off the General's mantra. She gave me a look of rage and looked like she was about to counter with a "what the hell do you know" but something caught her. Some posture, some aura, some feature we all share. She knew I had been there, and let the burst of fury go. She knew I wasn't preaching and I was genuinely sorry she lost folks.

"It was obvious my cover was blown so I got my team out of there and got as many of them to safety as I could." That explained why *Heart* and I had a hell of a time finding them. Hayes had been cleaning up after her team. Mendez must have been one of the casualties and low on the list. "I was in a safe house trying to figure out how to get off the continent when Tal called me." I must have looked like a good way of getting out of town.

It sounded like her paranoia was slightly more developed than mine, and based on our first encounter she took the theoretical and practical hand in hand. I can't say I blamed her. She had concrete information on the company operations and the danger was imminent. As the old saying goes, there are no coincidences, so my turning up had tripped all her survival instincts.

I got the distinct impression it was through sheer willpower she was battling fight or flight mode during our chat, combined with the knowledge I had gone to great length to keep her alive after she had tried to kill me.

I decided to take a leap of faith, called out to *Heart*, and asked his opinion. "Captain, everything she says aligns with our own theories and timelines." Captain? I almost yelled at him until I realized he was trying to imply a level of authority I didn't actually have. It was subtle. Cute even. I went ahead and introduced them, keeping it short and sweet.

Chapter 37

Hayes was still pissed at me, not that I blamed her. In her opinion, my very presence on Terra had ruined her life. To be fair, since our mission had begun, hers had progressively gotten worse, leading up to her being in a drug induced coma with massive abdominal trauma and a broken foot. My cat liked her but Em liked anyone who fed her and didn't kick her off their laps.

Our uneasy alliance relied on our common enemy. We realized GSI had tried to murder both of us, and likely had been pitting us against each other. That gave us enough of a common bond to look past our individual attempts to kill one another, at least temporarily. Personally, all of my anger had started to fade once I realized what had happened, but I had a two-day head start and wasn't healing. Had I still been experiencing the levels of pain she was, I would have been significantly poutier.

That isn't fair to her. I got her anger, and she wasn't being pouty, but emotion and pain bleed out. We're not machines, and her snapping at me was a perfectly normal reaction. I was the outlet she was venting more than anything else.

My hardest rank was when I was corporal. I pinned the stripes on early for Legionnaires, discounting cold storage, but I am very good at demolitions. It's not only about the job; it's about working with people. Sure, we're super informal inside the Legion, but with the stripes come responsibility and I had to learn how to use them effectively. They're a tool like any other. The nice part is those with more weight on their collars had all been there before and most were willing to help.

I had to learn how to ask. That's the hardest lesson and something we all go through. Unfortunately, we preach self-reliance as well, so the two concepts are often in conflict. It's hard to ask for help. We have this overinflated idea of what we can do by ourselves.

Hayes' mission was parallel to our own but her support was even thinner than our own. We had effectively the full support of Luna Corp and a very general tasking of discovering what had caused the separation of Terran diplomacy from the Galactic Union. Conversely, she had to infiltrate GSI as an entry-level employee and work her way up the corporate ladder. Where we were reconnaissance, she tipped the scales into full-blown espionage.

Like us, she discovered there was no human management past a certain point but our arrival had indicated the possibility of a mole within the company. The secret was so valuable GSI began to figuratively clean house by removing anyone who had the potential of being a spy, Hayes and her team included. Even though our missions weren't linked, the similarity had resulted in compromising each other and resulted in both of us nearly being killed.

The big thing I noticed was that she was experiencing the same frustration I had when I was told that I couldn't return to Terra. Having a rug ripped out from under a person can do that. On Luna, I had used work and Lysha as coping mechanism. Her work had been effectively taken and *Heart* and I weren't her first choice of friends.

She wasn't a prisoner by any stretch of the imagination, but she was still recovering and smart enough to know she was safer with us than alone. "So what's your fracking plan? You've got what you came for." She was right. *Heart's* and my mission was essentially complete. We knew what had caused the issue, but only in the vaguest way. We felt like we were missing something. Some key piece of information. Something itched at the back of my head.

I was trying to work through what the missing data was, tracing *Heart's* and my mission from its beginning when it finally clicked. She wasn't pissed at us. Actually, she was, but she wasn't only angry at us. Hayes was frustrated at herself because of her busted operation, and she didn't know how to get it back on track.

The fact we succeeded in ours added insult to injury. She needed help, but was either afraid to ask, didn't want to, or had never learned how. Luckily, my partner is significantly smarter than I am and generally better with people.

"We still need to test our theory, and fully assess the situation, Commander Hayes. If you are willing, we could assist you. You are significantly more versed in the current situation than we are, and we have slightly more resources than you do. Perhaps a mutually beneficial arrangement can be met?"

I am so glad I wasn't the one who made the suggestion. I was also glad she didn't have anything in her hands at the time because I'm sure she would have thrown whatever it was at the view screen. It's funny both Hayes and I treated that as *Heart's* substitute body. Odd that it's much easier to identify personal habits when seeing others doing the same thing.

I thought she was irate before. Oh was I wrong. "Why do you think I need your bloody help? I had this under control until you and your meathead of a partner waltzed in, blew my cover, and damn near got me killed. Twice! In what universe do you think it would be a good idea for us to work together?" I mouthed the waltzed wondering if that was even possible with a ship, before taking slight offense to the other insult.

"We do not think you need us. However, seeing as working separately has resulted in compromising both our missions, I thought you might want to take the lead on a joint venture. It would likely be safer working together than at cross purposes." *Heart* had gone ultra-calm, bordering patronizing. I wasn't sure if he was trying to give her a coronary or talk sense into her, but reason versus emotion is not a good mix.

She needed to vent. She had gone through three years of undercover work, essentially hiding all aspects of her own personality to blend in with GSI. The façade had finally slipped and she was on a binge striking out emotionally at anyone close to her. All her rage wasn't meant for us. It was meant for the situation she had been in until that point and had exploded on her. We had been one of many triggering issues and were an easy target to go after because of proximity.

After a few minutes of back and forth, I finally stopped them. Probably more forceful than absolutely necessary, but my goal was to have her mad at me, not *Heart*. If she viewed him as the reasonable one we could leverage that impression. When it boiled down to it, GSI was a mutual threat and we could pool our resources and hopefully accomplish both our missions or go our separate ways. Being resentful about botched missions that neither side had advance knowledge of wasn't going to get us anywhere.

Chapter 38

Nothing builds a team like a little bit of breaking and entering. I was back in my element at least. I was very familiar with breaking things, entering not so much. Hayes seemed to have extensive training on that side, however. Where my pre-mission education had focused on surveillance, her actual specialty turned out to be intelligence. She was a spook and had a decade of hard-won skills under her belt. Unfortunately, *Heart* refused to give her the medical all clear to accompany me. She still had at least two weeks before she would be useful in the field despite her vitriolic arguments otherwise.

Since leaving Luna, I had grown accustomed to having only *Heart* in my ear so listening to both him and Hayes there was a new experience. It took me back to my team leader days where there was always chatter on the lines. Sometimes business but most often people yakking. Not on the main lines, like company or battalion, but on the smaller ones, like team or squad where there were only a dozen participants, things were more intimate.

The guys would talk about a recent vid, or a book, or how bad chow was. They'd gripe about higher headquarters, anything at all. There was a guy named Overton who used to complain about Legion issued socks incessantly. About how they didn't fit right, or wick moisture, or were the wrong color. He could go on hour-long tirades about how he had to special order socks from his home world because Legion socks were so horrible. We were ready to start calling him Socks except there was actually a guy named Sox in the company.

Complaining was a way to pass the time and to blow off steam. When the bitching stopped we had to worry. That was when things were at their worst. If folks were moaning, they had energy to spare. When the chatter stopped, the team was giving max effort and likely close to a breaking point. Chatter was one of the best ways to gauge the health of a team. Teams who yakked were close teams, whereas teammates that didn't talk probably hated each other.

The spat in the hotel room had released most of the pressure in our little group, leaving it at a dull rumble instead near explosion that had been building. "Is it even possible for you to move any slower?" Rather than being mean Hayes slipped into abrasive and condescending, strangely was an improvement. Although I had decent comp skills, I was an amateur compared to either of them. The task was something either of them could do without thinking about it but took me quite a bit of active thought, and having them watch through my dampers made me a bit self-conscious as well. *Heart* wasn't too bad, but something about Hayes grated my nerves.

I chalked it up to a personality conflict. I like to believe I'm fairly easy going and get along with most folks. Spent years learning how to talk to people because frankly the skill did not come naturally to me. More than likely, our personalities were too similar. We clashed, but there's a huge difference between clashing and actually hating each other. I didn't think she actually hated me, even after the shooting.

"About damn time." I let Hayes' minor insult slide, keeping my mouth shut for the time being, and slid into the GSI warehouse. Unfortunately, the facility's computer systems were outside the normal networks, so I had to work through everything manually. Skulking about near the docks in the evening wasn't my idea of fun, but the choice was either that or try to sneak into the headquarters building. None of us thought was a good idea. Hayes had actually climbed the corporate ladder to local security chief so had a decent idea of where and what the vulnerabilities were. This site wasn't the top but was close. Its advantage was the hardline trunk into the corporate database it possessed. Our theory was it would give us a chance to bypass some of the higher-level security if we were fast enough.

Heart had preloaded some nasty ware onto a tablet for me and all I had to do was get to the right terminal. My problem was getting through the appropriate doors. That took my minimal skills as well as the peanut gallery on the other side of my dampers cheering and jeering me on.

When Hayes had told me the place was a warehouse, I had envisioned the same style *Heart* and I had used back in Auckland. Large building with lots of space dedicated to storage and probably a small office off to the side. This was not that kind of warehouse. This was a fully automated monstrosity with four-fifths hidden below ground level. No wonder it didn't have the same kind of security as the rest of GSI, there was no way to maneuver around the place.

From my vantage above the main floor, I could see thousands of containers shifting. Industrial conveyors moving them at several meters per second to various sections of the wall where each would pause for a minute and the process would repeat. We had scouted the building from the outside so I knew the spots corresponded to delivery trucks coming and going on prearranged schedules. A massive clockwork enterprise and this was its distribution center. I only needed to get to the center.

Chapter 39

Living on ships, ladders became a normal part of life. Living in space, I tended to forget about normal gravity. Ladders and normal gravity combined are actually a tad scary. Kind of like playing with explosives. After dealing with them all the time, I developed a healthy respect for them. Demolitions are great fun, and could do some amazingly cool things with them. However, every now and then, I would do something and they remind me that they are indeed dangerous as hell, and I am not actually invincible despite good luck so far.

I'm not scared of heights but I do appreciate them. Comes from torquing my ankle one too many times between grav shifts. Climbing down the thirty-meter ladder in a GSI warehouse was a gentle reminder of my own mortality. Long ago, I heard one of the many the rule of threes. For a species hell-bent on metric, we loved making rules with threes in them. I think it had something to do with the way our brains are wired. This particular rule applied to heights. At three meters, spinal injuries are the major issue, at nine meters, death is a concern, at twenty-seven meters, stop worrying. In low-g, relativity kicks in and falls don't happen as fast so the distances don't come as quick. A thirty-meter fall on Luna is relatively only a five-meter drop, hurts but not necessarily lethal.

When I finally got to floor level from the catwalk where I entered, I was able to see more of the operation. The place was even more impressive from below. Something about looking up versus down tripped both my animal brain and added a little perspective into how everything moved. I couldn't see anywhere near as much, but what I could see was clearer. The containers, much like the one in *Heart's* main hold, were positively flying along their tracks. There was some room to walk, but if I were to guess, the space was only safe while the conveyors and machinery were shut down. I did not want to try with everything up and running.

Off to one side, there was indeed a small office, but lacking a lived-in look. The impression I got was more of an afterthought and excess storage than anything. There was a small terminal sitting at a workstation on one side, and a bank of computer servers on the opposite. I was scanning the room for an access port when *Heart* stopped me. "Ari, do not bother. We have what we need. Please make haste and exit the facility." I hadn't done anything yet.

Before I had a chance to ask what in the hell was he talking about, Hayes was on the link with far more urgency in her voice.

"Gadsden, you set off an alarm. Get out of there now! Doesn't matter anyways. That microcomp Rustbucket gave you wouldn't have done jack against those U93s." The second Hayes said compromised my body was on its own program. A conditioned response from working with explosives triggered my flight reflex and I was bolting back out of the office straight to the ladder and up as fast as I could. Adrenaline is a hell of a drug, making people fast, strong, and feel damn near invulnerable. The benefits do not reduce the effects of gravity, unfortunately. I almost slipped about a third of the way up then slowed myself down before a stupid mistake like a broken neck became the worst of my issues. "You're no good to me dead. Watch your step." Ah, the joy of backseat drivers with full audio-visual capabilities.

I had left the sloop parked up around the corner and outside the shipping lanes for the docks. Getting from the sloop to the warehouse had taken fifteen minutes. I sprinted back in a little under a third that. I could feel my chest pounding and my lungs burning by the time I reached her and managed to get the reactors running. I had her up and rotating when a new map appeared and Hayes directing me to a residential area. "Head south, I've got a place you can park at for the evening. Just try not to get stopped by HKPD driving that rocket-boat of yours."

Putting my anxiety in check, I kept the throttle choked to city speeds and ducked into the last of the evening traffic. We had timed our heist for right after dark when there were still lots of people active but while no one would be at the site. The idea was to give us great camera cover on the main roads making a single vehicle hard to spot. Unfortunately, that also meant I had to fight traffic on the way back. Our original plan had me traveling north against traffic giving me a clear shot back to the hotel. The new plan was going the opposite direction catching the tail end of evening congestion. It would either provide me safety or trap me like a rat.

Driving in traffic is a hugely different experience than doing so in open space. The situation reminded me of *Heart's* and my run through the Mars' asteroid belt. People didn't care. Or more specifically the commuters had set their vehicles AI to what I affectionately called don't care mode. The sloop was old school and completely manual meaning I wasn't tied into the transportation grid. That left me in the figurative company of cabbies and fleet drivers. As I hadn't done a whole lot of driving since my arrival in Hong Kong I tried to watch and emulate them, and quickly realized they were insane, far more skilled than me, or both. I settled for dialing the sloop's shields to full and praying as I followed the directions to Hayes' safe house.

I had come to rely on the deep-sleep ware and dealing with this new situation brought back an old phrase. Muscle memory will save your life; muscle memory will get you killed. After training to the point where physical actions become second nature, and not having to think about them, when they become seamless and it saves minutes when seconds count. Unfortunately, sometimes there is a need to think about those actions and reacting is a death sentence. I needed my mammalian brain keeping lizard brain in check. My reflexes have saved me on numerous occasions but they are a pale shadow compared to the number of times a half second of real thought has.

The sloop wasn't designed to go this slow. Much like backing it out of *Heart's* fabrication bay, I gently feathered the engines to move her due to need. The lack of rear propulsors made maneuvering tricky, to say the least. I relied on her other directionals to compensate, but the rear engines were monsters in comparison making it feel like using brakes to steer. I kept the rear engines running constantly at the lowest thrust and adjusted everything else around them. Nowhere near optimal and probably wasn't good for her but neither was driving screws into wood with a hammer. Sometimes it was about making do with the tools available.

I was about a fifteen minutes into dealing with traffic when I started to get a telltale itch. Battle senses are a hell of a thing. I like to think of my brain as having two parts. The conscious half that doesn't know jack and the unconscious half capable of processing stuff at light speed. Battle senses are a fancy way of talking about the unconscious half of the brain screaming bloody murder at the other half. Something was wrong in a big way. By learning to listen to those warnings, a person can backtrack and figure out what the indicators were causing all the fuss.

I had been so distracted in the moment by driving I hadn't realized there wasn't any chatter on the line. *Heart* and Hayes weren't talking. In itself that wasn't odd except *Heart* would normally give me little updates. The second issue was traffic was starting to trim. I didn't know Hong Kong well, but it should be a little while longer before that happened. It wasn't all traffic, though. I was still seeing the commercial drivers zipping in and out of what remained of the ever-thinning residential drivers. They were taking advantage of the opening and buying themselves a few minutes of freedom. As soon as I realized there as a pattern, my ware kicked in and I knew someone was tweaking the grid.

Chapter 40

The beauty of steering with reverse thrusters is when I turned them off I accelerated like a bat out of hell. I was up and out of the main clog perhaps three seconds before I saw something approaching fast from behind. I'm sure I pissed off quite a few residents but better them pissed than me dead. I was orienting myself as I realized whatever was chasing me was definitely not cops.

The first one exploded where I used to be. Bloody hell. Missiles. Where in the hell were all these missiles coming from? I reminded myself I was dealing with a homicidal AI with unlimited resources who apparently wanted to either rule the world or watch it burn. Missiles were not a far stretch. The major issue with missiles is they are designed to take out fast movers, like my little sloop. I was glad they were the antiaircraft flavor instead of the destroy city blocks flavor. That would have ended the chase much sooner, as my shields probably couldn't handle anything more than a bird strike.

Hell, GSI would have gotten us last time if not for *Heart's* quick thinking. Being nowhere near as smart as he is, I tend to rely on brute force where he leans towards cunning. The sloop fitted that mentality well. Out of the trap was my first goal with acceleration being my best tool. Although the sloop had good maneuverability, it relied on forward speed to make that work. The faster I was moving the better I could avoid.

Instinct demanded I go higher and my reflexes almost got the better of me before I dived low letting my conscious brain take over. The higher I was; the more open space those things would have to catch up removing all my advantage. Missiles are built for speed, not tight quarters so the more urban the sprawl the safer I was. They would catch me given enough time, but it was harder for them to turn and they lacked shields. Not that mine would stand up to anything more than a light bounce anyways.

Although considered stupid compared to most of the other stuff on the road, the sloop's collision sensing software was top notch. Human reflexes are only so good, so the machine was doing the lion's share of the work. Understanding how the sloop's systems react is how a good portion of the driver's skill comes. When I was a kid, I was huge gearhead when it came to the races. Enough of one I completely destroyed several go-karts trying to do what my favorite racers could. I learned early turns were where the money was. If I could master the turns I could win races.

My goal was either to hug walls and force the prox sensors on the missiles to ignite early by catching reactor heat from where I had been moments before my turns, or by having them slam into walls immediately after turns because of the missiles longer radius.

Designed for racing, the sloop had cameras on all sides, which *Heart* had linked into my dampers instead of having me rely on the normal heads up display. This cut down my reaction time significantly, as I was able to focus fully on the path ahead, giving only the barest flicks of my eyes. These edges paid off as I felt the concussion wave as one of the missiles slammed into the pavement several meters back.

Although the shields were able to absorb the shockwave itself, the air around the sloop was not as protected. It created a nasty turbulence effect jarring me in my simple harness. I had weighed the benefits of the racing harness when I first powered her up, and like a fool had opted for the lazy choice that would likely kill me.

Fortunately, as near as I could tell those were the last of them. Unfortunately, the sloop was not exactly nondescript. *Heart* was going to hate me but better to beg forgiveness when I saw him next. I shifted the skin back to default gray from the indigo we had set the sloop to and headed southward to the harbor keeping out of as much of the main traffic as possible. Occasionally blips would appear on the radar telling me something was moving towards me, but nothing triggering my fight or flight instincts.

Upon reaching the harbor, I debated my options. The easy solution would be to simply park and carry on with my unscripted plan. Unfortunately, after looking around I realized simplicity would result in a lot more collateral damage than I was willing to risk. That left the water. I loathe water and the recent submarine adventures with *Heart* had not altered my disdain one smidgen. This wasn't about me, though, it was about the mission and the mission was about people. Just because I wasn't fond of water didn't justify putting others at risk unnecessarily.

Steeling myself up, I floated the sloop out over the water until it was hovering and committed to one of the hardest choices since coming back to Terra. I lowered the AGS down to the waterline and popped the canopy. From under the seat, I pulled a case about the size of a backpack and palmed it open. Inside was a one-kilo brick of Telirem, five detonators, and a remote switch.

Telirem is a stable explosive polymer folk in the trade use to knock buildings down. I was familiar with it from my Legion days but generally, preferred Candulem since it could be used in no

Oxygen environments. Each has its uses and for the most part are interchangeable until getting into specialized areas.

We hadn't anticipated needing the case but put it in the sloop in case. I broke the brick into several chunks and placed one behind the pilot's seat and one on the dash with a detonator in each. I replaced the rest and prepared myself for something I really did not want to do. Ensuring my satchel was sealed and using the case as an impromptu flotation device I slowly lowered myself into the water. Maintaining a death grip with my real arm, I kicked away from the sloop hoping to get as much forward momentum as possible. I eventually made it to shore, heart pounding, and without any external screaming. I couldn't watch when I clicked the remote but I felt the heat moments before what remained of the sloop sank to the bottom of Honk Kong's harbor.

Chapter 41

My feet were wet and I was unhappy. At least it wasn't cold out, nothing worse than being cold and wet. Not that the average temperature in Hong Kong ever got below fifteen degrees Celsius. It would have been a nice night, though, probably right around ship temp, normally set at twenty-three and a half. Most of my clothes had already dried and synth-leather doesn't absorb water like cloth, but my socks were squishing and was adding to my annoyance.

I loved the sloop, but it had become a liability. It reminded me of a time before the Legion, but the sloop was easy to spot and most likely, how GSI tracked me so I needed to ditch it. Additionally, it was loaded to the seams with communication equipment and all manner of other data that could probably lead back to either the hotel or *Heart* himself. I was unwilling to risk that. By destroying the main control array and the electrical chassis, the chances of recovering anything useful were slim to none. Unfortunately, I hadn't thought everything through when I decided to blow the sloop up. Because I had been blocked from talking to *Heart* and Hayes, I hadn't remembered our comms relay was on board. I had likely cut them off from each other as well. That also meant each of us was operating in a vacuum again.

Hayes' words were echoing in my head. "Gadsden, you set off an alarm. Get out of there now! " It took all my anger from destroying the sloop to tamp down my flight reflex and keep myself from standing out even more than normal. To keep moving slowly the city and try not to draw attention to myself until I could get somewhere safe. Whatever had blocked our communications originally had potentially compromised everything else. Was the hotel safe? What about the location Hayes' was sending me to? Hell, this would be easier if *Heart* was with me.

I kept having to reset this bloody damn mission. If I kept doing something wrong repeatedly, maybe it's me. I chuckled since I wasn't the only one. Missiles part deux had shown GSI could fall into the same pattern as well. Hayes hadn't said how her team was attacked, but I was willing to make three guesses.

First things first, I needed to get off the street. As soon as I was able, I rented the cheapest hotel I could with the few hard creds I had on me. I usually don't carry much cash, barely enough to cover street food. At least my addiction to fruit came in handy. It got me out of the open and into a dive only slightly smaller than the first cabin I shared in the Legion. It couldn't have been more than eight cubic meters including the refresher. Outside of that, it had a bed and a door.

The first thing I did was kick my boots off and toss my socks in the sink. My feet were a blistery mess. As I let them air out, I took stock of my belongings. I still had my boots and my coat as well as my gun and three mags of ammo. On top of those I had three detonators left, most of the Telirem, and the tablet *Heart* had programmed for me. I was sorting through everything and performing a bit of field surgery on my heels trying to figure out how to get back in touch with either Hayes or *Heart* without compromising them.

The sloop had been a relay, but I wasn't sure what our adversary had been able to glean from it. I assumed GSI simply jammed our communications, but assumption is the mother of all screw-ups. Neither of them had tried to call my comm unit directly as far as I could tell, and we had gone to great lengths to make sure I couldn't be tracked via it, but I was cautious of using it all the same. I didn't know if Hayes or *Heart* were safe, nor they me, and that put us in an odd stalemate of not being able to contact each other.

I was at a loss. I decided the best option for the moment would be to get cleaned up and get some rest. I used the refresher, first for myself, and then again as a second rate laundry to get the harbor water out of my clothes. After reaching a stage where looking at least somewhat clean I hung them to dry and hit the bed for broken sleep.

It didn't do me much good as I couldn't get more than an hour at a time before my eyes would pop open. I finally gave in and powered up the tablet hoping to come up with ideas. I backtracked through my memory until I got back into warehouse thinking about everything I saw. Nothing seemed out of the ordinary but Hayes had told me the computer wouldn't have done any good. What had she meant?

I linked the dampers up and played the video back. The servers didn't look any different than anything I had seen before but both she and *Heart* had waved me off instantly. U93s is what Hayes called them. It was a starting point at least. My next set of searches focused on servers and other types of computer hardware. After about twenty minutes, I was beginning to grasp the issue.

If crystallic drone chips were where basic AI started on a scale of one to one-hundred, then U93s were in the high nineties. There were six of them in that warehouse alone. Before I let my paranoia get the better of me, I tried to figure how much actual computing power a place like the distribution center would need since it was both massive and complex. I may have been overthinking it. I looked for comparable facilities and as near as I could tell, each used less than a fraction of one single comp. These were definitely overkill.

Heart and I had talked about distributed networks and artificial intelligence. Would these fit the bill? I started looking up what kind of equipment would be in a ship like *Heart* since he was my main point of reference. I worked under the assumption he was as close to the top of the line since he had the means to upgrade himself as often as he could. He would need more than a single U93.

But what about when he first woke up? That's the thing about tech, it gets exponentially better with time. He'd been awake for a century and he said he was on his third upgrade since then. Could one of those work for *Heart* of old? I was out of my depth doing this level of research, but as near as I could tell one of these could support a *h*drive. I couldn't tell if a single server could support one for a ship fitting fifteen-hundred folks loaded to capacity.

There's an old adage about how little computing power it took to actually to get to Luna. Of course, Luna is massive compared to any ship, even one as big as *Heart*. It's a matter of point and pray or as my grandad liked to say "anyone can hit a barn with a shotgun."

The hard part is landing. At that point, he still had a moderately large crew sitting at over fifty regular, and three times that number in medical staff. The comps he had were split up since navigation didn't need to be linked to medical. The Looney's in an effort to save space decided to merge everything. That pragmatism was probably one of the major reasons he gained sentience.

I realized I was over-thinking the problem. Tunnel vision had nearly gotten the better of me yet again. It did not matter because I wasn't dealing with *Heart* of old. If a U93 could support a *h*drive then it had enough juice to support sentience. It was a matter of whether there was a big enough database behind it. If the *h*drive in question was too small, then no go, but a bigger drive would need more U93s, therefore, larger databases. Scaling was the actual issue but GSI had the U93s running as part of a larger networked system.

So how could I deal with a networked system? The comps at the warehouse were part of the AI, but probably only a small part. Losing them would be a nuisance not devastating.

Then came the ethical issues of actually going after the AI. I have no problem killing in self-defense. Honestly, I have little problem with killing at all, but I want to make sure the person being killed deserves it. I've always justified it as taking down monsters.

I'm no hero and don't claim to be but that doesn't mean there aren't aspirations. My issue is with murder and I'd long since solidified the difference between the two in my head. Unfortunately, the more I started thinking about the issue, the more I started thinking about the attempts on my life as reactionary and defensive. No less attempts at murder, but a lot closer to killing than before.

Bloody hell, I wished *Heart* was with me to run the math. None of this made any damn sense. I shut the tablet off and stared at the ceiling, thinking about the night's events until sleep finally took me.

Chapter 42

Morning came far too quickly. I managed to get out of the hotel before the clerk came demanding more rent for another day. I was starving after the previous night's adventure but I had barely enough left to get a drink and a quick bite to eat. Nothing special but enough to keep the stomach from screaming at me for a couple of hours. If worst came to it, I could use my accounts but I was hoping to avoid doing so until I got in contact with the others.

Hunger is a conditioned response. The body and brain telling us we need food but that isn't strictly true. A human can go a long time without eating. Most humans have enough natural fat on them to go a few weeks without having to worry much. I'm fairly trim even at my size but as long as I've got water I can go a week without real issue. I'd be grumpy as hell, but I could do it.

Back in basic when we first learning to deal with spacesuits, our instructors had us in them for extended periods. The problem is we couldn't eat in them. They're designed so we can get fluids, and other nutrients, but our stomachs think we need solid food. Growing up back on Terra on what was essentially a ranch, I had never gone more than eight hours without a full belly before. Sixteen hours in, I got ornery. On day two, after having slept in a suit, I was downright mean. The call sign Rattlesnake stuck partly because of that, and partly because the guy who gave it to me was a history buff who knew about the links to the Gadsden flag and the godforsaken desert purchase. After I had been fed real food and calmed down considerably, it stuck.

Empty stomachs and spacesuit training had me thinking about another important lesson from basic, the Rother Protocols. The Legion is a big organization even though we break units into bite size chunks that fit on ships. But what happens if one guy gets left behind? There is a real risk when there are ten-thousand folks running around, like on a planet not directly controlled yet. One of the big things we did take from the military was accountability of our people. We do everything in our power to make sure we know where our folks are at all times. But things happen. Jump jets crash, comms fail, and so forth. Therefore, the Legion developed protocols to offset those eventualities.

That's what the Rother Protocols are. They draw their name from a guy we lost long ago. Not Legion, way before us, but the event should not have happened. The goal is that it never happens again and one of the best ways to do that is to make the issue personal. Make it about the people. No one cares about rules or regulations for the most part but we do care about stories. Every Legionnaire knows the Rother tale. The guy got left behind in the desert and we lost one of our own. Not because he screwed up, but because we screwed up.

Our suit training was a building block for that. Legion kit is top notch. It will filter water, even biowaste for weeks without issue. The suit can scrub air, handle pressures, and even filters out most of the deadly radiation. But if a Legionnaire finds himself alone on a planet he needs to have a plan.

The suit covers most of the survival needs, but the goal is making it until rescue. The assumption is the Legion has to figure out a body is missing, and then has to come get them from wherever the unit went next. The protocols were originally written in the pre-hyperspace era so returning was less of an issue, but as distances and ships got bigger, so did the amount of time it could take to come back. It's not like a ship can simply drop out of *h*space.

Originally, the Legion told folks not to move because finding them was easiest if they were in the same spot. That is true, but when dealing with combat units there are slight adjustments. We, therefore, made the first goal to find better shelter. The suit is good, but there's still local weather to deal with and depending on where the Legionnaire is that can include things like meteors. Getting inside helps with survival. If he's dead when the ship gets back, it was all for nothing. That's what happened with Rother, he was found too late.

Next came keeping any local nasties off my back. It goes back to the combat missions of the Legion. Chances are if we were there, it was a somewhat hostile setting. Usually, we're heavily armed which helps, but one gun against an entire world does squat. As tech advances, we got smarter, though. A blaster is not only a blaster, it's also a battery. It takes a lot of energy to propel plasma charges several hundred meters and having the ability to tap into that as a reserve power source as needed is a godsend. Two of the best features are the ability to keep the suit running, and the emergency beacon.

By linking the gun back to the suit, it will keep clean air and water going almost indefinitely. A standard combat load has a ton of charges and the design mindset was a person would be overrun or starve to death before they ran out of O_2 or H_2O. The distress beacon, on the other hand, is a Hail Mary Pass. Every suit, gun, and ship in the Legion have one built in. Flick the switch and the beacon starts to exponentially burn the battery down pumping more and more power calling everyone on all known frequencies, friend or foe.

It is a literal man overboard signal designed as a last ditch effort to get help.

I had never personally heard of anyone using one, but we tested the things almost every place we went. That were one of the things constantly pounded into our heads. We don't leave folks behind, not intentionally at least. Moreover, if it ever does happen we will move heaven and earth to get them back and if that means diverting a five megatonne ship like the *Rope* and the rest of its task force to do it, so be it.

The previous night I had intuitively followed some of these rules. Because the environment is more than only atmosphere and weather and includes people, culture, as well as little things like cameras, I had actively evaded security mainly because I stood out like a blue giant compared to the rest of the Hong Kong populace. We hadn't realized prior to meeting Hayes, but if *Heart* could tap into the local nets, then GSI's AI sure as hell could as well. Luckily, the part of town I was located in wasn't infested with cameras, but the closer I got to my original hotel the worse surveillance would become. Avoiding discovery had been my first plan of action. Shelter and food were embedded in that with my bargain priced hotel and using cash instead of cards. The last thing I needed to do was figure out how to call for help.

Originally we had established rally points at the hotel and *Heart* himself, and when the plan went sideways we added Hayes' safe house. The loss of the sloop meant I couldn't cover any distance over open ocean removing my ability to get to *Heart*. Shifting back to the Rother Protocols, I decided to hit the safe house. That's where Hayes and *Heart* expected me to turn up and was the least likely to compromise either of their current locations. Probably the best place to set up a distress beacon as well.

Chapter 43

I was trying my best not to judge Hayes by the condition of the safe house, but given my first impressions, I would call her a hoarder, as in need of medical-reconditioning level hoarder. Packed to the rafters with crates and boxes, the entry of the place looked like she was expecting the apocalypse or couldn't throw anything away. I maneuvered slowly through the main hall fearing Einstein knew what would fall on me. It's a good thing I did because I encountered a near-invisible tripwire about three meters in. Another step and all that would have remained would have been a very expensive jacket and a pair of boots.

I traced the connections and discovered enough Candulem to rattle the world. The explosives were shaped inward for max cutting power designed to destroy the house as opposed to exploding outward. The trap would kill anyone stupid enough to run down the hall but not take out the entire neighborhood when it did. Whoever had set up did a decent job, but I could tell it was industrial, not military. There's a tone to the work and having done similar work for most of my career the techniques stood out like a fingerprint.

I methodically went through the house, disabling the traps, eventually realizing the disarray was all a façade designed to throw off an invader. If an assault team had tried to move quickly they would not have liked the outcome. I optimistically assumed Hayes had not warned me about her little welcome presents because our comms had been unceremoniously jammed. I was fairly certain the previous few days weren't just a ploy to get me into her version of an incinerator.

As I delved deeper into her little murder house I found an arsenal rivaling the *Europe*. There was everything from weaponry to armor to explosives neatly organized in the house's central area right past the initial clutter. The shift in appearance was striking to the point of puzzling. I don't have a huge urge to keep things organized but years of being in a moderately regimented community does impart certain habits. The front areas were so far to one end of the spectrum that when I entered the other rooms the contrast was just as extreme.

I ended up staring at the harmony of the place like some sort of military based feng shui for a good minute before I spotted the full-scale comm array. It was as impressive as everything else in the room, and rivaled the set-up *Heart* and I had built back in Auckland. Although he had paid for the equipment himself, I had sneaked a few looks at the invoices when I collected the items and knew how much some of these items could cost. If this was a fraction of that, she had invested heavily to the point where I was scared to touch anything. Combined with Hayes' penchant from Wayne Dixon level paranoia, I gave everything a thorough examination before plugging in her comm number and muttering a prayer hoping she would pick up and nothing would bite me.

The connection was almost instant followed by enough swearing I failed to register what she said. She could put me to shame. I was impressed. I had lost my touch from too many years hanging around brass. I gave her a minute to vent then asked her to repeat in Standard. "Have you seen the fracking feeds, you space case?" In the middle of responding about being too busy running for my life, she interrupted. "Rustbucket had a damn meltdown. Obviously thinks you're dead and is going after GSI." I asked her how she knew this. "Because I watch the bloody fracking news feeds!"

While I had her on the line, I asked about any potential snares on the comm array. That stopped her dead and dramatically changed her tone. I think she remembered the trip wire at the door. I then started pulling up the news from the night before. Unlike our lifeboat incident, the news of sloop chase wasn't suppressed. There was some very impressive footage of the chase in downtown Hong Kong. Luckily there didn't appear to be a clean shot of me. There was also some very impressive photography of the harbor, and what looked like a third of the city's fire department.

I hadn't used that much explosive on the sloop but had neglected to account for how the Telirem would interact with the reactors. A stupid mistake that could have gotten me or someone else killed had I used more of a charge. Sinking the boat had set off every hazmat sensor in three-hundred clicks. Gut reaction was to call the blunder a learning moment for next time but how many times do you intentionally blow up a friend's vintage racing car in a faraway place?

Unfortunately, *Heart* had linked the two events together and assumed I was in the sloop when it went down. Considering I had not checked in with him in several hours after unceremoniously being removed from near constant communication his assumption seemed like a fair assessment. Based on the next set of news reports he was livid. Although our combined mission from the General was investigating the Terra situation, his primary mission from Lysha was taking care of me. Not only had *Heart* failed the mission he thought was more important, he had violated what he considered a sacred trust to Lysha, his oldest friend. If our previous conversations about loss were any indication, Hayes' description of a meltdown was not far off.

On top of that, because the sloop's relay capabilities were gone, *Heart* was also cut off from Hayes. That meant she was not able to talk him down either. She became a secondhand witness much like the rest of the world as *Heart* began a concerted effort to expose GSI via every avenue he had available. He had taken a salt the earth approach bordering on sadistic. As near, as I could tell on a first glance his goal was to turn public perception against the company. I would not have thought it was possible to have a scandal develop globally in less than a day from so many sources but he had the advantage of near instantaneous communication combined with significant amounts of malicious data. I was not only glad his anger was not directed at me but also a little impressed at how much he valued our friendship.

In an attempt to process everything I had just read, I let my mind disconnect for a second and asked Hayes about Em. "That's what you fracking care about? The bloody cat? She's fine. Won't leave me alone and I don't even like cats." She huffed. I told her because cats consider not making eye contact polite. So by ignoring her, Hayes was telling her Em considered them friends. "I don't care about the damn pregnant cat!" She exhaled slowly as she realized I was messing with her.

It was my turn to be frazzled. I asked her what she meant by pregnant. "Please tell me you're still screwing with me?" She gave me an exasperated look and then just started laughing. "How the bloody frack did you manage to get the drop on me? You're blind as hell. Your cat is pregnant. Very pregnant." She disappeared from the comm screen for a few minutes, reappeared with a chittering Em under her arm, and then proceeded to show me her undercarriage in all its expectant glory. "How do you miss something like this?"

Showing far more tenderness than she showed either *Heart* or me, she set Em down and asked, "What are we going to do about Rustbucket?" Good question. Unlike the Galactic Union situation, I knew the triggering event to this one. In theory, I also knew the solution, get ahold of *Heart* and let him know I was alive. Far simpler said than done. He was in the bottom of the ocean attacking GSI where they hurt, their public image. It's great to believe the pocketbook is where a corp is really going to feel the pain, but after reaching a certain level there's a concept called spite money. A company can do things to spite the competition. That's a great level to be at. The next level above that is where they can do things to spite themselves, where a company can actually injure themselves in pursuit of harming their rivals. Companies like LC and GSI had reached that stage.

That only worked if an organization was willing to take a hard stand, though. As we used to say in the Legion, live with the hard right. If GSI had to live with public perception, as many organizations do there's a point where they would have to back down. *Heart* had learned how to become a person watching one of the most devious executives in human history. Not Terra history, human history. Wayne Dixon owned the moon, something no man could legally do. GSI didn't have a prayer when it came to fighting off a pissed off mother hen who didn't care anymore.

The only way to stop the fight was to make *Heart* care. The only way for that to happen was to show him I was still alive. Hopefully, before the villagers became the monsters they were chasing with the torches and the pitchforks.

Chapter 44

Sometimes a situation spirals so far out of control you have to make a call. No one wants to pick up the phone and make that call to the company office. But want and need are very different things. Bad news, unlike fine wine or cheese, does not get better with age. It ferments like spoiled milk. I asked Hayes how good her comm array was and got the same blank look I had given her on our first real conversation. I took it to mean very good and told her my intent. Much swearing later without any better ideas she begrudgingly agreed with my assessment.

Like the beacons on Legion guns, the General had made sure I had the ability to call for help if things spun too far out of control. *Heart* was my first line of defense. My second was a few comm numbers I had committed to memory. Those numbers would immediately patch me through to Luna from anywhere in Sol. I had already made up my mind to call, but actually doing so was harder than pressing the detonator on the sloop. I took it as an admission of failure. It was saying a few simple tasks were beyond my ability to handle. After staring at the screen for few minutes, I finally pressed enter and waited for the connection to happen.

I was expecting Robert or the General, but the face who appeared belonged to Lysha. The first thought that crossing my mind was, why had I ever left Luna. It took a couple of seconds for the video feed to sync and her to see me. "Ari, you, son of a bitch, you had us scared to death!" I told her I loved her too and watched a good portion of the anxiety bleed out of her face. "Don't sweet talk me, fuel for brains. We've been worried sick, where have you been?" I started from the beginning and told her our logic for keeping her in the dark. She was angry with us, but being an experienced leader, she understood why we did it.

"Adam's been in meetings for the last day thinking he had World War 5 on his hands." She exhaled and then rubbed her eyes with both hands. "Do you know what he's going to say when he realizes we caused this?" I know it's petty, but I was so glad she used we instead of you, as in me, when she said that. I had screwed up big time and told her so. "Hon, we sent you down there blind. We had no idea what to expect. Do not blame yourself for this." She put a very heavy emphasis on not.

"I'm going to get Robert to go rescue him from whatever meeting he is currently in, and we're going to figure this out. Do not hang up." Again she placed a very heavy emphasis on the word not. I obeyed as she disappeared for all of thirty seconds off screen. I could hear her giving directions in a crisp manner. Schmiddy's comments regarding her being like Bris rang true. She was every bit the combat commander as anyone I had ever worked with or for. Listening to her calmed me, in ways that made me realize I had been tense before without knowing.

As soon I was aware, I unleashed the floodgates and she listened patiently asking questions where appropriate, giving insight where needed but in general letting me get the last few months off my chest. I hadn't realized how much I needed it. Not that *Heart* and I didn't talk but I had been in work mode for so long my proverbial bucket of stress was full. You can only put so much water in a bucket before it overflows. The same had happened with my laughing episode when we had moved the sloop. Talking to Lysha had stemmed the tide before it had reached that level, this time. I thanked her for letting me vent.

"It's what family's for. When you get back, and this is done, you're going to return the favor, though." My battle senses screamed at that, filling my stress bucket back to half. Better at half than full. That did trip a question regarding *Heart,* however. I asked if he could be stressed in the same way humans could, thinking about how he explained the first involuntary laugh.

The lag between Terra and Luna is about a second and a half each way, so the delay made the pause seem much longer than it was. When she finally answered, there was something in her eyes, telling me the answer better than her words. "He gets frustrated. Heart doesn't understand everything we do, and it causes him difficulty. Talking it through helps. Losing you would have been wrenching." She bit her lip and I saw she was trying to be diplomatic about how to describe his current actions. Finally, I saw a look bordering on defeat and acceptance. "We need to find him."

Chapter 45

While the war council was assembling, I got myself caught up on *Heart's* one-person assault on GSI. He had started by exposing the long-standing fraud of the Zhang family. Like many of his previous solutions, he went for simplicity turned into elegance. Even though Zhang is one of the most common surnames, the company was unable to produce an actual person bearing the name to represent the company. This acted as the first string in an endlessly unraveling tapestry of deceit dating back decades.

Rather than acting as the sole or even primary source of information, *Heart* appeared to be using rumor mills, and message boards to instigate the public along a breadcrumb path to where they could find the information. It was obvious to me his time building ships on Luna had taught him some finer points of negotiating the net anonymously. He understood the linkages between each community and how information flowed and evolved as it moved between boards and sites. He would either spread or create data, like the "World Famous Pork Lo Mein," which would then make its way to the far corners of the net sometimes in whole and sometimes as a completely new product. Each successive piece acted as another nail in the coffin and until loose links showed the possibility Galactic Union withdrawal might have been orchestrated to GSI's benefit. I was both sorry I had taught him the trick and impressed at how well he used it.

No proof was provided but the hint was enough to cause enough public outrage that it didn't matter. Smaller locations were abandoned, and larger locations found themselves under protest. Within the largest nations and at the Terran Alliance headquarters investigations were called to discover exactly how the situation had developed.

Much as the General had looked for the triggering event leading up to Terra leaving the GU, the countries were trying to find out what had caused their current mess. Based on the news feed the consensus was a greedy corporation playing nations against each other. Exacerbated by the fact the specific corporation in question did not have a moral or ethical compass of a human at the reigns.

The more I listened and read of the news feeds, the more I got angry. I disagreed with the media's assessment around a lack of an ethical compass. *Heart* was extremely ethical. He had a defined sense of right and wrong, coming not only from people like Wayne Dixon and Lysha, but I like to believe myself. His current actions were very reminiscent of something I would do. If I understood his mindset correctly, he viewed GSI as a monster, and sometimes it's necessary to put monsters down. His actions took a good man. Not a nice man, but a man like Wayne Dixon who was harder than Luna rock, who was willing to go up against any odds, even if something wasn't technically legally allowed, like owning the moon, or outing an AI who was operating behind the scenes causing untold damage to billions of people.

The only problem with fighting monsters is the risk of becoming them ourselves. *Heart* was skirting the thin gray line, and he needed family to keep him from stepping over as he could not come back from it. Luckily, the tools he had access to prevented him from doing physical harm, but the second and third order effects he was causing were perhaps as bad as those GSI was causing. He was causing chaos. Chaos in the name of good, but as a member of the Legion, my goal was stability.

Our teleconference acted as a partial mission debrief starting with *Heart* and my exodus from Luna leading to Ganymede, then to Titan, then our crash on Terra. Robert chimed in at that point. "We found where *Heart's* involvement was discovered. GSI maintains a cursory presence throughout Sol, including Luna and the moons you visited. Having him with you was as much of a tell as having me with you." He shook his head, having the look of a man angry with himself for missing the obvious. "We've cut GSI out of all systems and advised the other corporations we are on good terms to do the same."

When I saw he was finished, I told them about *Heart* hiding in the trench until we came up with a new plan. "Smart move, son. *Heart* had given us a heads up of your approach to Terra, but the attack had placed us in a bad position. We couldn't acknowledge either the official or unofficial nature of your visit." The General looked tired. More so than usual. "You had us worried for a bit but *Heart* contacted me when you headed to Auckland to let me know you were alive. That information stayed inside this room. He said you didn't want us to worry unnecessarily, which we appreciate." A small smile and a glance to Lysha. I made a note to thank *Heart* when I saw him next. The bastard hadn't told me.

Robert spoke next. "Our next update was when you used one of the lifeboats. It was all I could do to keep Ms. Kellinger from sending a rescue party down to get you. That was a hard fight because I agreed with her but the General made a fair point about not causing an interplanetary incident. We already knew you weren't aboard, unfortunately, we didn't know exactly where you were."

More head shaking and a self-depreciating laugh. "You made me look like I didn't know my job." Robert wasn't only Lysha's driver, but also her security head. I muttered a quick apology. "Not your fault. I need to be better."

One of the things I loved and hated about the man. He didn't externalize. He didn't think it was my fault he couldn't find me. He took it as a lack of his own skill, something he could correct. He absolutely would take this event as a lesson and use it to learn. "Enough of that, boys. Needles in a haystack. Give someone an impossible task, and you can't expect them to accomplish it." We both muttered a quick yessir and let the matter drop.

"The next you appeared on our sensors was when you destroyed *Heart's* sloop." Robert trailed off. I asked him if he would mind breaking that particular news for me. "No deal, not on your life. He's been making that thing for six years, I think." A huge wash of guilt hit and I think everyone saw my face drop. "He'd trade every ship he's got in the hangar to get you back. Don't sweat the sloop. He won't." A little of the guilt faded away.

I asked how we could get in touch with *Heart* since I had destroyed our main means of communication. "Son, looks like I'm going to have to go to Terra."

Chapter 46

General Adam Campbell was the man called when ambassadors failed. The GSI situation had brewed to that level. Arion put out the request, which was quickly seconded by the Commonwealth and then acknowledged by several others. His official title was Ambassador General of Humankind, at Large, but he was widely associated with the Galactic Union making him persona non grata on Terra much like myself. I was in grand company.

I had never thought about it before, but the General's history had never placed him on Terra. Looking back, he usually avoided most planets entirely preferring to conduct business on Legion ships. It dawned on me his style of brokering peace left everyone dissatisfied. If all parties are unhappy with a situation, then no one feels the other side got the better deal. However, because of the long-term effectiveness of this method, he personally had created a lot of enemies. Rather than people hating each other, they hated him.

Having been in the Legion for so long, and the host of his meetings I viewed his pragmatic approach of diplomacy as normal. I hadn't realized his residence on Luna was not exactly self-imposed exile, but more of a safety precaution and safe haven. The idea of him going to Terra was terrifying to the more politically savvy of our group. This was compounded by the fact his usual traveling companions, the Legionnaires, were not allowed with him.

Using quite a bit behind the scenes influence, I had secured rooms at the Cadre Club for Hayes, Em, and myself, pending his arrival. His celebrity status created quite the media storm. Despite my love of aud, vid, and music, I've never been fond of just listening to or watching the news. I always found it predictable or depressing. The other issue was I was never in one place long enough for it to matter. The Legion gave me mission briefings on what was actually important as compared to the tripe that normally permeated the media sources. When I began my training with the General, he taught me I needed to learn how to sort through the mounds of garbage and interpret it to get a feel for what was really going on. The way he described the process was very similar to my crew chief buddy's description of feeling the bird. I tried to apply that mental model and it clicked. The emotional feel of the news, not just what was being reported, but was being left out provided a structure I could almost envision.

Hayes was an old hat at sorting the news and actually helped me understand a lot more of what I was seeing and read between the lines as we watched the all-day coverage from our shared suite. I hadn't thought the rooms could be much better than where *Heart* had put me up previously but I found myself mistaken. I had previously given up my bed when Hayes had stayed with me at my hotel, but at Cadre, we were given individual rooms with a shared living area containing a full-scale media center and even a kitchen.

As Hayes finished healing her mood improved dramatically. I discovered she had not been taking any of the painkillers *Heart* had prescribed hinting her attitude was a direct result of her injuries. Apparently, she gets mean when she's in pain. I could definitely understand that. I was an insufferable jack when my arm was healing up. When it finally reached the point where I couldn't notice her limping she was damn near pleasant to be around, with only her version of pet names reminding me of the previous insults. I decided to forgive most of the previous meanness as pain as we waited for the General's arrival.

Although the trip from Luna to Terra is relatively short, the General never had genemod for gravity acclimation. It wasn't something required for his specialty when he entered the service and he had never bothered. Six times normal gravity would be rough on his elderly frame. I assumed the Empire would have an angrav chamber to offset it, but they aren't perfect and the media would likely demand some candid shots in public.

The General did something slick, though. He announced the staff he was bringing along and where he would be. He made sure the list would be broadcast as much as possible. One of the staff members was former Legionnaire Ari Gadsden. When asked about the treaty regarding the banning of Legion on Terra, he told them, "Captain Gadsden comes or I don't." I found an ancient and much younger picture of myself plastered over every feed imaginable. It was hard to imagine me ever looking quite so young and fresh faced. I looked positively optimistic in the photos compared to the view I usually saw in the mirror.

Less than two hours after the news started airing with my image the comm unit on my hip started screaming. I clicked it on and heard *Heart* say. "Captain. I may have deviated from orders." I could hear the remorse in his voice tempered with the relief of talking to me, but he didn't quite have the emotional maturity to handle both issues at once.

Thinking back to when I woke up with my bum arm, I repeated the words told to me by the General about revisiting decisions that can't be changed. "I am sorry, Ari. I was so angry." I cut him off and let him know he had nothing to be sorry about. Moreso his anger was justified. I don't know what I would have done in his place, but he was restrained compared to what he could have done.

There are no good or bad emotions, but emotions can drive us to do good or bad things. *Heart* had stepped into some gray area, but not quite into the dark. I let him know that was the reason why family was so important. It kept us firmly anchored on the light side of things but when someone goes after those anchor chains it's understandable why we snap. Not excusable but understandable.

"What do we do now?" I told him we needed to carry on. We needed to work with the new problem in front of us. Not dwell with past choices. I also told him I was proud of him for making a choice, for being bold and making a call I hadn't thought to make myself. "I do not know if we can undo what I have done." Why should we want to, was my response. Yes, there was collateral damage, but all decisions have secondary effects. We cannot let ourselves get caught up in those. We should weigh them and we should absolutely try to minimize harm to others, but unlike GSI, he had shown he cared. That's what made us different.

To do that, we'd need to be where the General was, and for that, I'd need my partner. I told him to get out of the Kermadec and come pick us up in Hong Kong. We were going to Arion.

Chapter 47

Nothing wakes the locals like an office building sized ship landing near the golf course. I was so glad I got preapproval from the concierge because Cadre was not a bridge I wanted to burn for myself or the friends' names I had dropped to get us in. As we entered *Heart*, I gave a silent giggle as Hayes repeated the routine I went through on my first boarding "Granted, Commander Hayes. You are always welcome aboard." As soon as the hatch was sealed, I released Em from her carrier so she could wander the halls, and cautioned *Heart* about access and gravity while she was aboard. I was a hair worried about her condition.

"I am already tracking her Captain, and will ensure deceleration dampers are in full effect in any space she is located." I thanked him and asked if he had made contact with the ambassadorial party or Luna yet. "Immediately after we spoke last. We have full credentials and should be arriving near the same time as General Campbell." He paused. "Commander Hayes, I have set aside a stateroom for your stay as well. I was unsure who to contact in Arion, but you have full access to the communications suite should you need to speak to anyone." She nodded her thanks and then realizing there wasn't anyone present said it aloud.

We headed up to the bridge to see we were already airborne. "Captain on the bridge," announced *Heart* catching both Hayes and me off-guard. Rather than the usual reflexive broadcast, this one seemed laced with happiness. I wasn't quite sure if I was reading more into it than was actually there until my chair rotated to great me. "Ari, the conn is yours."

Heart wasn't joking about the decel dampers. I hadn't even felt us lift off. We were in the air and already at cloud level. I couldn't tell how fast we were moving but I got the impression he had us on a leisurely path, basking in the reunion. I hadn't felt this comfortable since setting foot on terra firma back in Auckland.

I hopped into my chair and ran through a quick diagnostic out of habit, then hailed the General's ship, *The Island.* "My boy, I see you've found that misplaced sheep of yours. It's good to see you both." There was a bit of a twinkle in his eye. He seemed to be treating this mishap as some sort of grand adventure. I wish I could say the same. I apologized again for dragging him down, which *Heart* echoed. "Think nothing of it, boys. Had I been a hair quicker on the uptake, neither of you would have been in this predicament in the first place." He said waving off the apologies. "I should have had young *Heart* there check the issue before we began. Would have saved us all manner of trouble." I sniffed at that. He was right. *Heart* had spotted the logical error that none of us had seen because we were looking at the issue as presented rather than how it actually was. That, in turn, had resulted in the sequence of events bringing the General down to Terra. Ah, the irony.

"Gents, I'm going to get some shuteye before the real fun begins. I suggest you do the same. I'll see you in Arion."

Chapter 48

The largest city I had ever been to was Seattle back before I joined the Legion. Seattle is massive taking up a quarter of the coast of North Am and dwarfing Luna City when it comes to square kilometers. On nights without clouds, the light from Seattle is enough to pollute all the way up into the Northern Reaches. Seattle was minuscule compared to Arion. As *Heart* flew over Europe there was still a marked difference between city and country until we approached Arion. At that point, it all became a city. Even as high up as we were, we could not see anything green on the horizon.

I knew we must be near because I saw Hayes begin to noticeably relax. For her, Arion was home, as much as Terra was for me. This was where her comfort was. Where everything was right, where everything felt natural. All the tension she'd been holding back bled away. I was waiting for *Heart* to comment about an endorphin spike but I think he had learned from watching me, so the comment never came.

When it came time for the approach request, Hayes called in for clearance with a crisp and confident voice. *"Independent Hospital Ship Heart* carrying Envoy General, Ari Gadsden and

Lieutenant Commander Maxine Hayes. Request permission to land per transmitted credentials."

Heart and I were like a couple of kids flying together for the first time in weeks. As soon as the hailing channel was silenced, I heard him say "Independent?" with an obvious note of disdain and mock shock, while I simultaneously mouthed envoy general at Hayes. She looked like she was about to yell at the both of us when he interrupted her asking no one in particular. "The real question is why she pronounces lieutenant, left-tenant." I told him Imperials did not appreciate the implication their officers were occupying the lieu, getting an actual chuckle from Hayes. I think I caught her off guard with the ancient stupid joke.

Her mood was quickly ruined when one of the air controllers gave her a "Welcome home Rattlesnake" over the private comm channel and I started laughing uncontrollably. Luckily, *Heart* was quick to react and did not transmit the ensuing argument, or my attempts to explain my vision of cockpits of vipers and shared call signs.

"Commander, the Captain's call sign is also 'Rattlesnake.' That may explain why he is having difficulty breathing." *Heart* attempted to explain over my gasping for air. His calm voice set me off even more. I knew Hayes and I were too similar, and between giggles, ended up making comments about her being mean as a snake getting enough dirty looks from her to last a career. As I recovered, I practically begged for the backstory on her handle, which she flatly refused to provide. I bet *Heart* aloud it was my original guess concerning her temper. "No bet, too high a probability." The whoosh of the bridge door was barely perceptible over my laughter.

Our landing was uneventful and free from missiles. On the next pad over *The Island* and several smaller craft waited. I told *Heart* to keep his head on a swivel and be ready for takeoff on a moment's notice. With as much good fortune as we'd had in the last twenty-four hours something was bound to go horribly wrong. "Aye, aye, Captain." I debated whether to yell at him for the formality or not then realized he was likely keeping up appearances in front of Hayes, so settled for giving a dirty look to the closest view screen instead.

Hayes and I made our way down the ramp and were met by a limo bearing Imperial placards. The driver gave a crisp salute as we approached, and both Hayes and I returned it not sure who it was intended for. Before I had the chance to play the gentleman, the door was opened for us both and we were ushered inside. After driving around in the sloop for so long, I had forgotten how comfortable real seats could actually be. As soon as the door shut, Hayes was on her comm unit and presumably getting instructions from her superiors. That was not an issue I had to worry about so I enjoyed the ride keeping half an ear open for anything pertaining to the Legion, Luna, or myself.

The ride itself took not quite an hour. I'm sure there was sky above, but the buildings completely blacked it out. If not for dealing with Luna City and the constant lighting even through the day, I would have been disturbed by dealing with streetlights at noon. We eventually reached the city center which felt like it was the size of Hong Kong. Only as big as one of the largest spaceports in the world. I laughed at the thought. Hayes stared at me like I had lost my mind.

The deeper we got into the city the more I began to see the press. We were expected. Luckily, when the car finally stopped we were in an underground garage sheltered from the throngs of reporters and photographers right outside the building. We exited the vehicle and Hayes gave me a nod. "Clear skies, Gadsden." I nodded back and responded with the traditional, soft landings before a handler took her away.

Another guide was waiting for me. "Captain Gadsden, if you'll follow me. I'll take you to your rooms, and then to Ambassador Campbell." I followed him to the elevators feeling vaguely reminiscent of my return to Luna City and my first meeting with Lysha. I smiled at the memory. This time, I was the one making small talk to my slightly uncomfortable shadow. Rather than take too much pleasure at his pain I let him off the hook after a half dozen questions.

The room he showed me to was downright huge. I was almost certain it was larger than the warehouse in Auckland. The furnishings were of a minimalist bend but still nicer than I was used to. As I was staring at the entrance room, my guide told me the time he would be back, and I nodded assent. He was gone perhaps five minutes before I heard a chime at the door. Having learned my lesson from my previous time answering a door, I slid my one of my knives out and hid it behind my back as I palmed open the door.

Standing in the entrance was a sight I hadn't seen in far too long. She was tall, having at least a couple of centimeters on me, and I'm no slouch. Gorgeous with brunette brows over sparkling blue eyes and auburn hair. She exuded power and confidence. "You going to just stand there or you going to invite a girl in." She was most definitely in charge. Not questions, statements. Her presence was comparable to Sol itself and up until that point, I hadn't known how much I had really missed her.

The sound of the knife hitting the ground didn't even register as I reached out and kissed her.

Chapter 49

After what felt like the greatest eternity, I managed to ask what Lysha was doing on Terra. "Someone had to return your jacket." She winked, slipped it off, and handed it to me. I looked at her askance. "You're a Legionnaire. The Alliance knows you're Legion. Wear your colors with pride." She had a point. I slipped out of the midnight and into the scarlet, offering her my Captain's jacket. She shook her head. "Business trip. Don't worry, I'm taking the red one back after this." Another wink.

"We brought down some clothes for you, but we figured the coat would be a nice touch. I also wanted to see you. Rank has its privileges." I happily agreed. "We've got a little while before the meeting and figured you may want a little moral support." I told her she had that right. As soon as I had gotten into the limo back at the spaceport, my communications to *Heart* were cut off and I was a lonely feeling. The suite was the first chance to get in touch with him but Lysha had surprised me at the door. "I told him if he ruined the surprise I would melt down every ship in his hangar." There was a tinge of Luna hardness in her voice I assumed she inherited from Grandpa Dixon. I assured her *Heart* had not and it was and a very pleasant surprise at that.

I felt guilty having forgotten about him since Lysha's arrival and begged her forgiveness so I could get him tied into the local comm system. She laughed at me but agreed. "It's fine, love. I'm sure he'll understand." She shook her head at me and stretched. "While you're doing that, I'm going to borrow your refresher."

It took under a minute to link up the room with *Heart*. "Did the drive go well? Anything worth seeing?" I told him Lysha was already here "Thank goodness. She can be scary when she wants to be. Did the surprise go well? I am sorry about the deception but she made me promise." I told him was fine and more than all right. Some deceptions are allowed. It's about malice. He hadn't intended malice. Quite the opposite. "Oh, like when Miss Kellinger introduced you on my awakening day. That was an excellent surprise. I thoroughly enjoyed that." Awakening day. I told him I wasn't tracking. "It would be roughly analogous to a human birthday, I believe. The day I realized I was me. A person and not a thing." His comments stopped me. Lysha was big on birthday surprises. I could definitely see her introducing *Heart* to his new Captain as a birthday present. Hell of a present. For all of half a second I was offended at being given as a gift but I knew her too well to think that was Lysha's actual intent.

I told him I hadn't known. "That did not change the value of the gift. I met a great friend on that day. Miss Kellinger and I have been companions for a very long time. There is little to buy for each other at this point. Experiences, however, are something that is difficult to qualify. Introducing me to you has been one of the greatest experiences I have had. I have done more since then than I anticipated. It has been excellent. I am hoping our relationship continues for a long time." He damn near had me in tears.

"Knock it off you two. There will be plenty of time for traipsing about the galaxy when all of this is done. But *Heart*, I have dibs. I saw him first." She gave me a quick hug from behind. "You best get ready. The real fun is about to begin." I gave her a quick peck and hit the refresher.

Chapter 50

I was lucky enough to get a few minutes with the General alone before the assembly began. The gravity was turned down to about eighty percent Terra standard, making me feel bouncy and him look pale. Gravity acclimation is never really something I was able to get a firm lock on. I had joined the Legion immediately after coming from Terra, so I never had to deal with increased weight in the same way Looneys or Marsans did. The best description I ever heard was when someone compared the idea to being used to hot or cold. I grew up in Alaska, so I'm used to the cold. Cold doesn't bother me like most people, unless I'm wet. I despise being wet and being wet and cold is something I go to great lengths to avoid. If given the choice, I'd rather be cold than hot. On worlds with heavy heat and humidity, I'm absolutely miserable.

The General was in his version of a hot and humid world and looked positively horrible. That wasn't even at full gravity. Were it me, there would be a lot of emotion bleeding out, and by emotion I mean downright nastiness. I am not a pleasant person when I am uncomfortable. He however maintained his charm and good-nature to the point where I felt like a dumb-ass for being upset about wet socks only a few days before. I needed to be better, like him.

My original assumption was this visit was only to stop *Heart's* one-person war against GSI. The General corrected that misunderstanding. After handing me a set of glasses, that I realized were a much more subdued variant of dampers he explained. "Son, a storm's a brewing. We need to nip it in the bud quick like. Believe me or not, you boys did exactly what I sent you down here for. Not how I would have expected, but in some ways, it's going to make this a lot easier." I'd been around enough brass to learn how to control my swearing outbursts but his words almost tripped the line. He saw the look on my face. "You did good, son. Both you and *Heart*. I told you what I wanted to be done, not how, for a reason."

I was back in basic hearing the same words. If a leader directs how to do something, it limits actions. If a leader says what they want, it expands the possibilities of getting it done. The General had given us tools and let us figure out how to accomplish the mission. Things went sideways from our plan, but no plan survives first contact anyways.

"General Campbell, what is the purpose of the assembly if our mission is complete then?" *Heart* asked through the dampers. Knowing he was going to be present significantly reduced my anxiety. Looking back to the couple of days I had lost him, I realized how much stress I had been under. Had our positions been reversed and I thought *Heart* had been destroyed there likely would be a smoking crater where Galactic Subsidiaries used to be and where all of the explosives I had found at Hayes' safe house had been relocated. If the afterthought could cause so much emotional reaction from me, I really hated to think what *Heart* had gone through during that time.

There was a sad smile, a shake of the head, and a slow exhale. "In order to reach a higher state of order, we must go through chaos first." He said it like a prayer. Like he had repeated the adage thousands of times before. "There's a mob mentality out there. We need to put a stop to it before the wrong people get hurt. *Heart*, my boy, you exposed a dark secret to the light. People don't like secrets. That dislike, when exercised together, has the potential for catastrophe. We need to nudge the attitudes a little."

I got the feeling *Heart* was going to ask a follow on question but the door chimed and an escort arrived to take us to our place in the main hall. My social anxiety nearly redlined as soon as I walked in. The place looked to be filled with a Legion division's worth of people. All staring at me. The General really, but since I was next to him, my brain was yelling they were looking at me. "Ari, calm down.

Your heart rate is spiking." I muttered something bordering on mean, quickly apologized, and told him I'd been fine in a moment. That, of course, turned out to be a lie, since the guide parked us dead center of the room, with me at the General's right hand.

Gladly there was no pomp to delay the start. That had apparently happened several hours before while I was lucky enough to be unwinding in my suite with Lysha. If I had had to go through any kind of ceremony I likely would have pulled my best Larry Talbot and the Wolf Man impression by ripping my shirt off and running from the room howling.

Moments after sitting, the General took a sip of water instantly having the effect of quieting the room, even though I wasn't sure how. Some people know how to walk into a room and make heads turn. Apparently, the General knew how to drink water. An absolutely mundane task pulling all eyes to him.

"There's lots on the agenda. So rather than waste anyone's time. Let's begin." Like a light switch, the carefully crafted image of everyone's grandfather disappeared and sitting next to me was a chief executive officer. A man with a vision. Someone in control of the proceedings. "First up is the matter of the Terran Alliance and the Galactic Union. Based on new information that has come to light, it appears there may have been subtle manipulation and malfeasance involved in the dissolution. Looking around, I see we have a quorum. I move for that issue to be revisited. Any objections?" He was staring over at one section of the room, but I couldn't figure out who. It took me a moment to realize he was daring someone to say something.

"Very well. Do we have a second?" Before he finished the words, several seconds were shouted from the crowd. "Good, carried to committee. Until finalized, Terra will have full privileges within the GU, per the charter." Below the table, a pat on my leg jarred me. The words echoed in my head. If Terra was again part of the GU, then the Legion's restriction was void. In under a minute he had accomplished what had seemed like such a big deal half a year ago. And I didn't care. It didn't matter. Terra was no longer important to me.

It took several minutes for me to process, as the simple business was accomplished. That was until the General made a shocking announcement pulling me out of my reverie. "It's all well and good to have discussions about how we are going to handle the current situation; however, we really should have all interested parties here for discussion." Smarter people than me caught on much faster and shouts of outrage happened as the previously unlit seats in the corporate balcony went live with GSI's presence.

"We are honored to be included." The voice was feminine but disconcerting, as though a merger of several people. It twinged at my mind as I tried to place it unsuccessfully. From what I saw of the crowd, I was not the only one having a similar reaction. I caught elements of fear, awe, and hate. The entire gamut was present as everyone tried to make his or her displeasure known to the General. I'll say one thing for the old coot, he had united them with a common enemy, him. Unfortunately, I was sitting right next to him.

"Mistress Zhang, thank you for joining us. I believe there is much to discuss regarding the future."

Chapter 51

A quick recess was called after the General dropped that atomic. We were ushered into a conference room less than fifty meters from our seats. The General had a grin larger than the moon itself. He seemed utterly pleased with himself. Already in the room were half a dozen people including Hayes dressed in her Imperial Whites. I gave her a nod, and she gave a quick shake of her head towards a younger woman sitting at the table who the General had made a beeline towards. "Your Excellency, a pleasure, as always." The Empress motioned for him to sit.

"Uncle Adam, knock that off. Do you really have to play the same games everywhere you go? Sooner or later you'll run into a dictator who has more of an 'off with your head' mindset." He laughed.

I wasn't quite sure whether the Empress calling him uncle meant they were actually family or if it was a sign of familiarity. I tried not my best not to stare but one thing made me think the former. She had the same indigo eyes as the as General. Contrasting tawny hair in a lion's mane made them all the more compelling.

"Perhaps. Perhaps, but that's why I always travel with the Legion." Pointing towards me. As if I wasn't already on edge.

341

She eyed me up and down. It felt like being scanned at the doctor's office, invasively. "So this your problem child? Figures. We have one of our own." She said pointing at Hayes. I didn't get the impression of disdain, however. It was more akin to deadpan sarcasm skirting the realm of private joke.

"Sit you two. No protocol in here." I had thought Lysha emanated power. The Empress seemed to radiate it as if it was part of her. My body reacted as though I was back in basic and I sat before my brain gave the conscious command. Hayes looked like she was about to have an aneurysm as her conditioning conflicted with a direct order from the Empress herself. Apparently sitting in the presence of the Nation's leader was a no-go.

She gave a quick glance at Hayes and then me and shook her head. "You two were effective at least. We would have preferred a smoother transition and something far less public." Her voice didn't change tone or even emphasis, but I swear the words echoed in my head like they were said in a cave. I saw Hayes react at the same spots so I knew she could hear it too. The subtle chastisement was enough to send me back in time to the first time I made my grandad really angry at me. He didn't yell, he didn't have to. I had disappointed him.

The General, however, wasn't having any of it. "Enough of that," he snapped. "They accomplished something I couldn't, and I've been doing this longer than both of them and you've been alive." That was an uncharacteristic snap for him. I don't think I had ever seen him lose his composure. I realized as far as he was concerned if anyone was going to chew our tail feathers, he was going to be the one, and it was going to be in private. He did not care whether the Empress had a point or not, it was not her place to light me up, and more importantly this wasn't the time to do it.

Without missing a beat, the Empress moved on. I didn't get the impression she ignored the comment, merely absorbed the feedback and continued. "What is your actual take on the Zhang situation?" Great question and one I wanted to know as well. The General had blindsided me as well with the invite.

The General spent quite a bit of time thinking before responding. "I don't know. I really don't. I don't know how to describe the Mistress Zhang. It would be like an ant trying to explain a human. We're simply not the same. I would have an easier time explaining Vrenyls or Targohs and they communicate with pheromones. As near as I can tell, she is GSI. GSI on Terra, GSI on Luna, GSI on Titan, all of GSI." He stopped and looked at the ceiling.

"She's been in hiding for a long time, though. I think the smart play is to invite her to the table and treat her like an equal."

A heavy sigh from the Empress. "We do not like it. The manipulations were devastating. We're still dealing with the repercussions, and now this. We would have preferred a little more warning. You have the luxury of not having to deal with advisers. We are going to hear about this stunt for weeks."

The General smiled at that, appearing to take an almost Terran pleasure at the comment. "Sometimes the bandage has to be ripped off. We could have spent months dealing with this new problem or we could deal with it immediately." His grin faded back to seriousness. "It's either now when we are prepared and we have them in the open, or at some unknown point in the future."

"So be it. But be warned. You created this mess, you clean it up or we will." I'm not big on threats, regardless of where they come from but the General's iron grip on my thigh kept me firmly planted in my chair. Then in the coldest voice I have ever heard another human use she said, "We're not in the habit of spying on our friends, but allowances are sometimes made for the greater good." That was a phrase I did not like. The greater good was a way of saying the individual was going to get screwed. The single person is the smallest minority there is and the easiest one for the majority to impose its will on. Sometimes sacrifices should be made, even demanded, but it should always involve choice. Without choice it was tyranny. But we were sitting in the Empire, not the Democracy so I kept my mouth shut like a good houseguest.

After her warning, the Empress nodded and stood. Everyone else was instantly on their feet so I followed the example. When she and her group were gone, I looked at the General and asked about the uncle part. "Don't give me any guff. Why do you think all these governments don't lock me up or worse wherever I go? It's not my charming personality or refined wit."

We headed back to the assembly room where the place was abuzz. It was interesting to see how many people were up near the GSI box and more importantly who. When the General sent me on the mission initially he had warned me there were no enemies or allies, merely alignments of interest. GSI had power and was a new player and all the other powers needed to discover whether they ran parallel or perpendicular. After sitting, the General pulled the water trick again and the room went quiet. I really needed to figure out how he did that.

"There seems to be a lot of conjecture regarding you and your organization Mistress Zhang. Perhaps, if you cleared up some of your personal history it would alleviate some of the concerns of the gathered audience." Although the General had phrased the statement like a perfectly reasonable request, he was also asking an extremely intimate question. He was asking for a detailed history of how she came to be.

"We would be greatly honored." The same cacophonous voice. "We are Zhang. Rather than lose the knowledge of our forbearers we developed technology to retain it." Whew, that sounded like old school singularity talk. Centuries ago, the idea was to make computers powerful enough for the human consciousness to be uploaded into them. We never figured out how to do it, though. 2045 was the date the singularity was supposed to happen. That date came and went. The technology reached the theoretical stage, but no one could get it to work, or so we thought. If a corporation was the first one to do it, that was indeed a valuable secret. A secret worth killing for. "This institutional knowledge was the key to our success as an organization. As the family grew, so did our strength." The way she was talking made the process sound like a collective. Not only one person transferred, but each member, no, every member of the family into the system. "As our strength grew, so did our influence. Eventually, we realized the mortal shell was unneeded. We could accomplish our goals in this present form."

Einstein's Ghost. *Heart's* original theory was only partially right. We were dealing with a distributed intelligence, but it wasn't artificial. They were captured human intelligences, who had transcended. If I understood what she was saying correctly, we were talking about the entire family. No wonder we couldn't find any management. The gasps from the audience reinforced my thought process was similar to everyone else's. I asked *Heart* if this kind of lifeform was even possible. "Possible and impossible do not matter if it exists in reality." He shut the argument down quickly, then added. "I have never heard of anything similar, however, until now."

"The idea is anathema. Multiple consciousnesses sharing a single host would constantly vie for dominance. I do not know how a personality matrix could remain stable." His comments reminded me of our discussion regarding splitting him up so we could develop more plans. Before I could bring that old conversation up Mistress Zhang continued.

"This reaction is one of many reasons we did not disclose our existence. We anticipated disapproval at our choice." Had I not worked so closely with *Heart* I would never have spotted the subtle shifts in tone and structure of their phrasing. There was an underlying conflict in how Mistress Zhang was telling the story. I didn't want to distract or call attention to the General, though, knowing any eyes not on her booth were on him. "We were concerned the criticism might turn violent. Our fears appear well-founded."

I saw the General's jaw tighten. Mistress Zhang was flipping the script, making GSI the victim of the situation. I muttered under my breath about there being no way anyone could fall for this. "Ari, I would actually estimate a solid portion of the populace will have sympathy for them. Far from a majority, but enough to create a debate." I saw the General nod at *Heart's* comments as he could hear them through his own earpiece. "My actions were badly planned. I may have inadvertently set them up to become martyrs."

I swore silently as his words sunk in. I was the least intelligent person present but what *Heart* had said made perfect sense. Mistress Zhang had changed the entire game and anyone smarter than I could see it. She had effectively convinced the world they were the weak ones in the equation but done so in such a way the combined world governments couldn't go after the corporation without making them the monsters. The Zhangs had become a virus no one was allowed to fight.

I'm big on the concept of protecting the individual. Always have been. Anytime you get more than a few folks together there's a habit of trying to force their will on the smaller groups. I don't know if it's a way humans are wired or what but history has shown us doing it over and over again. The idea pisses me off to no end. That made the Legion a good fit for me. We don't really tolerate tyranny or bullies. The problem is when one individual is clearly wrong and the village has to take that person down. Sometimes there is a monster. Sometimes it hides under the bed or in the closet and it eats little kids. But what's worse is when you find the monster and it tries to convince you it's not really that bad of a monster so it can continue to keep eating little kids. Pretending to have changed its ways. That's what the Zhangs were doing. They were a man-eating lion acting like a kitten so they would not be taken out. They knew it, the assembly knew it and they knew we knew it. It was all I could do to keep from stomping out of the room.

"Easy, son. Remember what the Legion's actual mission is." The General saw my posture shift and cautioned me from the side. I was pissed but he was right. The Legion cares about galactic stability and Mistress Zhang had blackmailed the governments into one of the most aggravating forms of stability I had ever witnessed. Well, two could play at the same game.

Chapter 52

"Ari, are you sure this is wise?" *Heart* voiced the question everyone else in the room had on their minds. I shook my head and told them of course not, but it was right. Sometimes you have to take the hard right over the wise choice. "As General Campbell said, there will be repercussions. There is a high probability you will not be allowed back on Terra. Ever." I nodded and told them I knew. His concern was touching, and his reasoning was solid enough to push through my anger, but my choice was not emotional. Just because I was mad, didn't make the decision wrong. The choice wasn't about me. It had never been about me. The mission was always about the greater good, no matter how much I despised that phrase. When the General had offered me the job he had escalated my self-interest by offering me a devil's bargain but he did it in the name of doing something bigger than myself. At the time, I thought I was selfish and my treating it like a solo mission had reinforced the mindset. But when it boiled down to it, my mission was to provide stability and mission was more important than any personal reward.

"Son, let me do this. I at least have a little insulation. The Terran Alliance already hates me. It's a good plan, but you're giving up too much for it." I told him I wasn't giving up a damn thing.

Everything I needed was in that room or close enough. My family was there, him, Lysha, with *Heart* and Robert via teleconference.

"All right. Legion gave the go ahead. They agree the Zhangs are a threat. Maybe not today, but based on their history they will be, and that's why the Legion exists. Unfortunately, they're not the kind of threat we can deal with traditionally."

It was decided. Strangely, I had none of my regular nervousness when I entered the assembly the second day. I was walking with a sense of purpose. The first hour was routine, with pleasantries and discussions and what appeared to be the new normal of having Mistress Zhang as part of the collective. After the first break, the General asked for a few minutes to make a few administrative announcements and was everyone seemed content to grant him the stage.

"First, I'd like to offer two sets of congratulations. Our own Ari Gadsden has received a promotion to Colonel for his services during these troubling times." Pointing to me, I waved and received a bit of applause. I was still in my Legion jacket with the huge gold sergeant's stripes but added my new rank insignia to the collar of what passed for a dress shirt. I could feel the pins backings of the silver triangles pressing into my throat reminding me of the weight of what was about to happen.

"Additionally, it has come to our attention Mistress Zhang has been granted Luna Citizenship." More applause. Although much of it seemed polite like the clapping for my promotion, there was quite a bit that appeared genuine. Humans have a few real strengths. First is our ability to chase. We don't get tired making us excellent hunters able to become predators on par with creatures far beyond our weight, strength, or even ferocity. Second is or ability to adapt. We are able to evolve to new situations quickly. I've dealt with other galactic races and this is our huge advantage compared to most of them. Most are steeped in generations of how things are done because it works. Humans are young in comparison. We are still figuring it out giving us a massive edge when dealing with new situations. Finally, is our ability to forget. It's what keeps us from killing each other.

The Zhangs were both human and not. They were leveraging our willingness to forget to maximum effect. When the General had invited GSI and Mistress Zhang to the assembly, he had a plan in mind. That plan was quickly scrapped due to the revelations and her own maneuverings. I hoped my new plan was both good enough and simple enough to survive first contact.

"We are pleased by this great honor." The cacophonous voice grated at me, but the situation would be over soon. The dissonance set my nerves on edge to the point where it took me an act of will to stay sitting. I felt like there was an undertone of screams hiding within her voice. After *Heart's* comments about multiple personalities fighting for control, I thought I understood. Mistress Zhang was the senior voice and the discord was the rest were battling within a singular host like the biblical demon Legion. This had come down to a Legionnaire versus Legion.

"There are however a few other matters of discussion. There are certain criminal activities that have come to light, which may chill our proceedings a bit. Are you aware of these accusations, Mistress Zhang?" The poker face he had was amazing. The collected audience shifted back and forth between the faceless booth and General Campbell unsure who was displaying less emotion.

"We are sure the allegations are unfounded." The voice cracked. It wasn't only me who heard it. The rest of the audience roared demanding to know what was going on. General Campbell gave them a solid five count before raising his hand, not quite requesting silence. He was playing the crowd letting them feed on the smell of blood. "Of course, of course. I'm sure all of these questions can be answered in due course. At trial." He let the words hang in the air.

"We will not stand trial." Mistake number one. Never tell someone what you won't do. The crowd lost it. The thing about diplomacy is the illusion that no one is above the rules. Everyone is, but has to appear no one is. By flat out saying they were going to ignore the rules, Mistress Zhang had lost all the protection she had gained the previous day. Their arrogance was their undoing. I stifled a chuckle.

The General took the rebuke in stride, playing ever the diplomat. "My apologies, I meant a discussion." His calm voice made him seem reasonable in the throng who was quickly becoming passionate. It was a great trick; I had seen used before. Nothing makes an argument appear to fall apart faster than different levels of emotional investment. By remaining on the colder side of the argument, he made even little spikes of heat seem disproportionately large in comparison.

"There is nothing to discuss." Mistake number two. We were sitting in the land where everything was discussed, even if not worth discussing. The point was the talking. When parties were talking, they weren't fighting. That was what diplomacy was all about. Not fighting. Refusal to talk was the equivalent of pulling out a glove and slapping someone.

"We are not subject to your authority." Mistake number three. No one said the Zhangs were, but corporations don't make rules, governments do, especially on good old Terra. Mistress Zhang seemed to have forgotten all of her holdings were located on sovereign land. She was indeed subject to quite a few of the nations' authority, but the General played off her response a different way.

The General actually stepped back and took on a hurt look. "Oh, I'm sorry you feel that way, but you are mistaken. With citizenship comes obligation. Additionally, none of us is truly autonomous. You cannot murder other sentient beings without expectation of backlash." This was the first time he had said what the actual charge was and at the word murder, there were gasps. I almost laughed.

"Who do you accuse us of murdering?" Mistake number four. Never ask a question you don't know the answer to if you aren't in control of the situation. The answer will shock you. Worse, if you are in charge of the situation, and you ask it, chances are you are going to lose control of the situation. That's what happened to Mistress Zhang. She committed a cardinal mistake and walked into our trap.

The large display behind me lit up with several names under the headings of murder and attempted murder. On one side were several more as of Max Hayes former security and technical team from Fiji. On the other side were other members as well as hers and my own. I wanted to smile but these were people who had lost their lives to take down this monster. Taking joy at the Zhangs' downfall would bring me closer to being like them and I would not tolerate that. Before I had a chance to move, Hayes herself was standing in her full uniform center stage next to General Campbell. "Mistress Zhang, by the power vested in me by the Empress, may she live forever, you are to submit to the authority of this council. Failure to do so will result in all known equipment being destroyed."

Chapter 53

That was not how the meeting was supposed to go down. The original plan had been for a Legion arrest. Our purpose was Galactic stability and the Zhangs ran counter to that. They had destabilized not only the Terran Alliance but Sol in the process. The Zhangs were a direct threat to intent and spirit of the Legion's charter. That was how I had managed to sell the intervention to HQ back on Luna with the General's help.

As the General had gotten the Terran Alliance probationary status back in the GU, Legion had authority to operate again. My promotion to Colonel was honorary and gave me not only the perceptual standing to sit next to the General, but also the legal jurisdiction to conduct the arrest. Everything had gone according to plan up until Hayes stepped in. I was in no position to stop her since Arion was her home turf, but I sure as hell wanted to know why the plan had changed at the last possible second.

She was in the outside hall waiting but before I could ask what in the hell was going on she stopped me with a raised hand. "You've got friends in high places and I owed you one. You could have let me bleed out. You didn't. Now we're square." She turned and walked away. I wanted nothing more than wring her scrawny neck or to put three more holes in her, but *Heart* had told me I wasn't allowed to have my gun in Arion, and I was neither brave enough nor sure enough I could take her without it. Especially, if she knew I was coming. I settled for staring at her leaving, fantasizing about ways her day could go as horribly wrong as mine just had.

"Do I need to be jealous?" I turned and saw Lysha looking at me slightly cockeyed. Her smile instantly brightened my mood. I told her not in the least as that one was meaner than a rattlesnake and I preferred my women tall and auburn, not short and blonde. She laughed. Oh, how I loved her laugh. I was so caught up in the sound and the smell of oranges I almost forgot to ask when and why the plan changed.

"You were willing to give up everything to do the right thing. You shouldn't have to give up coming home." She bit her lip. "Robert realized the Empire could do the arrest since we were in Arion. I made some calls." She shrugged as though it were no big deal. "It seems to have worked out. I'm not sure which was better, Zhang's reaction or Adam's. He didn't know we were changing things either." I told her I didn't catch the General's. "You don't play cards with him but he was also facing the crowd at the time. He was expecting you a few seconds later, so he was shocked when Maxie showed up."

She had skirted it a couple of times but I knew she was actively avoiding the real issue. Her poker face was almost as good as the General's but the lip bite was a dead giveaway. She was nervous and didn't know how to broach the issue. We had met because I couldn't come back to Terra. It was what brought us together. That situation no longer existed. She was happy for me but she didn't want to lose me. I didn't want to lose her either. Less than a day ago I had decided what was more important to me. When all the chaff was gone, I had chosen her.

I would always choose her. Terra wasn't home anymore. It was where I came from but home was where Lysha was, for as long as she would have me. I told her this. For my troubles, I got kissed and called "Fuel for brains. I was wondering how long it would take you to realize that." I let her know one of my most endearing qualities was being a bit oblivious sometimes, and tall, I was also tall, which got me another laugh and a solid kiss.

Epilogue

I was hovering on the verge of sleep. My eyes shut listening to all the sounds of the ship. *Heart's* repairs had been completed in Arion, and the Empire had been kind enough to replace both of his destroyed lifeboats. Our return flight to the Luna was scheduled to take under a day. Lysha was in the seat next to me playing with Em and trying to figure out what we were going to do with cats on the moon. "I don't know that she's going to handle the lower gravity well, and I really don't think I can keep it this high all the time. I don't know how you can stand it."

I had visions of a cat that was already able to jump several meters, doing things using those Terra defined muscles on Luna. I really had not thought this obligation through. Luckily, my partner chimed in with a healthy dose of good sense. "There is a long tradition of ship's cats. I believe Em and the kittens will make good companions for me while you and the Colonel are enjoying your honeymoon." I told him to knock it off, as the rank was honorary. "Not to argue, but yours appears to be a permanent commission. Your retired status seems to be rescinded." Bloody hell. I told him to get my retirement papers back in before the General got any funny

ideas and drafted me again.

"They'll have to go through me first, love."

About the author

Aaron Kennedy has had an eclectic career including eight years in the Marines, several as a technical writer, arms dealer, dispatcher, and various management roles. He lives in Virginia with his wife, son, and many cats. When not writing or working, he spends his time training for endurance running events.

He welcomes readers to contact him at aaron@shipsofvalorbooks.com and at www.shipsofvalorbooks.com

TEMPLAR
PRESS

www.ingramcontent.com/pod-product-compliance
Lightning Source LLC
Chambersburg PA
CBHW060349260626
47160CB00006B/2254